HEATHER BLACKWOOD

THE SOUND OF WINGS

A TIME CORPS NOVEL

The Sound of Wings

First Print Edition: 2014

ISBN-13: 978-0-9888054-4-6

Cover and Formatting: Streetlight Graphics

CHAPTER 1

HUGINN WAS AN AMNESIAC RAVEN, but he was not an unobservant one. He understood that something had gone terribly wrong, even if he couldn't remember what it was. He and Pangur Ban sat high in the pepper tree overhanging the street in front of the Time Corps safe house. It was one of their favorite spots, away from the humans and their endless chatter. A breeze rustled the branches, providing the only respite from the August heat. Huginn heard a shout from inside the house as a car slowed and turned into the driveway.

"They're back," said Pangur Ban. "I hope they have information."

The white cat stood and stretched, digging her claws into the bark, then leapt down to the ground and made her way to the cat door that led into the kitchen. Huginn flew up over the house and through an entry hatch that the Professor had built into the frame of an upstairs window. He joined Pangur Ban in the living room, taking his perch on the back of a wooden chair.

"I think something bad has happened," said Huginn, as people shouted upstairs and a woman named Hazel rushed into the kitchen, a phone in her hand. "What is it?"

Pangur Ban looked at him, unblinking. "Do you not recall?" There was no reproach in her tone. There never was.

Huginn clicked his beak, a nervous habit that occasionally helped him to clear his mind. It didn't help.

"Elliot is trapped in the Library. Do you remember Elliot?" asked Pangur Ban.

"Of course. The young man with blond hair. Though sometimes he's older."

Time travel meant that members of the Time Corps aged asynchronously with each other. Huginn was used to meeting people out of order and he remembered Elliot.

"Yes. And the Professor and Felicia have been trying to find a way to get him back. They've been gone a few weeks, but it could have been longer on their personal timelines."

"And now they have returned," he said. "That is good."

"They are calling Astrid right now."

Huginn remembered that Astrid was Elliot's cousin. She was not a member of the Time Corps, but as a Door, she was their greatest hope of getting Elliot back to their world. She was capable of opening Doors between worlds, but so far, she had been unable to reach Elliot.

"I remember a little more now," he said.

Pangur Ban did not comment, but she was not given to idle chatter. She jumped off the chair and glided into the kitchen, lean and graceful. Huginn wished he could be as elegant, but it was impossible when flapping around the innumerable obstacles inside a human house.

A tall, lean man with black hair dragged a trunk upstairs, careful not to bang it on the way up. That was the Professor, the man who had invented the time machine in the 1800s in another world.

"The Professor doesn't look like he's happy," Huginn said to Pangur Ban when she returned.

"No one is happy," the cat said.

Twenty minutes later, Astrid rushed into the house looking desperate but a little hopeful. She was young with short blonde hair and blue eyes, like her cousin. The other members of the Time Corps gathered in the living room.

Huginn recognized Neil Grey, Elliot's partner and closest friend. With both Neil and Astrid trying to get him out of the Library, why wasn't Elliot already free? He would have to ask Pangur Ban later, as he hated the pitying looks he received when others knew he didn't remember things properly. Today was a particularly bad day and he knew it. He would remain silent.

"Well?" said Astrid. "How do we get Elliot out?" She wore her work uniform from Luna Park, the local boardwalk. Her hair was wild and windblown and her cheeks were red either from exertion or the heat. Even with the windows open, it was swelteringly hot inside.

The Professor glanced around, and Huginn watched him take a mental roll call. He leaned forward in his chair, leaning his elbows on his knees and clasping his hands in front of him.

"We can't get him out yet. From everything we've found, it's a one-way trip into the Library."

"There has to be something," said Astrid. "You can't just leave him there."

The Professor sighed. "No one said we're leaving him there."

Astrid looked miserable, but then so did the other humans.

"We're doing our best," said Felicia, who sat beside the Professor on the sofa. Huginn noted that she was sitting very close to him, with their legs occasionally touching. Interesting. They had not shared such close physical proximity before they had left. He also noticed that the Professor's hair was longer and shaggier.

When Felicia Sanchez was younger, she had accidentally slipped through one of the Professor's time rips and after all this time, she had not been able to return to her home world. She had assimilated well into the Time Corps, but of their number, she was the only one who wanted to leave some day. Huginn supposed that on her personal timeline, she had spent about three years with the Time Corps, perhaps more. That would put her in her late twenties, while the Professor was a little older.

"Have you made any progress on creating a Door?" Felicia asked Astrid. She said it gently, but Astrid visibly stiffened.

"I've done everything. I've made Door after Door, and none of them go to the Library, not for more than a moment or two. And I can't be sure, but it could be any library. I can't tell. Sending Elliot there was a one-time thing. I can't replicate it."

"Perhaps the other Doors can help you," said Neil Grey. "You're not the only one."

"Well none of them has contacted me. So I'm stuck with needing you all for help. And you haven't been able to do a thing."

"Now, that's not fair," said Felicia.

"You want to know what's not fair? My cousin is trapped because of me and because of you. And now—"

She stopped, staring at Felicia's lap. Glittering on her left hand was a simple gold band.

"You got married?"

The Professor's expression softened as Felicia took his hand.

"We were going to announce it later," Felicia said. "But there were more important things to discuss."

Astrid shot from her chair and took a few steps, then turned and plopped back down. Huginn thought it was a useless movement, inefficient and so very human.

"Elliot is trapped, and you guys are getting married!"

"It won't affect his timeline at all, not even by a minute," said the Professor.

"Why didn't you invite us?" asked Hazel Dubois in a wounded tone. She was the closest thing the Professor had to family, as he had raised her from a young age. Both of them were from the same home world and shared the peculiar deformity of the feet that all people from that world possessed. She was also the captain of the ancient Viking ship Skidbladnir.

"You were all there," said the Professor. "Or, you will be, rather. But right now isn't the time for nuptial celebration."

"No, it's not," said Astrid, glaring at Hazel. Huginn had never seen her so upset before. She must have pinned all her hopes on Felicia and the Professor returning with useful information. Huginn would never have made that mistake, but Astrid was still young.

"We're all doing our best," said Neil Grey, Elliot's partner. He was in his forties at this point, which meant he had been in the Time Corps for about twenty years. Huginn could only guess as to how many of those years had been at Elliot's side. Like Huginn and Pangur Ban, the two of them almost always worked as a team.

"It's been weeks," said Astrid. "Who knows what's happening to him."

"The Library exists outside of time," said Pangur Ban. "For him, time may be shorter."

"Or longer."

Pangur Ban dipped her head in assent. Huginn knew that Elliot would escape from the Library eventually, as he had gone in a young man and Huginn had met him when he was older. Many of them had. The thing was, he could be imprisoned for years, miserable and tortured. No one could be sure as older Elliot had always kept quiet on that point.

A girl who was Astrid's duplicate knelt beside her. They were technically identical, though anyone seeing them together could easily tell them apart. The girl had chosen the name Sister, though Huginn understood that it was not a typical human name, and thus she would have to choose another at some point. Sister had longer hair than Astrid, a scarred face and a timid, skittish manner. She had once been a slave to the Unseelie, one of the types of beings called sidhe or fair folk. They had cut out her tongue as a child.

Sister touched Astrid's hand gently, but Huginn saw the angry set of Astrid's jaw and knew that her fury was directed inward as much as outward. She had been the one to send Elliot to the Library to save his life.

"I know," muttered Astrid to Sister. "We'll find him." She turned to Felicia. "Was the entire trip a waste?"

"Not completely," said Felicia. "We did find one thing. It's a long shot, and it's not about the Library, but rather about the Librarian himself."

CHAPTER 2

Some nights, Astrid dreamed of the void, the place between. It was not frightening or strange in the way that places sometimes were in dreams. It was empty and silent and dark. She loved it, this place between worlds that was neither beginning nor destination. It felt like home.

The void was normally soundless, but this time, she heard a tiny whimper, like an animal. It came again, and she felt the sudden swooping sensation of slipping back into consciousness, then there was the twist of blankets around her body, the glow of the light against her eyelids. It was Sister who had made the noise.

The girl slept on the floor between the bed and the window. Astrid had to remind herself that Sister was the same age she was, eighteen, though she seemed younger. Sister moaned in her sleep and Astrid slipped out of bed to wake her.

Kneeling beside her, Astrid could not help but study the girl's face, an exact duplicate of her own. They were not twins, nor were they related in any way. Sister was human, and Astrid was not. Astrid was the changeling, the fey child who had been substituted for Sister when they were infants. Sister had then been spirited away to the Unseelie world to be raised by Astrid's biological mother. There, she had been raised to be a slave, nameless and tormented.

Sister opened her eyes and for an instant, her face registered confusion.

"You're with me. You're safe," said Astrid.

Sister rolled face-down and heaved a heavy sigh. Astrid touched her shoulder, and the girl flinched at the touch. She had been in the human world for a few weeks and the transition was not going well. She was unable to sleep in a bed, preferring a spot on the floor against the wall. Everything seemed to either confuse or frighten her, including television, the noise of Los Angeles traffic and the garbage disposal. Astrid would have thought that escaping a life of cruelty and slavery would have improved Sister's life, but instead she was miserable.

"Do you want me to make breakfast for you?" asked Astrid.

Sister shook her head, then sat up and pulled her hands free of the blankets.

"Is Santiago here?" she signed.

"No, he might come by later though." Astrid hoped he would not. She didn't like Santiago. He was one of two people who could communicate with Sister when she had first arrived, though the rest of them were learning her unique form of sign language and Sister was gradually learning American Sign Language. Santiago was Coyote, an ancient being native to the California, Arizona and Nevada dessert. He was also a liar and a womanizer. Sister was completely devoted to him, and though he was kind to the girl, Astrid didn't want Sister to become too attached.

Sister looked like she was about to cry. "What about Elliot?"

"No, he's still trapped in the Library." The thought of her cousin brought a wash of pain. "Come downstairs and I'll make you pancakes before I go to work," Astrid said.

Sister seemed to be considering it. "Can you call Santiago?"

Astrid sighed. "He's probably asleep. You'll be all right without him."

Santiago was probably sleeping off a hangover after a night of partying. Thankfully, he didn't often stay at the Time Corps safe house. Sister glanced at the clock, and Astrid watched as she paused to make sense of the numbers.

"Here," said Astrid and pulled some clothing out of the closet for each of them. Of course, they were the same height and build, but Astrid tried to keep their clothing separate, hoping that Sister would get used to the idea of personal possessions. Since she was used to wearing a slave's robes, Sister preferred long skirts, loose tops and no shoes. Astrid tossed a skirt and blouse on the bed and then turned her back to Sister while she put on her work uniform, khaki pants and a polo shirt with the embroidered Luna Park logo.

When Sister entered the kitchen fifteen minutes later, the first thing she signed was "I want you to call Santiago."

Astrid poured pancake batter onto the griddle. "Yukiko will be here soon. You can talk with her."

Sister considered it. "I told Santiago about the dreams before. He understood them."

Astrid knew about Sister's dreams, the nightmares that had plagued her ever since she had escaped from Unseelie and entered the human world. But Santiago apparently had some comforting insight that Astrid did not. Sister sat down at the table looking utterly dejected. She heaved a sigh.

"Elliot was in this dream," signed Sister. "Santiago will understand it."

"Fine, I'll text him," said Astrid. She hoped he would not reply, but within moments, he answered that he would come over soon.

Sister was just finishing her pancakes with blueberry

syrup when Santiago came in the back kitchen door without knocking.

"I was just coming in from hunting," he said. "I was hoping to get some sleep."

He didn't look tired. He never did. Astrid wasn't sure exactly what he was, a nature spirit or an old god. He never answered questions of that kind. But whatever he was, he was unnaturally good-looking with tawny hair, tanned skin and a physique of a swimsuit model. It was occasionally distracting, and right now Sister was looking at him expectantly. Without an invitation, he poured himself a cup of coffee.

"Bad dreams, eh, pet?" he said gently to Sister. She nodded and looked down at her empty plate. He didn't press her for more information, and Astrid got the feeling that they wanted privacy. Though she was Sister's doppelganger and she was close with the girl, she knew that Sister needed other friendships. She couldn't spend her life only talking with Yukiko and the other members of the Time Corps.

"Tell me, Astrid, how is the psychopomping going?" Santiago asked, sliding a few pancakes onto a plate and adding two thick pats of butter.

"Nothing yet," said Astrid. She was a new psychopomp, a companion who led people's souls from life into death. She was a Door. Aside from that, she knew nothing. She had only performed her function once, on a sentient kitten. His two siblings and their mother, Pangur Ban, were around the house somewhere, probably lounging in a sunbeam or chasing lizards in the backyard.

"I've never been friends with a Door before," said Santiago. "You'll have to tell me all about it once you start your work."

"I have to get to my real job." She filled a water bottle, threw a frozen bean burrito and a soda into a paper bag for lunch and headed for the door. As she was picking up her purse, Sister padded over and put her hand on her arm.

"He'll stay, you know," she signed. "When the rest of you go, when you go to art school in New York, he'll still be here."

Astrid hugged Sister good-bye, knowing she was correct. She wished there was a way for the girl to have regular friends, but explaining a scarred and toungeless twin was impossible. Sister would remain at the Time Corps safe house, where her peculiarities did not draw any special notice. Perhaps one day she might become one of their agents, but for now, she needed to learn basic human skills.

Astrid headed down the street, toward the commuter train that took her to work at Luna Park, the only boardwalk in Los Angeles. The park had been partially destroyed by the Wild Hunt a few weeks before, but thanks to a hefty insurance policy that the owner, Mr. Augustus, had taken out only a few months earlier, most of the place was up and functioning once more. Astrid knew better than to question how Augustus had known to buy the policy. Like his eleven siblings, he was privy to information that the rest of humanity was not.

Astrid took a seat on the train. Sister was correct about Santiago staying around while everyone else might leave. As far as Astrid knew, the Coyote never left the southwestern part of the country. With Elliot trapped in the Library and with her heading to Columbia for art school, who would care for Sister? The three of them were family, if Astrid counted Elliot as her cousin, which she still did. It wasn't right to ask anyone else to watch over Sister. Even Yukiko, who Sister was fond of, would eventually go her own way. She wasn't a member of the Time Corps, not in any official capacity anyway.

Astrid needed to check in with one of the members of the Time Corps to see if they had yet managed to get

Sister a birth certificate and Social Security number. Perhaps, eventually, she could learn a trade that didn't involve speaking.

Astrid had to rethink her plan to go to Columbia in the fall. It was selfish to leave Sister on her own. Perhaps she could learn to make Doors from New York to the Time Corps safe house in Los Angeles. That way, she could stay with Sister and still attend art school on her scholarship during the day. It might work.

She sighed. She had thought that moving out of her mother's house and getting a scholarship would solve her problems. Instead she was an inexperienced psychopomp without any guidance or direction, her cousin was trapped in the Library in another dimension and her duplicate needed almost round-the-clock mental health care.

The commuter train did nothing to relax her as it slid along the tracks, bumping rhythmically, buildings streaking by the window. The Time Corps house was her temporary home, but she understood now that she was a creature of the between places, of the passages separating one from another. She would never truly belong anywhere, and she had made a sort of peace with the idea. But she was not content to see the people she loved imprisoned or helpless.

She walked from the station to the boardwalk. Luna Park was already filled with sunscreen-scented visitors eating sticky frozen treats and sweating in the August heat. She headed for her accustomed spot, her pretzel cart. She was born an Unseelie, but because she was raised in the human world, she was immune to knots and salt, unlike other sidhe, both Seelie and Unseelie. The girl who was running the cart went home for the day and Astrid shoved her purse under the cart and checked her stock.

The arcade nearby beeped and buzzed with activity and riders screamed as they flew down the drop on the wooden roller coaster. Out on the beach, a group of teenagers played volleyball. She had chosen this, this human life, a life of minimum-wage work and ordinary problems. But she had not chosen to be a Door, nor had she chosen the sentence imposed upon her cousin, Elliot, who had been sentenced to death by the Seelie for the crime of tampering with time.

If he had not interfered in her childhood, the Unseelie and their cousins, the Seelie, would have possessed a Door who could allow their kind to move in and out of the human world, just as they had centuries ago. But Elliot had tampered with events just enough to let Astrid make her own choice. The sidhe courts had sentenced him to death, but with a little quick thinking, Astrid had sent him through one of her Doors into the Library instead. Any non-human being who heard of the place quailed at the thought. Even Santiago was frightened of it.

A couple purchased two salted pretzels and two lemonades from her, walked away and paused to look over the boardwalk railing, out over the beach and toward the ocean. A crowd of young people passed by, enjoying their summer, and Astrid sighed. If Elliot was a time traveler, why hadn't he thought to leave a nice big deposit in her bank account for her? Or at least enough to cover a few months of living expenses until she started school?

When the crowd cleared, the couple who had purchased pretzels no longer stood against the railing. Instead, they were on the ground. The man crouched, his hand on his chest, while his wife slid her arm around him. Astrid yelled around the corner of the arcade for the employee staffing the prize counter to call the paramedics. A crowd gathered, obscuring her view, and a minute later, two Luna Park security officers arrived and pushed the crowd back.

She moved forward, wanting to help and also knowing that she could not. She had no medical training and didn't even know how to perform CPR. She ought to help keep the crowd back. She wore the park uniform, so the crowd might listen to her. She headed for the group, but something caught her eye to one side, just beside a blue and white covered trash can with the park name on it. It was a twitching movement in the air. In an instant she knew precisely what it was.

The air had shimmered. She had only witnessed such a thing when she had been present at a death, though the Time Corps members assured her that it also occurred when a time rip opened between one time and another or between worlds. The air shimmered again, a few feet from the ground, then the air grew into an opaque, foggy disk. The center of the circle opened, revealing a mirror-like surface. Passages to other worlds allowed one to see the other side. This was true in all cases but one. This was a Door, the thing she created and the thing she was. It was a Door into death.

She hurried toward the Door, noting only briefly that paramedics had arrived, pushing an empty gurney. The man, the dead man, walked toward her, as solid as he had been when his hand had brushed hers as he paid for the pretzels and lemonade.

"I think ... I thought something happened," he said. "I thought it hurt."

Astrid wasn't sure what a proper psychopomp ought to do. She was supposed to accompany a soul to the afterlife, but she had no idea how exactly to accomplish this.

"I'm not sure, but stay here, with me." She wasn't sure why she wanted him to stay, but if her job was to be an escort for the dead, she couldn't very well let him wander off.

"Something happened over there," he looked back. "Where's Sandy?"

"She's fine," she said, moving closer. He was sunburned and balding and his tee shirt was faded black with a football team logo. He was also clearly frightened.

"Look, I need to tell you something. I think you passed away," she said.

"No," said the man.

She wasn't sure how to respond to that. "I mean it. You died. Over there. Your body is over there, and you have to go through the Door over here."

"No. No, I can't go without Sandy. She was here with me." He craned his neck, looking for his wife, but she was obscured by the crowd.

"You can't stay with her anymore," Astrid said. "It's time for you to go."

She felt like an idiot saying these things. Was she supposed to tell him he was dead? He didn't seem to believe her. Should she inform him that a better place, like heaven, waited through the Door? Was that the truth? Or would he move on to another body, another life?

"Yes, I have to go," he said, and Astrid relaxed. Then he turned and headed for the crowd, back toward his body.

"Wait!" Astrid cried, but he did not look back.

As she watched him leave, she noticed something. A small dark-skinned boy, about eight years old, stood at the edge of the crowd. But instead of trying to see what the commotion was about, he was watching her. Then he turned, followed the dead man's spirit, and a few moments later, they emerged from the crowd, hand in hand.

"Are you sure she's there?" said the man. "I haven't seen her in fifty-three years. She died so young."

"She's there. And your parents and grandparents. I promise that Sandy will be along soon too."

The man and the boy stopped a few feet from the Door and the boy looked up into the man's face and gave him a small, reassuring smile. The man released his hand and stepped through the Door, which then contracted, like a pupil, and was gone.

The boy turned to Astrid. "That wasn't your Door," he said. "It was mine."

CHAPTER 3

When the sickening spinning finally ended and the weightless, falling sensation abated, Elliot found himself face-down on a cold stone floor. The place smelled like wet rock, earthy and moist, and though only a few lamps burned on the wall, the place was bright. Diffused light poured in through high windows of translucent white stone. Alabaster, he thought. Piles of scrolls and tablets filled parts of the room, and through a wide archway, he saw rows and rows of bookshelves filled with volumes of varying sizes. He pushed himself up.

An instant earlier, he had been standing with his cousin Astrid in front of a crowd of angry Seelie. Astrid had made a Door to death, and then another location, and he had stepped through. Now he was in this place, not dead. At least he hoped not.

It was a library. Astrid had sent him to an old library. Okay, then. It could be a lot worse. He was, as far as he could tell, safe from the Seelie who wanted him dead. Now, he simply had to find a way to get back home to his fellow Time Corps members, Astrid and Sister and his partner Neil.

"Ah, there you are!" A giant tortoise lumbered in on all fours and tipped its head to one side, examining Elliot with one beadlike black eye. "I thought someone had arrived."

Elliot was no stranger to talking animals, and he felt a moment of pride as he responded without horror or shock, as if a giant talking tortoise was nothing out of the ordinary. "Where is this place?"

"The Library, as you can surely see. I take it you're not a great scholar."

"There's no need to be nasty, I only asked a question."

"Then you are not a scholar?"

Ah, so he was seeking information. Elliot wasn't sure how he ought to answer. "And what if I am?"

The tortoise blinked. "You're not." He sighed. "Just another accidental arrival. You're the third one this year. Come along then."

The tortoise led him through corridors and rooms, too many to count, all of them filled with books or scrolls, stone and clay tablets or electronic reading devices. Columns painted in bright red and blue, gold and orange held up a high ceiling, sometimes made of plaster, and in other rooms of warm sandstone. Statues stood here and there, depicting hippopotamuses and crocodiles, jackals and peacocks. Some rooms had plain walls and were filled with soft chairs. Elliot wondered what was stored there, as every other room was crammed with reading materials in every form imaginable. As they walked, the tortoise spoke.

"I won't make the same mistake twice, you see," said the tortoise in his low, gravelly voice. "I'm going to show you the reality of your situation, put you to work, and that will be that."

"Put me to work? No, I need to leave. I need to get back home. Just show me the exit, and I'll be on my way."

"Just come along and we'll get this over with." He led him up a curving marble staircase, which the tortoise navigated with remarkable agility.

As they climbed, Elliot remembered having climbed this staircase before. Déjà vu, but not the typical sort. He remembered waking up in his trailer just after dreaming of this place. His spirits lifted. He had a rare ability, according to the Time Corps, to detect things that were not solidly attached to a certain place, or when timelines slipped slightly off from where they ought to be. For the most part, it was a useless skill, though Neil and the others had assured him it would come in handy. If the timelines were off in this library, then that information might prove useful.

After twenty minutes of walking through rooms both ancient and modern, they arrived at a simple wooden door. Elliot wasn't sure if he should open it for the tortoise, but any concern he had over propriety ended when the animal reared up on his hind legs, his blunt claws reaching around the knob.

The room beyond was dark, unlike all the others which were illuminated by the high-set alabaster windows. It was empty save for a wooden chair which sat just beneath a shuttered window.

"Go on and open it," said the tortoise. "You'll see where we are."

The tortoise's tone gave Elliot pause. But wherever he was, whatever time or whatever world, he would cope with it. He was a Time Corps agent. He unlatched the brass hook holding the shutters together and opened them.

Outside it was black. It was a dark beyond night, beyond the photographs he had seen of deep space. There were no buildings below or in the distance, no horizon, no clouds, no stars. It was simply emptiness. Elliot leaned out over the windowsill, looking down where the walls of the Library ran down, down, down for floor after floor. He could not see the base of the building, but little rectangles of light shone from within the library, descending endlessly into the dark. They glowed with the same pale light that lit the library inside. The light seemed to have no discernible source. Odd.

He looked upward to see the same thing, an endless windowed wall rising forever. The place around the building was quieter than silence. Not only was there no sound, but even the sound of him breathing was muffled, absorbed. He squinted into the distance, trying to pick out anything, any variation whatsoever. The blackness was absolute. It pulled color and light and everything into itself, leaving nothing. It was the absence of everything, all matter and even, Elliot had the sudden notion, thoughts.

Looking into the darkness, he felt something tug at a thread in his mind, like a fish pulling on a line, present one moment and vanishing the next, leaving a little swirling hole. The tortoise walked up beside him and raised himself to look out the window beside him. He was glad for the company, as looking into the black gave him a deeply uneasy feeling.

"It is said that if you look too long, you'll go mad," said the tortoise. "But it's not true. I've looked into the void plenty of times."

"The void. Is this the void?"

The idea gave him hope. Astrid was a Door, and she was able to make pathways through the void. Surely she would find him.

"It is. And now you see where you are. We are outside of time and place and whatever world you came from."

"Earth."

The tortoise waved a paw as if what Elliot said was irrelevant. "You are here now, and here you will remain."

Elliot wasn't so sure about that, but while he waited for Astrid to make a Door or for Neil and the rest of the Time Corps to find a way to this world, he would make the best of his situation.

"I didn't introduce myself," he said. "I'm Elliot."

"Malachy."

"Are you the librarian?"

"I am a librarian, but not the Librarian. Him ... him you would not wish to meet."

CHAPTER 4

"I'M JUST HERE FOR THE files on the Librarian," said Captain Hazel Dubois.

She didn't reach for her gun, even when Kurzen's guards moved up to flank her. They were huge, and she was small, even for a woman. And though her gun was a great equalizer, they could take it from her in an instant. Mr. Escobar, a capuchin monkey and her first mate, shifted uneasily on her shoulder.

"We agreed on the price, Kurzen. I have the devices on my ship," Hazel said. "The deal stands."

Kurzen was a slim man, too young to have amassed so much wealth and power without inheriting it. Hazel had heard of his father, but preferred to deal with lower profile individuals.

The situation had seemed ideal. Kurzen possessed a file with images of a cave painting from a place somewhere in the Mediterranean. Hazel had a time traveling ship and could provide him with hundreds of the newest implantable electronic devices a month before they became available to the public. She couldn't understand how twenty-first-century electronic devices were constantly being redeveloped, making older ones obsolete within such a short time. In the mid-nineteenth century, when she was born, even fashion hadn't changed so quickly.

"What I don't understand," said Kurzen, "is why these files are so valuable to you. The price you agreed upon was far too high for some digital images of crude paintings."

“The cave collapsed, or so I understand,” said Hazel. She had no idea where the cave was located, or she would travel there herself, arriving before the collapse. But even if she could see the cave, she did not have the academic commentary on the images from a now-deceased scholar. If she knew his name, she could find him before he died. But Kurzen had all of that information in one neat package.

“Yes, the little coastal cave is gone,” said Kurzen. “Collapsed and swallowed by the sea. Which makes these files the only ones of their kind.”

“That's why I offered a high price,” said Hazel. “A price that you agreed to.”

“A price that could go higher.”

“I only have so many devices. I can't get more. The new versions are being announced next week, and you can be there to sell them during the initial frenzy. There's plenty of profit to be made here.”

“Look, Captain Dubois. You're cute with your little monkey and I hate to disappoint. But I didn't get where I am by letting valuable information slip through my fingers. Someone will be willing to pay for these files, either one of the big museums or a wealthy private collector.”

“It'll take you months to find them and negotiate a price. And there's no guarantee that they'll pay you more than I will. Besides, if you give the files to me, I won't publicize them. They're for personal use only.”

How could she explain to him that she would take the files back to Los Angeles for Julius and Pangur Ban to study and that they'd never be made public? If he desired, Kurzen could sell them twice or more, not that he'd get a good price. Hazel was the only one who wanted them. But she couldn't tell Kurzen that without explaining why she needed them.

A man entered and whispered something in Kurzen's ear.

"My associate informs me that the sample of the device you provided is real, not a knock-off."

"Why do you care if you don't want to deal?"

"Unload the cargo," said Kurzen to one of his men.

"So you are going to deal?"

"I didn't say that."

She turned for the door and the guards moved in, blocking her way. "Excuse me, gentlemen," she said, giving them a sweet smile. Occasionally, people would act politely if presented the opportunity. She didn't sense that this was one of those times, but she was a Southern woman, and old habits were hard to break.

"Take the goods off the ship," said Kurzen.

"Don't you go near it!" said Hazel, spinning on him.

Mr. Escobar leapt from her shoulder, slipped between the guards' legs and dashed out the door. Skidbladnir, Hazel's sentient Viking ship, would listen to the first mate's instructions to move out of range of Kurzen's men. And, failing that, her crew would stop them. They only looked furry and sweet. Even if Kurzen's men were armed, and they certainly would be, hers were not helpless.

Two men held her upper arms, but lightly. She didn't struggle, nor did she try to pull away. The situation was not so bad, really.

"Why are you smiling?" Kurzen asked her.

"Did you wake up with something strange near you this morning?" she asked.

He tried to hide his reaction, but she caught the flicker of apprehension in his expression.

"What was it?" she asked. "Nothing too frightening, I hope."

"It wasn't too bad, was it?" said a voice behind them. Neil Grey, Hazel's bosun and friend, came through the doorway. Then he also came in through the back door, followed by four other versions of himself. Others appeared behind the first version, all wearing identical clothing, blue jeans and a black duster. All of them were of medium build with brown hair and eyes. Ordinary looking and forgettable, Neil never drew attention to himself, except in times like these.

The two men released Hazel, preparing for whatever the Neils had in store.

"It was a letter opener," said the first Neil. "Right beside your pillow. And if you don't wish to wake up with it though your eye, you'll give us what you agreed upon and we'll be on our way."

"What the hell is this? How the hell do you have clones?"

Hazel knew that here, in 2072, clones in common use did not exist. It would be decades before the emergence of the duplicate hordes. Kurzen was only confused and trying to make sense of the impossibility that confronted him.

"Call off the men you sent to my ship," said Hazel. She caught the eye of one of the Neils across from her. She did not know where he fell in the spawning order of the group, but by the time she and Neil met up later, he would remember it. Typically, in these dealings, the Neil who did the talking was the oldest of the group, as he would have the memories of all previous versions.

"I'm not doing a damn thing," said Kurzen. "You all leave right now. Leave now and we'll let you go without any trouble. You keep your goods."

"You're going to give us the files, and then you're going to receive your payment. A straight transaction. All fair," Hazel said.

Kurzen appeared to be thinking it over. "And if I don't?"

It was a foolish thing to say. There were ten Neils now, according to Hazel's count, though there might be others outside. And Kurzen only had four burly goons plus his own skinny self. Why would he try to refuse them?

"There's no need for any unpleasantness," said Hazel.

"See, here is what you do not understand," said Kurzen.

"If a dealer could simply appear with more firepower or manpower and take what's mine, I would not be running this section of town. I'm not giving you the files. No deal. Now leave."

Hazel made eye contact with the Neil in charge. She did not need to say anything, as she knew that he'd understand her thoughts. She liked this part of their deals, when they didn't need to speak.

"Check your back left pocket," said Neil to Kurzen.

"What do you mean?"

"Just check it. Your answer is there."

Kurzen reached into his pocket, pulling out a piece of paper. He unfolded it and Hazel watched his eyes dart over the lines.

"What the hell is this?" he cried and threw the paper onto the desk as if it were alive.

Hazel glanced at it. It was an exact transcript of everything they had said since the Neils entered the room. She tried not to laugh.

"Here is how it will work," said Neil. "You will give us the files, immediately. If you do not, you will wake up with something worse than a letter opener beside your pillow. Remember this morning, how you wondered why your toothbrush was on the bathroom counter instead of propped up in the cup? Why your clock was ten minutes fast, when normally it keeps perfect time? I can come visit you any time I like. We don't take kindly to those who won't honor agreements."

Kurzen glared at them and told one of the guards to call off the men. Apparently dealing with them was more trouble than it was worth.

Five minutes later, all but one of the Neils dispersed to return to their original times and Hazel walked back to Skidbladnir beside the remaining one.

The ship waited a quarter mile offshore, its red and white sail hanging loose and the crew of monkeys lined up along the railing, waiting for their captain. Mr. Escobar must have taken the ship out to prevent Kurzen's men from boarding it. No guards waited at the dock. The place was eerily quiet.

Mr. Escobar sat high up in the ship's rigging, watching. At a wave from Hazel, the ship turned its dragon-headed prow toward shore, the row of round, spiked shields along its sides glinting in the afternoon sunlight. Hazel shoved her hands in her pockets and watched Skidbladnir approach, admiring her beauty.

The dragon was sentient and could move herself along independently, but a crew at the oars or sails was necessary to make good speed. The monkeys rowed the ship up to the dock and then lowered the gangplank. They unloaded the boxes of implantable devices, leaving them on the dock where Kurzen's men could retrieve them.

"We should hurry," said Neil. "I hear someone coming."

An instant later, the crew must have heard it too, because they leapt back onboard. Hazel didn't hesitate, but took her place on deck. They pulled away, and as the dock receded, eight armed men appeared.

The men took aim and Hazel shouted a warning as she flattened herself on the deck. The crew leapt to the deck as bullets struck the wood siding of the ship and the metal shields along its sides. The crew pulled at the oars and Hazel pulled out her pistol and lined up a shot.

Neil touched her shoulder. He did not need to say anything. The men were lowering their weapons as the ship moved out of range, and Hazel had no need to kill them. The ship sailed on until they were in open water.

"I don't think we'll be able to deal with Kurzen again," she said to Neil as they sailed north along the Chinese coastline.

"Likely not." Neil pulled a tiny device from his pocket. It contained the files on the Librarian. "That trick only seems to work once. Then they hire better security for their living quarters. I'll miss visiting Kurzen though. He's adorable when he's asleep."

It was one of Neil's rare jokes, and Hazel smiled. He offered her the data storage device.

"You keep it. We'll look at it once we're away from the coast." She gave orders and the ship moved eastward.

"I wonder how you do it," she said. "How you can appear beside yourself."

No one else in the Time Corps could exist within ten miles of themselves. They had tried, many times, but always hit an invisible wall. They could only exist once in any geographical area. If they had not been limited in this way, they could travel back in time over and over again, just as Neil had, and change the course of history. As it was, only Neil could do it.

The two of them had no secrets, not since she had told him about the strange lettering that she had spotted on the roof of his mouth. Since he was now in his forties, on his personal timeline, that was twenty years ago. For her, it had been five.

"He's dead, you know," she said to Neil, knowing he was thinking of his former boss, the man who somehow had been able control him with a word.

"I know."

"And you're not what he wanted you to be."

That would be a murderer. Neil had worked as a time-traveling assassin, tricked by Mr. March into thinking he was only killing murderers and people who bent the course of history toward evil. He had killed evil people, but there had been others who may have been innocent and Neil had refused to continue.

Neil sighed and looked back toward the coastline, shrouded in early evening fog. They had been traveling together for weeks, seeking the information that might help them get Elliot out of the Library. She was a Southern girl from Louisiana during the Civil War who should have been married by now. He was a strange creature of unnatural strength and speed who thought he had been born in the 1970s, though he had few clear memories. Like the rest of the Time Corps, circumstances and strange events had thrown them together.

"You never told anyone, did you?" Neil asked. "About the letters in my mouth?"

Hazel glanced at the dragon head on the ship. Skidbladnir was alive and always listening. Hazel's quarters were below decks, and no one would hear them there. She tipped her head a fraction and then had a word with Mr. Escobar, giving him instructions, before she headed down the steps into the dark of the ship's interior. Technically, the ship was too shallow to have a below-decks. But her ship was not ordinary, and possessed a few small rooms and a cargo hold.

"You should ask Yukiko," said Hazel. "She might know what the letters mean."

Yukiko was an on-again off-again member of the Time Corps. She was also a Kitsune, a Japanese fox spirit who had lived most of her life in California. She was young for a Kitsune, but old compared to humans.

"Don't you dare tell her," said Neil. "No one can know."

"One of them might know what the letters mean. Pangur Ban is old as well, and well traveled. Julius does nothing but read all the time. One of them might have a clue as to what it means."

"It doesn't matter. Mr. March is dead, and I'm free."

While Hazel turned on her computer and inserted the data device, Neil picked up a book from Hazel's shelf and flipped through it. The book was from her own time and she had brought it with her from the nineteenth century. It sat beside an e-reader, an ancient stone statue with unreadable words carved into its base, pieces of driftwood and other oddments of a life lived asynchronously.

"If you're free, then how can any knowledge be harmful?"

she asked. "It might help you understand why you can't remember so much of your past. It might give you peace."

"It won't. All I'm going to learn is that I'm a killing machine or a monster. And what then? What happens if Santiago tells someone at one of his parties? Or if the Seelie or Unseelie or psychopomps or whatever the hell other supernatural beings are out there find out about it? What if I'm something worse than just an assassin?"

"It won't matter! Because we know you and we love you. Me and Elliot especially. He's your partner, and neither of us cares what you were made for, only what you are now."

She went through the files, glancing at the images. There was only one painting, photographed at various angles. An enormous pair of white wings with black tips folded around a man. Or she thought it was a man. The only part of his body visible were two clawlike hands, reaching in anguish to the sky. Flames surrounded him, engulfing him.

For a moment she thought of Lucifer, the angel cast down from heaven. But if that was what the painting depicted, then the whole trip was for nothing. She glanced through the commentary. This was supposedly an image of the Librarian and the woman who painted it was described alternately as a seer, a prophetess or a madwoman. She hoped that Julius would have more luck deciphering any clues in it since it didn't seem to have any usable information on reaching Elliot.

"I think I know," said Neil. "I know why I can travel within the same space as myself."

His tone was different, and she knew they were on dangerous ground. Hazel's stomach dropped and she took in breath to interrupt him. A thought had occurred to her once in a while, but she had tossed it aside. Neil loved art and music and reading. He was kind and good and ethical, most of the time. He had friendships and loved people. He had even kissed her once.

“It’s because of Mr. March,” she said with more assurance than she felt. “He must have done something to you. Back when he blurred your memories and tattooed the roof of your mouth, it must have been then. It’s just because—”

“No. Stop. We both know why. It’s because I have no soul.”

CHAPTER 5

THE BOY'S NAME WAS GOPAN, and he explained to Astrid that, like her, he was a psychopomp and a Door.

Astrid only stopped to grab her purse and leave the pretzel cart cash drawer with the man running the arcade prize counter. She then left the cart abandoned, its pretzels spinning on their metal hooks in the orange glow of the heat lamp. If Mr. Augustus, the man who ran the park, had a problem with that, he knew where to find her. His brother, Julius, owned the Time Corps safe house in Los Angeles.

"Not every death requires a psychopomp," said Gopan. "We'd be far too busy if they did. Some souls are, how should I put it? More sticky. We keep them moving. We keep the gears lubricated. We exist for people who might have become geists, so it's a win-win for them, for people, for stability of the world and the barriers between worlds. Healthy doors open and close at the appropriate times, regulating passage."

"And that man back there was a sticky soul?"

"Apparently, or I wouldn't have needed to come." He looked around as they walked, and he asked her for money to purchase an ice cream sandwich. She gave it to him.

"Where are your parents? Are they around here?"

"No, they're back in India. I live there too. I normally handle most deaths around my area, so it's nice to be visiting this part of the world. Normally, the only part of the United States I see is in Nebraska."

"Why Nebraska?"

"That's where Jeff's bookshop is. He's our supervisor. We'll go meet him in a little bit." He checked his watch and counted on his fingers to account for the time change. "Yes, we still have a while before we have to go."

"How many of us are there?"

"Right now, including you, there are five. Jeff owns the bookshop and generally runs interference between us and the higher-ups. Robin is from Ghana. He and Graciela are good friends. She's from Argentina."

"Does that mean I'm in charge of North America?"

"Not precisely. Jeff is in North America too, and I can't do all of Asia by myself, as there are just too many people. We all get jobs all over, but we tend to stay in our geographical area."

"But I only speak English."

"When we're on the job we can speak to anyone. Off the job, and we're on our own."

He paused in front of the Tilt-n-Whirl, cocking his head to one side. Astrid hoped he didn't want to ride on it, as she wanted to meet this Jeff person and learn everything about being a psychopomp, including how to open Doors to other places. Places like the Library. Gopan turned and walked down the boardwalk, toward the exit.

"Pardon me for asking," he said, "but do you have your aspect yet?"

"I'm not sure I even understand what that means." She didn't mention that she had heard the term before, from a being called the Piper, who informed her that she would receive her aspect soon. He had also told her that she had the sound of wings about her.

"Ah, it's an alternate form, often an animal. It's useful in a variety of ways. It'll come to you in your sleep, most likely."

"What's yours?"

"You're new, so you don't know, but it's considered very rude to ask someone what their aspect is."

"But you just asked me."

"No, I asked if you had one, not what it was."

Astrid thought it was a distinction without a difference. She didn't want to be rude, but curiosity got the better of her. She would never get the opportunity to ask again.

"Since I'm new, can I ask what yours is?"

"You're looking at it."

"You're not really an eight-year-old boy?"

"Not hardly," he said and finished off his ice cream sandwich, stuffing the wrapper into a trash can.

"But you said an aspect is an animal."

"Most of the time it is. Mine is a child. I find it useful because almost everyone loves children. We're nonthreatening. Hopefully yours will be useful too."

Astrid wondered what sort of thing she might be. What animal did she resemble? She was introverted and shy, so perhaps a rabbit. But that would be a totally useless aspect.

"Some common ones are black dogs, horses and various kinds of birds," Gopan said.

"Why is it rude to ask about someone's aspect?" she asked.

Gopan got a thoughtful look. "Your aspect tells you about yourself, and it tells others about you. It's a part of your nature that's on display for others to see. If your aspect is, for example, the traditional black dog, it means you might be loyal and dutiful."

Astrid caught Gopan looking at her from the corner of his eye.

"It's more than just a piece of your personality," he continued. "It's sort of like appearing naked. In a way, your aspect is more you than you are. Your face, your body, you inherited them from your parents. Your aspect is about your interior self, your soul."

Astrid's face and body were merely copies of Sister's. When they were infants, Sister was in danger of death and the Unseelie had swapped Astrid for Sister, making her into an exact copy of the infant she replaced. She had no idea what she had looked like before that, and her Unseelie mother had informed her that her current appearance would be hers for life.

"So, you see," continued Gopan, "to ask about an aspect or to reveal it is to reveal a part of oneself that is invisible and secret, like the human soul."

"You're very philosophical about it."

"My aspect is a human. They're like that."

CHAPTER 6

HUGINN WOKE FROM HIS NAP with a start when Pangur Ban spoke.

"Yukiko is home," said the cat from her seat in the living room front window.

While Huginn, as a raven, preferred the best perching spots around the house, Pangur Ban, like all cats, enjoyed sunbeams and windowsills. Sunlight backlit her white fur, illuminating her long, lean shape. Her two black and gray striped tabby kittens were somewhere about, most likely tearing toilet paper off the roll or climbing the bedroom curtains. They were old enough now to be mostly independent and were still learning to talk. He tried to remember their names, and it took a few moments. Diego was the male, and Frieda was the female. Astrid had named them after two of her favorite artists, Diego Rivera and Frieda Kahlo. Yukiko came in through the front door and tossed her purse onto the entryway table.

"Any word on the Library?" asked Pangur Ban.

"Nothing," sighed Yukiko, dropping into a stuffed chair. "Red Fawn has asked a few people, but no luck. Julius isn't having too much success either. Elliot is good and stuck."

"I have an idea," said Huginn. "Why don't we consult with June in San Francisco? If Augustus, Julius and Red Fawn don't know anything, maybe she does."

Yukiko gave him a strange and pitying look. Pangur Ban said, "That was where Yukiko just returned from."

Huginn searched his memory, but he could not recall. “Have we asked all of the Twelve?”

“All the ones who we can trust,” said Pangur Ban.

Huginn tried to count the members of the Twelve in his mind. There was Red Fawn, who had once been called May. She ran the Chumash Legends show at the Luna Park boardwalk. Then there was Augustus who ran Luna Park but used to have a music shop in New Orleans in the nineteenth century in Hazel’s home world. His sister, September Wilde, had lived there with him and was there still. Julius owned the safe house in Los Angeles in the hub world while June had a house in San Francisco. There were others, and he strained to bring them to mind.

“I’m going to talk with Astrid again,” said Yukiko. “All she has to do is make another Door to the Library and we’re done. I don’t think she’s trying hard enough. I think she’s afraid.”

“You would be afraid too,” said Pangur Ban, “if you had to go to the Library. I don’t think she’ll be able to make a new Door, but it’s not out of fear. I’ve known Astrid since she was a child, and she’d do anything for her cousin, even at great risk to herself. Oh, it looks like someone is coming.”

Yukiko rose to look out the window, and her shadow fell across the carpet.

“What happened to your tail?” asked Huginn. Yukiko was a Kitsune, a fox spirit, and even when she was in human form, her tail cast a shadow.

He knew immediately from the look Pangur Ban and Yukiko gave him that he had said something wrong. “You’re still young,” he said, trying to be diplomatic. “You’ll get one after a century. Isn’t that the way with the Kitsune?”

“Shush, Huginn,” said Pangur Ban.

He flapped over to the back of the sofa, looking out the window. Outside sat a familiar car, the one belonging to the Coyote, Santiago. He opened the passenger door and a young blonde woman in a long skirt and shawl stepped out. Yukiko grumbled something and returned to her chair.

Something stirred in Huginn's memory at this image of a man and a woman walking together up the front walk. He held very still, watching them, waiting for the memory to come. When the girl looked up at the man, he felt a memory break loose, like a chunk of melting ice cracking and falling into the sea. The memory bobbed into consciousness, and he remembered a place in the cold North, his homeland. It had been dark for a large part of the year. He remembered a young couple walking together outside a building. Inside, celebrating people feasted, drank and sang songs in a language old and now forgotten. There was no more to the memory than that.

"What are you thinking?" asked Pangur Ban.

"I remember a festival, or a feast. There were people from long ago, from the cold North."

Pangur Ban did not say anything, but he knew she was considering what he had said. He relied on her to remember things for him, and he wondered how this piece of information might connect with others she knew.

The man and young woman entered the house without knocking, and Huginn remembered that the girl, Sister, lived there. She waved hello and then headed upstairs. The man, Santiago, glanced around, and finding only Yukiko, Pangur Ban and Huginn, he addressed Yukiko.

"You need to help Sister," he said.

"You seem to be doing a decent job of that yourself," said Yukiko. "You spend an awful lot of time with her."

"Jealous?" he said, with a sly grin.

"Hardly. I'm just worried about her. She's young, and we all know how you are with women, especially inexperienced ones. She's too attached to you."

"I'm trying to help her. The poor child lived a lifetime

in slavery. I thought you, with your rigid code of morality, would find my assistance commendable."

"I would, if you were actually helping her. Instead, she's just becoming more dependent upon you."

"I agree."

Huginn watched Yukiko as her lips parted in surprise. For Santiago to agree with her was rare. The two of them were always at odds. Huginn imagined it was because they were both canines, and were territorial. Thankfully the other people around him were not so irrational.

Santiago sighed. "Sister is struggling. She needs someone to help her survive in human society."

"I'm not human, in case you forgot," said Yukiko.

"I'd never make that mistake, Kit. But you're more human than I am."

Huginn thought that his words made no sense. Both of them were canines who lived among humans. Sure, Santiago was much older, but Yukiko, tailless as she was, was still a Kitsune.

"I told Sister that I'm leaving town for a little while," he said. "I need to make sure there's someone to look after her, who will stay with her and not leave. Will you do it?"

"I'm not planning on leaving any time soon, but why are you asking me? There are plenty of other people around."

"Yeah, an amnesiac raven, a talking cat, a pirate queen who comes and goes, a new psychopomp who will probably get sucked through one of her own death Doorways and a professor who is fascinated with digital watches. Not to mention whatever the hell Neil is."

"Felicia is human and sane. She's reliable."

"Sister doesn't need humans," he said.

"I disagree," said Pangur Ban. "The other day, Sister referred to my kittens as her littermates. And she still hasn't chosen a proper name for herself."

"See, that's exactly it," said Santiago. He then turned Yukiko. "Since you're a Kitsune, you have to concentrate to fit in with the humans. You have to consciously remember their rules and customs. That's why you can help Sister. She has to learn the rules, because she doesn't automatically know them."

Huginn was surprised at Santiago's understanding of human nature and of Yukiko's as well. Perhaps he was more insightful than he seemed.

"She needs someone to take her out shopping," said Santiago. "To learn to use money, and she needs to learn more American Sign Language, not this weird one she brought back from the Unseelie world."

"Sounds like you have this all planned out," said Yukiko. But Huginn knew that she cared about Sister. Now she was just resisting Santiago out of habit.

"I need someone I can trust," said Santiago. "You'll do it?"

Huginn then understood something. Santiago did not need to leave for a few days. He was ancient, and though he generally stayed in Southern California, sometimes heading as far east as Las Vegas or into Arizona, he was never forced to go where he did not wish to. Without admitting it, perhaps he agreed with Yukiko that Sister was becoming too attached to him. That must be why he wanted Yukiko to help Sister instead of doing it himself.

"I'll do it," said Yukiko, "for her sake. Not for yours."

"Oh, I'd never ask you for anything for myself, Kit."

CHAPTER 7

At a knock on the door, Elliot slapped his book closed. A small stack of its companions sat beside his bedroll. He wasn't supposed to take books, but since he had not removed them from the Library, he did not consider his temporary ownership of them as theft. He was not sure if Malachy agreed with his assessment, but the tortoise had not objected to his collection.

"They need us downstairs," said the woman named Imee from outside the door.

"You can come in," he said and she cracked the door.

"It's late. What do they need with us?"

"There's a delegation of Greeks. They want coffee."

"Fine, I'll be down in a little bit."

Imee disappeared. She was also a human refugee and his only friend asidc from Malachy. Elliot sighed and shoved the door closed with his foot. The small upstairs room, more of a closet really, contained his bedroll, an old-fashioned wooden milk crate, a round window looking out into the void and another one on the opposite wall that let in diffused light. The space was tiny, only slightly larger than his bedroll, but he was glad of it. There was no reason for anyone to come visit him or want to share his quarters.

He pulled a shirt and pair of pants from a pile inside the milk crate and changed, tossing his pajamas onto his bedroll. When he had first arrived, Malachy had provided him with a few changes of clothing and a bedroll, but no shoes. Servants went barefoot. It was some sort of traditional rule.

Three weeks had passed since his arrival, and feelings of déjà vu still occurred regularly, but he had learned to ignore them. He already knew he was outside of time and space. Over time, he had settled into a routine. The Library kitchens were huge, and various people came and went, but the core staff remained. He was one of them. He spent his days peeling potatoes and carrots, washing dishes and carrying the garbage to a covered hatch a few floors down that emptied into an unknown place. He thought it might drop into the void, but he wasn't sure.

Heading down the dark, narrow servants' staircase, he entered the kitchen. It was a strange anachronistic mishmash of modern equipment, like a microwave and walk-in refrigerator, and older things, like a wood-burning stove and iron pots and pans. An ancient metal coffee pot called an ibrik hung on the wall and was used with a coffee grinder that resembled a huge pepper grinder with a geometric pattern of decorative dents covering its metal surface. He took the grinder from the shelf and set it on the counter.

"They say we have fifteen people in the delegation," said Imee.

"Why do they have to come in the middle of the night?" he grumbled. But he knew the answer. The Library did have set mealtimes for visitors, but it existed outside of time. Night and day did not exist here. The humans, Elliot and Imee among them, preferred to live by a twenty-four-hour clock. Other beings, like Malachy, kept their own hours.

"How's your book?" asked Imee.

"There's nothing in it," he said, knowing she would understand. Both of them were trying to find a way out of the Library, and neither had given up hope that a way out could be discovered through exploration and research.

After spending weeks exploring every nook and cranny they could discover, and finding the Library limitless, they had turned their focus toward research. Still, in their spare time, they continued searching the corridors and rooms, opening doors and exploring hidden spots, hoping for an exit.

"Did any of the members of the delegation look promising?" Elliot asked Imee.

"I haven't seen them yet. Malachy told me to get coffee and cakes ready."

Visitors, almost all of them scholars, came from the outside world to visit and research. It was Elliot and Imee's job to cook for them and serve them in a large dining hall adjacent to the kitchen. Since these individuals returned to their homes eventually, Elliot and Imee had tried repeatedly to find a way to travel back with them. This, of course, would only work with humans, as they did not wish to be taken to the worlds of the Unseelie, Seelie or one of the various lands of the otherkind. They had asked many scholars, but all assured them that they could not go back with them. It was impossible.

Imee sniffled behind him, and Elliot wondered if she was coming down with a cold. After the third sniffle, he turned to look at her. She was crying silently and staring into the pot of boiling water.

"It's okay," he said. "We'll find a way home. The Time Corps is searching for me. I know it. And my cousin is too. I promise I'll take you with me."

Imee was from the Philippines in 1972. From their conversations about history, including the first man on the moon and dates of wars, they had concluded that they were from the same home world. That made things easier. She could simply return with him and he could take her back through time to her family.

One of the oddities of traveling between worlds was the lack of human duplicates. Imee would never find her family in any world but the one of her origin. Each individual person existed in only one world, so one could never meet one's alternate version. Duplicates simply did not exist. But some people, typically ones who were significant to history, existed in similar versions. For example, Lincoln was president in most worlds during the Civil War, but they were not the same man. Jacob Lincoln, Abraham Lincoln and Obadiah Lincoln were all elected president, while Ezekiel Lincoln had been poisoned before he became a senator.

It posed an interesting set of questions about the universes. Why were some events and personalities fixed while others were flexible? And did that imply the existence of a power controlling it all? Just as Neil could travel within ten miles of himself while the rest could not, some things were difficult to explain.

But right now, none of that mattered. Imee would not care about the intricacies of time travel. She simply wanted to get home.

Imee sniffled. "My grandma used to make coffee every morning and it just got to me, that's all."

He put his arm around her shoulders, not sure if she wanted the contact or not. She was reasonably attractive, if a few years older than he was, but Elliot could only think of her in unromantic terms. She seemed content with this arrangement, and though they spent many hours working side by side, their relationship remained platonic.

"You never asked me how I came here," she said.

"I wasn't sure you'd want to talk about it."

Any time they had broached personal topics, Imee had grown quiet and sullen, so Elliot had stopped asking. She shrugged, and he took his arm away, removing the pot from the stove. He found a cloth napkin and gave it to her to wipe her eyes and nose. Some girls looked pretty when they cried. Imee was not one of them. It made her seem even more pitiful.

"I was visiting Manila," she said. "I grew up an hour away from the city. My girlfriends and I all went to the city for a weekend trip, just for fun. There was this curio shop full of silly tourist knickknacks and we went in. I had to use the restroom, and I went to the back of the shop. When I opened the door, it was just an ordinary restroom. So I flipped on the light and closed the door, and the instant the door closed, the room changed. I was in the Library, in a room far, far upstairs from here. And right next to me was a door, right where the restroom door had just been. I have checked that door over and over, hoping it would open to the curio shop. But it never does."

Elliot put together trays of food and brewed the coffee while Imee patted a cold, wet cloth on her eyes. They served the Greek delegation in the dining hall, Imee bringing trays of cakes and Elliot pouring steaming cups of coffee for all of them. He listened in on their conversation as he worked.

Most of today's scholars were so ordinary looking they would not merit a second glance from anyone in Elliot's world. Some could easily hide their physical differences, if they so chose. At the end of one table sat a small man with a forked serpent tongue, conversing with a woman with a third eye at the base of her throat. She closed it and pulled a gauzy green silk scarf over it when she caught Elliot watching her. Other non-human scholars were easier to spot, like the gray-skinned girl in a giant feathered hat and tailored purple suit who ate six little cakes within the first five minutes. Elliot served each person, listening to everything.

Imee and Elliot continued for two more weeks, exploring, reading and listening. But every time they found a new area of the Library or a promising book, they came up empty.

One day, Imee stood alone beside him in the kitchen, chopping leeks and singing softly under her breath in

Tagalog. Elliot understood the words, as all languages were comprehensible in the Library. It was a cheery song about a bird.

"Malachy said I'm to go to the market tomorrow," she said, smiling. "I'm supposed to do more of the meal planning."

"Well, congratulations," he said, not knowing how else to respond. If she wanted to make the best of her situation, taking on additional responsibility and finding some joy in it, then who was he to rain on her parade? "I hope you'll enjoy it."

"You're dumb sometimes," she said. "I don't care about the shopping, though it will be nice to get out of this building now and then. See, there's a passageway. That's where most of the scholars enter, at the end of the bazaar. I've heard them talking."

"And you think you can get through?"

"I won't go without you," she said. "I'll just take a look. I'll see how it works."

Elliot was skeptical, but any new idea was a good idea. He hadn't learned anything new in weeks, and if the row of market stalls held some secret, he was as eager as Imee was to discover it.

The morning of market day, Imee entered the kitchen with a wide-brimmed straw hat and an old, hand-pulled rolling cart. One of the other kitchen staff, a boy who had been raised in the Library, washed cups at the sink. They could not talk about the market in front of him, and Imee adjusted her hat and grabbed the handle of her cart, giving Elliot a wink. He went about the day, serving, cleaning and listening with a lighter heart.

After his duties were completed and he lay on his bedroll, reading by the light of the alabaster window, there came a knock at his door. He jumped up and yanked open the door, eager to talk with Imee and discover everything she had learned. But instead, Malachy blinked up at him.

"I had a friend, a man, like you," Malachy said. "He came to the Library after I did. And he wanted to get out, to return to his wife. I told him that he could have a good life here. I have lived here many years in contentment. But he would not be satisfied. He went to the marketplace one day, to the very end. And I never saw him again."

"What happened to him?"

"He was gone. He did not come back. You can have a good life here, Elliot. You too can be content."

"I want to go home. You know that."

Malachy looked past Elliot, toward the small round window facing out into the void. Elliot tried not to look through that window, as it pulled at his mind in an uncomfortable way.

"You need to understand," said Malachy, "this place is not like other places. Like water flowing downhill, all information flows to the Library eventually."

"I'm not concerned with that. Tell me what happened to Imee." But Elliot's insides twisted. He already knew.

"The market day job is now yours."

CHAPTER 8

"IS THERE ANYWHERE WE CAN go where we won't be observed?" Gopan asked Astrid. "I need to make a Door."

Astrid took him to an empty hallway near the boardwalk staff lounge. He created a Door, identical in appearance to the Door to death, but instead of a mirrored surface in the center, Astrid saw an alley, complete with a trash dumpster with a dark, fetid puddle spreading beneath it. Without asking her permission, Gopan grabbed her hand and pulled her through.

"It's better to come through in an alley or back room, where we're not noticed," he said. "We can pop in and out among people, and for the most part they don't notice. But this way guarantees we won't startle them."

"What happens if they see us when we come through a Door?"

"Nothing. They just see us, but generally don't notice anything amiss. It's similar to the way we can understand any language. We get some protections when we're on the job."

He led her down the street, and they stopped in front of a bookshop, complete with a swinging wooden sign overhead depicting an open book with old-fashioned letters spelling out "Marginalia." The wooden window frames were old and cracked, but the glass was clean. The window display included some newer books as well as older, more tattered volumes.

"This is Jeff's shop. It's all used books, but no truly valuable antiquities. Mainly old paperbacks, Reader's Digests, Encyclopedias. No one comes here, for the most part."

"Then how does he make money?"

"He does a decent business selling used books online. And he does get a few customers in person." He checked his watch. "We have a few minutes until the others get here. Everyone will be happy to meet you. It's not often we get a new member."

"Do you only get a new psychopomp when an old one dies?"

Gopan gave her an assessing look. "God, it's not anything morbid like that. We do die, after a while. But we retire at age seventy, so typically we don't die while we're still working. No, you just happen to have come of age, and you get to join our merry band."

Astrid thought of what death meant for a psychopomp, to travel through that mirrored Door, to see what was on the other side. She was curious to know. Where exactly did they send the sticky souls? What waited beyond?

Gopan opened the door, an old-fashioned one with dark green paint and square panes of glass on the top half. A little brass bell rang overhead and Gopan called out Jeff's name. The shop was small and cramped, smelling of dust and old books with volumes crammed into every space, piled on top of the shelves and teetering in uneven stacks on the floor. Yellowing handwritten cards identified each aisle as Romance, Science Fiction/Fantasy, Reference, Biography and others.

"The shop's empty," called a man's voice. "It's just us."

A bearded, middle-aged man appeared from between the bookshelves. Curly brown hair surrounded a round, thoughtful face that lit up at the sight of her. His eyes were magnified by his glasses and she saw him look her up and down. Oddly, she was not offended. She sensed that he was just trying to learn about her, not make any sort of judgment. She still wore her Luna Park uniform, and her hair was too long to be neat and too short for her to pull it into a ponytail.

"I'm Jeff," he said, and held out his hand. She shook it.

"Astrid."

"Come on in. I have doughnuts in the back."

A room at the back of the shop contained an old table with five metal folding chairs surrounding it. At the center of the table sat a pink cardboard box held closed with a piece of scotch tape. A coffee pot gurgled on the counter as it brewed. Gopan pulled open the pink box, selected a rainbow sprinkled doughnut and turned the box toward her.

"Graciela and Robin both like the bear claws, so we leave those for them."

"Tell me what Gopan has told you so far about being a psychopomp," said Jeff, taking a glazed doughnut.

Astrid took an apple fritter, poured a cup of coffee and took a seat opposite from Jeff. It felt strange that something like a Door into death was discussed like any ordinary thing, as if being a psychopomp was similar to joining a book club. These people were like her. They were Doors. They could understand what she felt and thought and could answer her questions. These were her people.

She told Jeff what she knew, leaving out how she was Unseelie and had opened Doors between the human and sidhe worlds. He seemed pleased with what Gopan had told her and nodded to the boy, who took another doughnut and smiled.

A minute later, a slender woman came in. Graciela looked like she was in her early thirties and when she embraced Astrid, she smelled of expensive perfume. She wore tight jeans, high-heeled shoes and lots of jewelry. She was not bookish like Jeff or slightly odd like Gopan, nor was she gloomy or strange, the way Astrid would have imagined someone associated with death. She pulled out her phone when it dinged to report an incoming text and told the group that Robin was on his way.

Graciela told Astrid she was from Argentina and worked in a clothing boutique, though she did a little modeling on the side. Astrid felt conscious of her ugly uniform, her scruffy hair and old shoes. Even dressed up, she'd never look like Graciela.

Robin, a black man in his forties, arrived, and as he entered he received an enthusiastic hug from Graciela and then took a seat beside her. The meeting, if you could call it that, was nothing more than a chat session, with Robin and Graciela engaging in a few side conversations of their own while Jeff and Gopan filled in some of the holes in Astrid's knowledge.

They were the only five active psychopomps on earth, Jeff told her, and one was born about every decade, give or take. They became Doors around the time of adulthood, which in modern culture was around age eighteen, though it was earlier in previous centuries. When a sticky soul needed an escort to the afterlife, one of the psychopomps felt a tug inside, which all of them insisted that Astrid would not mistake for anything else. He or she would then make a Door, walk through to the soul, escort it through the mirrored Door into the afterlife, and then make another Door to return home.

"There's no pay involved," said Jeff. "But we save on airfare, as long as we can hide our Doormaking from others. All of us have regular jobs, but you have to find one that lets you leave at a moment's notice. Most of our jobs only take a few minutes, so you can escort a soul during a coffee break.

"Or a bathroom break," said Robin. "You make a Door in a bathroom stall, make a Door, help the soul, then return to your job."

"What makes the souls pull us?" Astrid asked. "And what's beyond the Door? Is it heaven?"

Gopan slowed his chewing and watched Jeff.

"None of us know, and that's the truth," said Jeff. "None of us have gone through a Door to death, as we wouldn't ever come back. And I have very limited contact with the higher-ups."

"Who are they? The higher-ups?"

"Well, there's only one I talk to regularly. And he's not a higher-up really, so much as one of us, but retired and very old. So occasionally I'll consult with him, but he's shy and doesn't meet with everyone together. We're a naturally occurring phenomenon, and as such, we operate more by natural laws than by hierarchical ones."

Astrid would have to think that over. Doors, she knew, were born. They were people. But a Door could also open on its own. She had heard of people who had stepped through Doorways that were not made by any living thing. They simply appeared. And then there were Doors made by technology, as in the case of the Professor's time machines that ripped holes between places, times and worlds. Three types of Doors, each different.

"Can our Doors go through time?" Astrid asked.

Jeff looked displeased, but only for an instant. Astrid thought he might be the sort of person who could not hide his emotions well, which would be useful. She wanted more information than instructions on being a proper psychopomp. She wanted to get Elliot out of the Library, and it supposedly existed outside of time.

"No. Our Doors are only in our own time. We live just as ordinary people do, one day after the other," said Jeff. "And we can be killed just as easily as everyone else. We've lost people to pneumonia, influenza and car crashes."

"Can we marry and have children and everything?"

"Sure. We're just like everyone else. We just have an extra duty to humanity."

"It's nighttime back home," said Gopan, checking his watch. "I need to be going."

"I'll see her home," said Jeff, and Astrid was glad that she didn't have to figure out how to make a Door to Los Angeles on her own.

Everyone made sure they had Astrid's phone number and she entered all of theirs into her phone, adding a note on the time differences in their home countries.

Graciela and Robin gave her a hug, then left together. Gopan simply said good-bye, not offering to shake her hand. Once they were gone, Jeff cleaned up the coffee and doughnuts.

"Robin and Graciela are a lot alike," said Jeff. "There's no romance between them, if you got that idea. They're just twin souls, in a way."

He handed her the pink doughnut box and told her that she should take them home.

"You're skinnier than I am," he said. "And I bet you have more questions. So now is the time. Ask anything."

"I want to know about aspects."

"I won't tell you mine. But I'll help you with yours, once you get it, and if you choose to reveal it to me. It should come any time now."

She thought of asking Robin's and Graciela's aspects, but decided against it.

"Why are you the boss?" she asked. "Do you give us orders or anything?"

"I'm only in charge, nominally, because I'm the oldest. When I retire, then Gopan will be the leader. I'm just like the rest of you in my abilities and knowledge. I'll coordinate your training, help you along. You'll train with each of us, so someone will be with you for all of your early jobs until you know what you're doing. All of us have something to contribute, and don't discount Graciela because she's the youngest. She has things to teach too. We each approach the job in different ways, and your way will be unique to you."

Astrid tossed out the used coffee cups, not sure how to ask him about finding a way to the Library.

"I have a question for you," said Jeff. "You're Unseelie, I know that. And I know you've been to the void. I'd recommend not going back. It's very dangerous."

"I liked the void. It was comfortable. Like coming home after a long day."

"I know. Being what we are, that only makes sense. The void is part of our nature, a thread among many in our being. But don't go there again. There are things there, void wyrms, and they'll kill you. Don't ever take people through your Doors either, unless they're sending them to death. It destabilizes things. Now, when we're on the job, we can pull threads in people's minds and touch their thoughts. That's fine, but whatever you do, never use other people's minds as passageways again."

"How did you know I had done that?" She had once used many minds to find her way back from the void.

"The old one I talked to. He can feel things we can't."

"He's not human either, is he?" she asked.

"I doubt it. But the thing you need to know is this: You can destroy people. Their minds are delicate and strong at the same time. Some pieces are more fragile than others, and when you travel through, you can bump those pieces and unbalance someone."

"They'd go insane?"

"Maybe. Or a personality change, a violent outburst, anything. Or it could also give them a brilliant idea for an invention, reform a criminal, cure an addict. There's no way to tell. Just stay out of minds."

He wiped down the table, cleaning up crumbs and coffee circles.

"You don't know me, so you probably don't trust me," he continued. "And from what I've heard of your home life, the human home life, I'm surprised you're doing as well as you are. But I can help you. We all can. Once in a while, there will be a bad psychopomp, one who won't do his duty or who is just a jerk. This is a good group, a stable group. Now, with that said, I know you come with some baggage with the Seelie."

"They're angry with me because I sent my cousin to the Library instead of death," she said, hoping that Jeff truly was trustworthy. They were family, in a sense, and she could use all the help she could get. Heaven knew that the Time Corps had not been very helpful in saving Elliot. A little stab of anger gnawed at her at their incompetence, followed by remorse. They were only trying to undo her act, after all.

"And that's what I wanted to discuss," said Jeff. "Our higher-up negotiated as best he could, and instead of having to turn you over to the Seelie, or be in their service for three full moons or whatever crazy thing they dream up, you have to perform three tasks for them. Then your debt will be paid."

"That sounds like something out of a fairy tale."

"I think there's a reason for that. They're unpredictable and erratic, but in some ways they're more hidebound than anyone. Besides that, the Seelie are bad people to be beholden to. On their own, they're a pain, but it's those among them who are sympathetic to the Unseelie that really worry me. Those people would gladly force you to open a Door to Unseelie to free their separated brethren. Part of the negotiations involved not forcing you to open a Door into or out of the Seelie or Unseelie worlds. I wish you hadn't gotten into trouble with them at all, but what's done is done. So do your three tasks and be done with them forever."

"Did this higher-up say anything about the Library?"

"There's nothing you can do for your cousin. Now, I like books, but not even I would venture into the Library."

"But there's nothing stopping me from making a Door to the Library aside from my inexperience. Once I learn, I could do it. It's possible, right?"

He sighed. "I'm not your boss, and I have no power to force you to do anything. But if you went to the Library, then you could no longer be summoned to escort souls. And that affects our work, so it involves me. The soul would suffer and it would upset the balance of life and death. It's serious.

"And that reminds me of another thing. From what I understand, a while back you opened Doors to the Seelie world in your sleep. I heard that a few slaugh came through."

"My cat killed them." Astrid didn't mention that her cat could also speak and was a member of the Time Corps. "It hasn't happened again."

"Good. I suspect that's because you're growing into your position. Our abilities are natural, like breathing, and once you can control them, you should have no problems with unintentional Doors. Now, it's time to get you home. Let's have your first lesson, making a simple Door."

For the next quarter of an hour, they worked at the back of the shop until Astrid could reliably open a Door to the backyard at the Time Corps house. Jeff handed her the doughnut box and came with her through the Door, wanting to see where she lived, in case he needed to come visit her.

"Ah, Los Angeles," he said. "It feels different here. Can you tell?"

Astrid said she couldn't.

"Maybe that comes with age and experience. Or maybe it's because you grew up here. It's a funny place, unstable. Did you ever wonder why there are no subways here?"

"We have a few. I suppose we don't have more because an earthquake would collapse the tunnels."

"Earthquakes are a reason but also a symptom. It's

because things can live in tunnels, catacombs, subways. It would be a city beneath a city. Like it is in London, Paris and Rome."

She thought of New York, where she'd go to art school, and its extensive network of subways. Jeff stuck his hands in his pockets and looked up at the sky.

"This place, the City of Angels, was created without an underground. It's a failsafe, of sorts. It forces things into the light. But it's not foolproof, for evil has its illusions, and this city, of all in the New World, is the city of illusions and make-believe. There's one thing you need to know." He turned and looked straight at her. "We're on the good side. Death isn't evil, it's natural. It's unfair sometimes, but natural. Imagine the opposite, if everyone lived forever. That would be the truly terrible thing. Or if sticky souls stayed here, going mad, tormenting the living. We are the last people they see before they pass to the afterlife. Our job is sacred and we take it seriously. I want you to understand that about us. About yourself. We're with the good guys."

He said good-bye, made a Door back to his bookshop and was gone. As Astrid carried the doughnuts into the kitchen, she realized that Jeff hadn't questioned her about the worlds of the sidhe, her Unseelie family or anything else aside from the minimum he needed to know to keep his group safe and functional.

She still didn't know if she could trust any of the psychopomps, though she very much wanted to. They must have their agendas, their needs and goals, just like anyone else. They were people, just as she was, hopefully decent and good-hearted. They were as ordinary as anyone. But what had she expected? Of course death was as familiar as the face of an old friend.

CHAPTER 9

HAZEL FOLLOWED NEIL AS HE descended below decks to check their cargo of fancy mead. They were approaching the small Mexican coastal town where, with luck, their trade would go smoothly. The deal was unrelated to helping Elliot, but Hazel owed the recipients a favor, and tried to keep the goodwill of the few people she knew in various times. After dropping off the mead, they would sail up the coast, using the time machine to travel to the early twenty-first century, where they would arrive at the Time Corps house in Los Angeles.

At the bottom of the cargo hold steps, Neil turned to her and stopped abruptly, causing her to bump into him in the dark. Her eyes had not adjusted to the lack of light, but she could see him looking down at her.

"What? What's the matter?" she asked, stepping back so she didn't have to crane her neck to look at him.

"I need to ask you something." He paused and looked over her shoulder, at the steps.

"What is it?" she whispered. "Is it something with the crew?"

She saw him shake his head in the dark, and now that her eyes were adjusting, she could see that he was watching her.

"Remember back at the safe house? When you first came to this time?" he said.

She did. She remembered the first meeting of the Time Corps, five years ago by her personal timeline. She and

Neil had eaten vanilla ice cream and Neil had kissed her. Then he had taken her for a driving lesson. It had been a disaster, albeit an exciting one. Then Neil had gone his way and she had gone hers, spending five years meeting him in various times and doing jobs for the Time Corps. Once she learned that Elliot had disappeared, she and this older version of Neil had joined up.

She wondered why he came now in his timeline, in his forties, instead of earlier, but knew better than to ask. Since that kiss, he had been distant, as if he knew something she didn't. Undoubtedly, he did. That was the way of asynchronous friendships. He never made another romantic overture again. She accepted that the kiss was a lapse on his part and that they would remain as close friends. The thought still stung though, even after all this time.

"How—" then he spun around toward the cargo hold and Hazel saw what he must have heard. It was a man, emerging from the darkness. The entire crew was made up of capuchin monkeys, so there was no mistaking an intruder. They were still miles from shore, which meant this person was a stowaway. How long had he been on board?

"My Emmett," said the man to Neil, and came closer. He was dark-haired with grey at the temples and his eyes were a pale gray blue. He couldn't be a stowaway, as they had been at sea for days and his slacks were crisply creased and she could detect the fresh tang of his cologne.

Neil was motionless, and Hazel wondered why this man was calling him by a strange name.

"I'm Captain Dubois," she said, inserting herself between the man and Neil. "Who are you and why are you on my ship?"

The man ignored her, his gaze fixed on Neil. "You failed me," he said, so quietly that Hazel almost missed it. Neil would have heard it clearly, as his senses were far more keen than her own.

She heard rather than saw Neil's physical struggle. It started with him taking a breath, and as the man approached, she knew that she had never heard the sound before. It wasn't that he didn't breathe, but he was such a silent person, moving about the world without drawing the slightest attention. The next moment, as she heard him exhale a ragged breath, she knew what was happening. Neil was resisting the man.

"You leave him alone!" she cried. The man reached for Neil, who stood immobilized, and Hazel drew her pistol. It was an older weapon, an antique in this time, though by its own timeline it was only a few years old. Neil had taught her to shoot with it during the Civil War, and she was more comfortable with it than with newer weapons. She pulled back the hammer.

"Stop there, or I'll kill you again," she said. She had not recognized him, but now there was no mistaking who he was. This was Mr. March, formerly Neil's boss, and a being who could control Neil's actions, when he so chose.

March looked at her from his new face, handsome, yet severe. The light from the overhead hatch let her see a tiny scar bisecting his cheek. The last time she had seen him, he was lying dead at her feet, a thin, older man with very fair skin and light hair. Mr. March was one of the Twelve, and now she understood why his siblings, September Wilde and Julius, had not been too upset about March's death. He could return from the dead.

"The bullet will not reach me, you understand," said March, never taking his eyes off Neil.

What he said was true. March had the ability to create warrens in space and time, some of them just large enough to redirect a bullet. She had seen it happen before.

"Why are you here?" she asked. "Leave Neil alone. He hasn't done a thing to you."

Mr. March placed his hands on either side of Neil's face, as gentle as a father caressing an infant. Neil opened his mouth, and Mr. March murmured, "I love you." He kissed his forehead.

Before Hazel could do anything else, Mr. March rubbed his thumb along the roof of Neil's mouth three times and turned away. He blinked once, and Hazel saw tears shining in his eyes. He took a step away, and then was gone, vanishing through one of his warrens.

Neil hadn't moved, and Hazel holstered her weapon and grasped his hand, but his skin turned rough and cold.

"Neil!" she cried and touched his face. Why hadn't he started to move again? Why was he simply staring into space? His face became coarse under her palm and she grabbed his shoulder, which was hardened beneath his shirt.

What had Mr. March done to him? His eyes lost their luster, and as she watched, his features crumbled inward, just slightly, becoming rough and as still as death. Only his clothing remained soft.

He teetered sideways, and she threw her arms around him to hold him up, planting her feet and leveraging her weight to keep him upright. But his bulk was too much and he fell backward and to one side, crashing to the floorboards with a sickening explosion of dust, pulling Hazel to the ground with him. She blinked through the dust, her mouth filling with the ashlike grit as she knelt and tried to make sense of the shape before her.

The light from the hatch illuminated him completely now, his face a frozen mask of death, his mouth slightly open, exposing teeth like tiny headstones. His nose was nothing more than a nub, his eyeballs blank stone globes in their sockets, sightless, his entire body transformed into hardened earth.

CHAPTER 10

"THERE'S A MAN IN OUR backyard," Pangur Ban said. The cat sat on the bedroom windowsill, and Astrid stroked her as she looked down into the yard. No one else ever petted Pangur Ban, but the cat had been Astrid's friend and wordless companion through much of her childhood. And as the cat had never objected to being touched, Astrid had continued their old familiar practice, even after discovering that her pet cat was a sentient being.

"That was quick," Astrid said. "That's Jeff, the head psychopomp."

"Interesting," said Pangur Ban, but did not elaborate.

Astrid headed downstairs and out back, passing the living room where Pangur Ban's kittens, Frieda and Diego, watched a children's movie. As close as she could tell, they seemed to be about the equivalent of preschoolers in their understanding and verbal abilities. Sister sat to one side, looking through a children's book. Huggin perched on the back of her chair, teaching her to read. His memory might be shot, but his intelligence never failed him.

"I'll be out for a few hours," Astrid called, and Sister raised a hand, one thumb up, in acknowledgment.

"Ready to go?" asked Jeff when she emerged.

Without waiting for a reply, he created a Door, one tall enough for both of them to step through comfortably. In the center, she saw a middle-class living room with cream carpet and high, bright windows.

"We need to go quickly," said Jeff. "I want to be able to grab lunch before I go back to the shop."

Astrid stepped through the Door after him into the living room of an American tract home. Bland paintings of flowers hung on the ecru walls beside antiqued wooden wall hangings with the words "Love" and "Laugh." Framed family pictures, some of them in black and white, crowded for space on the mantle and the cinnamon scent of store-bought air freshener hung in the air. The place was both cloyingly artificial and homey at the same time.

"I'd like to start you on an easier one, some elderly person," said Jeff. "But this looks like a young couple's home."

"Is the person already dead?" Astrid whispered.

"You don't have to be quiet. Even if there are people here, they won't see or hear us. We don't even leave DNA evidence, which is darn handy when there's a murder. When we're on the job, most of the time, we're undetectable."

"Most of the time?"

"If we want to be seen, we can. And animals and very young children sometimes see us. That's where Gopan has an advantage, because he's little and cute. And to answer your question, the person will be dead or dying within a few minutes. We try to get here quickly, or the soul lingers and gets frightened."

They entered the kitchen and Astrid stopped. "They have a high chair. It's not the baby, is it?"

"I hope not," said Jeff and, after making a quick circuit of the deserted downstairs area, they climbed the stairs.

Jeff looked through the master bedroom door before Astrid did, and he put his body in between her and the doorway.

"This might be rough for you," he said. "But we'll do it together, okay?"

"Oh God, it's the baby."

"No. It's the mother."

Astrid looked into the room where a woman was lying down on the blue and white floral bedspread. She was in her late twenties with a brown ponytail and nicely pedicured bare feet.

"Is she dead?"

"She will be soon."

"But she looks healthy. How will she die?"

"No way to tell. Heart attack, aneurysm, stroke, the ceiling could collapse, a poisonous spider could crawl across her pillow."

"Can't we help her?" she asked.

"There's nothing we can do. She can't see us yet, and if we tried to grab her or talk to her, she'd be frightened. Also, she'd die either way."

An instant later, the woman rose and stood beside the bed, watching them. Astrid suddenly felt very much like an intruder, standing in this woman's home, watching her as she lay on the bed and simultaneously stood beside herself. Then she saw it, the Door. Fog swirled and then parted in front of the master bathroom entrance, leaving the mirrorlike Doorway in the center. Astrid knew she had made that Door, and now she had to convince the soul to go through it.

Jeff stepped just behind her, close enough to speak quietly into her ear. "She sees the body," he whispered. The woman looked at herself on the bed. "Notice how her spirit looks younger than the body. That's valuable information for you. But also see how she's not as pretty as her real version. Perhaps that's also useful."

Astrid didn't see how this could be important.

"Now look around the room," he said. "See the photos? Also, did you notice the family photos downstairs? She's connected to her family."

A baby cried from a room nearby and the woman raised her head and rushed out of the room, brushing past Astrid and Jeff with a gust of icy air.

"Why doesn't she see us?"

"She does and doesn't, it seems. She saw us clearly that first moment, but now she doesn't. That's also a useful piece of information. It means she's reluctant to go, not acknowledging that death has come for her. All of these pieces of information let us help the soul, they're threads in a tapestry, making a picture for us."

They followed the woman into the baby's room, a confection of pink and lace, with bins full of blocks and stuffed toys. A little girl, about a year and a half old, stood in the crib, holding her arms up to her mother.

"The baby sees her," said Astrid. "She can see her mommy."

She felt Jeff's hand on her shoulder, giving her a reassuring squeeze. "This is a tough one. I'd have rather taken you to escort an old, sick person. But by definition, none of the souls we encounter want to go. An old person can hang onto life just as tightly as a young one."

The mother tried to lift her child, only to have her arms pass through the little girl's body. The baby wailed and shook the crib railing.

"First, move the Door in here," said Jeff.

Astrid had moved Doors before, but she had been in fear for her life at the time. This time, she found it easier, and the Door materialized in front of the child's closet door.

"Do Doors always form in front of other doors? The last one was in front of the master bathroom."

"Good observation. They don't have to, but like attracts like, and since you envision them similarly, it's not surprising. You can move them any time you want. But look, the woman sees us again."

She spun toward them so quickly that Astrid felt a stab of terror as the woman's eyes met hers. She was looking into the eyes of a ghost, a dead person, while her corpse lay in the other room.

"What are you doing in my house?" The woman came toward them. "You get out of here!" Astrid leapt back, banging into Jeff, who pulled her aside as the woman charged forward.

"She can't hurt you," he said. "But she's a mother and we're in her territory."

"Wait!" Astrid said, as the woman glared at her, looking like she wanted to do violence. "We're here to help you. Your arms went though the baby. You saw your body. Remember that."

The woman looked down at her hands, which, to Astrid, appeared solid. The baby watched from the crib, eyes round.

"I'm sorry, but you're dead," Astrid said.

"Not the most poetic, but effective," muttered Jeff.

"Oh, come on," Astrid muttered. "I'm doing the best I can."

"Now comes the tricky part," said Jeff. "Think about her mind, see it as a series of strings, all woven together, and see if you can touch one."

"Why?"

"You're going to convince her to go through the Door by using her own thoughts. Remember the pictures? She is a family-oriented person. That makes her a pretty easy case. It means she has loved ones who are dead, and she feels attachment to them. Use that."

Astrid reached out, imagining the woman's mind. It wasn't as hard as she would have guessed. She felt the woman's interior landscape.

"I'm dead?" said the woman.

"Yes," said Astrid. "And now you have to go to ... to the next place."

She hesitated to use the word "heaven," worrying that it might be a lie.

"No," said the woman. "No, I have things to do here. I have Krystal and Mike and tomorrow is my Zumba class."

Astrid took a step toward her, slowly, as if approaching a feral animal. "See that Door?" she said, indicating the swirling fog and gently undulating mirror, reflecting the pink and white of the room back at them. "That's where your family is. They're waiting. You can't stay here."

"But Krystal," she said, looking at the baby.

"You can't be with her any more. Your body is dead."

"I can still stay! She can see me!" the woman cried, and Astrid considered touching her, to try to ease her pain, but she did not. The woman approached the crib and looked down at her little girl.

"She won't see you forever," said Astrid. "When she's older, she won't see you at all."

"I'm not going! She needs me."

When her mother drew near, Krystal raised her arms again, making a little sound.

"Reach into her mind," Jeff said. "It won't be a specific memory. It'll just feel like a certain thread is stronger than the others. That's the one you're going for. The powerful one."

Astrid obeyed, feeling gently until she detected a stronger thought. Then she pulled and the woman turned toward the Door.

"Mom?" she said.

Astrid looked, but saw no one.

"She heard her mother's voice," said Jeff.

"She's waiting for you," said Astrid. "She's waited a long time to see you."

She had no idea if this last bit was true, but Gopan had said something similar to the man on the boardwalk. The woman looked from the Door to the baby. Astrid reached in and pulled the thread in her mind again, then searched and found two other strong ones and pulled those as well.

The woman moved toward the Door, listening to whatever voices from her past beckoned. Little Krystal's face crumpled into a scowl and she looked like she was about to cry. Jeff slipped over to her and distracted her by making his hand into a makeshift puppet and talking softly to her while Astrid pulled another thread in the woman's mind.

Slowly, the woman moved toward the Door, and at the last instant, her face grew joyful, and the years fell away from her, leaving her a young woman of about twenty, her face radiant with absolute joy. She stepped through the Door, which then contracted and vanished.

"Not bad," said Jeff. "I typically pull one thread at a time, but your method is effective too, if a bit crude."

"You make it sound like I'm a big brute. I tried to be gentle."

"Don't worry about it. We all have different approaches, and as long as the soul goes through the Door unharmed, we've done our job. Oh, and if you ever need to know, you can physically force a soul through. Hopefully none of your early jobs will involve that. But you can do it. You're strong enough and they can't hurt you."

Krystal looked from Jeff to Astrid and back again, then screwed up her face and screamed.

"Let's be on our way. No need to leave any weird memories with the child." He headed down the hall.

"We can't leave her home alone. Who will take care of her?"

"The woman is married, and I'm sure the man will be home in a few hours. The baby might get hungry, but she'll be all right."

"Is it bad for her to see her mother die?"

"She won't remember. And she came into the world fairly recently. Not so different, really."

"Are there Doors to—to wherever baby souls come from?"

"Not my department. I think they just show up. But who knows? There might be spirit midwives somewhere out there."

"That sounds better than what we do."

Jeff was partway down the stairs but he turned toward her, lifting a finger. "Now don't think like that. We're not bad or evil or dark. We don't wear black and harvest souls for Satan or anything like that. We help souls go where they're supposed to."

"Fine, but what would have happened if we couldn't get that woman to go through the Door?"

"She'd have hung around the house for a while, maybe a few years, maybe a decade or two. She'd be able to visit with her daughter for a little while, sit in the same room, follow her. But eventually, the girl would grow up and would lose the ability to see her. Then, the mother would go gradually insane. Watching her husband date and her daughter live without her wouldn't cause it. Being in the world of the living would do it. It would be bad."

"How did she die? Is there any way we'll know?"

"Not without an autopsy. She was lying down beforehand, which meant she probably felt unwell. If you want to try to figure out what killed her, you can, but it's best to just move on. Knowing the cause of death doesn't make this easier."

"Was all that stuff true? Is her family waiting for her?"

"That I don't know. There's something on the other side. That we can be sure of, or there wouldn't be a Door. If no one had a soul or if souls blinked out of existence at death, then there'd be no need of us. As to what's on the other side, your guess is as good as mine."

CHAPTER 11

"THERE'S NOTHING!" SNAPPED HAZEL, SLIDING her chair back. "Not in this time or any of the others I've checked."

"Your websites and files do not hold the collective knowledge of the ages," said Mr. Escobar, her first mate. "Perhaps you should check other sources, other people."

They sat together in her quarters, Hazel at her desk and Mr. Escobar on the shelf above her, perched between the Global Positioning Satellite device on one side and a brass sextant and glass-faced compass on the other. Nearby sat a stack of books, a few interestingly shaped shells and an old mechanical toy jackal with green jewel eyes. Various navigational devices both ancient, modern and, to Hazel's way of thinking, futuristic, crowded her shelves. All of them were useless to her right now.

In a cargo crate against one wall lay Neil's body. His clothing was still intact, but the outer layer of his skin was crumbling. Beneath the surface, he seemed to be solid stone, though Hazel hesitated to do anything more than scratch him lightly with her penknife. The crew had wrapped him in canvas and laid him in straw, carrying him to Hazel's quarters at her insistence.

She had managed not to cry in front of the crew, and thought once they were gone, she would give in to her emotions. But instead of feeling grief, she had experienced a dark determination. Killing Mr. March again would be so very gratifying. Oh yes. It would. But the act would be useless. Instead of hunting him, her time was better spent discovering what Neil was and how to bring him back. It gave her something more important to engage her thoughts than mourning. He didn't have to stay dead. This world, the hub world, was filled with strange beings and rules that did not exist in her home world which was ruled by science. If March could come back from death, perhaps Neil could as well.

"I haven't just been looking online," she told Mr. Escobar. "I've e-mailed a number of people. Iceland, Wales, Botswana, Paraguay. Anyone I thought might know something."

"And the Twelve?"

"We'll be in Los Angeles this afternoon. Julius is my best hope."

"Because he is a learned man?"

"Yes. If he doesn't know, perhaps he knows someone else who does."

Hazel would talk to the Twelve, to Santiago, Yukiko, Astrid, any and every weird being she could find. Someone would know what could turn a man to stone. Someone would know what the strange lettering on the roof of his mouth meant.

She reset the settings on the temporal uplink that the Professor had installed on her computer. It allowed her to receive signals through time or when she was out of typical wireless range. Depending on what time she was in, the device could be incredibly useful. Like she had done so many times before, she searched the net for images of letters from various languages. There were so many from so many cultures through so many times. But who was to say that the letters in his mouth were even in a human language?

Mr. Escobar hopped lightly onto the desk and touched her arm. "We will help him," he said. "And if he is permanently deceased, we will give him a fine burial at sea."

CHAPTER 12

THE LIBRARY CONTAINED THE COLLECTED wisdom of the ages, which was useful if one knew where to look for it.

After all this time, Elliot still did not.

Imee was gone, dead if Malachy was to be believed. Elliot didn't think the tortoise was lying, but he might be mistaken. Without a body, Elliot clung to hope.

He pulled his rolling cart through the enormous iron library gate and toward the long stone-paved street that ran the length of the marketplace. The row of booths somehow attached to the Library at specific times, allowing goods and people to come through in both directions. Elliot wasn't privy to the schedule. Malachy had told him to go to the market, and he went, without money but with the assurance that anything he purchased would be paid for by the Library.

People of all sorts crowded the marketplace, some pushing and haggling loudly while others glided silently through, pointing at items and slowly removing coins from concealed locations on their persons. Clothing varied from gauzy robes to canvas pants, long, fur-lined coats to nothing much at all.

The first stall at the edge of the marketplace sold glass vessels in sizes ranging from giant bowls, large enough to hold bathwater, to vials tiny enough to fit inside a locket. They glittered cobalt blue, blood red and grass green in the light, some of them dangling from strings, swinging in the breeze. A nearby vendor sold rugs, another, exotic fruit. Elliot paused and consulted his list. Yes, he'd need more fruit than usual. A group of twelve scholars was scheduled for arrival that evening, all of them subsisting solely on a diet of fruits, vegetables and fermented liquids. He wouldn't purchase anything just yet though. He had more important work to do.

Looking up past the long corridor of stalls, he studied a low mountain range in the distance, misty and indistinct. There was a world outside of the Library, and this street through the marketplace was a pathway to get there.

He dragged his empty cart along, crunching over a pile of spilled nuts and bumping past shoppers. He passed a bookseller, a fruit juice stand, a shop filled with colorful knit hats, a dress vendor and a pair of brothers selling wooden musical instruments. Hazel, who loved music, would have liked that stall, while his cousin Astrid would have enjoyed the collection of tiny sketches on flat stones at another booth. Neil would have stopped to listen to the man playing a whistling tune on an ocarina, and the booth full of tiny clockworks would have fascinated the Professor. He wished they were there with him.

But his friends had failed him. Astrid hadn't created a Door and Neil hadn't arrived with a time machine. Out of all of the members of the Time Corps, not one had come. He knew they were trying, that he wasn't abandoned, but why was it taking so long? Well, he wouldn't sit idly by. He would take events into his own hands. If he had to get himself out, then so be it. He was no helpless princess locked in a tower.

The booths flashed by as he hurried, eager to find the doorway or ship or whatever waited at the end. Malachy had told him that Imee had simply gone to the end of the market, and was gone. That answer was unsatisfying. Imee was human, like Elliot, but he had one thing that Imee did not. He could sense time disturbances, and if she had gone through some kind of portal, or even a Door like the ones the Professor or Astrid could create, then he might be able to sense it.

He kept on until he passed another booth, selling glittering glass creations, some swaying on strings. He stopped dead in his tracks. A rug booth stood next door, and he had seen both before.

It looped. The marketplace looped back on itself. A woman bumped him from behind, muttering an apology in a brutal, clipped language. He dragged his cart to one side and looked back, only to see the huge iron entry gate through which he had come. It was still ajar, and beyond it, an Egyptian garden stretched, sprawling and elaborate. The sand-colored Library loomed high, imposing and lifeless. It appeared to be parked, settled on land with a sky above, as ordinary as a free-floating inter-dimensional library could be. He knew that it was only an illusion, and that anyone looking out from one of the Library's many windows would see only the void.

If the marketplace looped, then how did anyone get through? And why hadn't Malachy told him? Well, if this was the beginning and end of the marketplace loop, then he now had one more piece of information than he had possessed before.

"Hey, watch this for me a minute," he said, shoving his cart up against the side of the glass stand without waiting for a response from its proprietor.

He moved down the aisle again, trying to recall what booths he had seen just before ending up back at the glass booth. There stood the familiar man playing the ocarina, the clockwork booth, and now another, selling fine, nearly transparent paper. That was it.

"Is this the end of the marketplace?" he asked the man at the paper booth.

The man nodded, not looking up from a box of tiny

paper fragments, so small that Elliot thought they might be confetti.

"Did a woman from the Library come by here a week ago?" he asked.

"Lots of people come here. I wouldn't know if anyone was from the Library." The man took a silver spoon from his sleeve and scooped a few spoonfuls of paper fragments into a silver bowl.

"What about scholars? Do they come past this spot?" Elliot knew that this was one of the entrances that visitors used when coming to the Library. He did not know the others, but had listened to enough conversations in the dining area to know that most of them used this path.

"They do. Some scholars came earlier today."

He must mean the new group of twelve scholars that Elliot was preparing for.

"I'm trying to find out if anyone left from the Library," said Elliot.

"There were Greeks last week. Some left, and fewer returned." The man set the silver bowl on a display shelf and set the box of paper fragments under the table.

Elliot looked through the end of the marketplace to its beginning. The space between this booth and the glass booth was seamless and undetectable. His wooden cart still leaned against the glass booth and the gray mountains still rose in the distance. He studied the air, the ground, the people, and detected no time slips, no anomalies. The booths and people did not change, the same pile of spilled nuts lay on the ground, just as it had on his first trip. Nothing indicated that this wasn't an ordinary corridor in an ordinary bazaar.

Fewer returned, the man had said. But the Greek delegation had not grown smaller. All of the same people had been at every meal before Imee left and after. The missing person was Imee. It had to be. And if she had been with the delegation, then he knew whom to ask.

He almost sprinted for the Library, but without anything to serve to the Greeks and the new group of scholars, he would be punished. There were worse things to be tasked with than cooking and serving, and he did not intend to lose his opportunity to speak with the Greeks. He purchased the items on his list as fast as he could, not bothering to shop for the best deals. He even purchased an expensive bottle of vodka from a man wearing a bear skin. If the Library kept him hostage, then it could very well pay extra for the privilege.

That evening, while serving stewed fruit, green salad and rice wine to the new scholars, he stole glances at each member of the Greek delegation. They seemed to enjoy the novelty of their fried chicken with corn on the cob. He had even baked two pumpkin pies for later. Well-fed scholars were cheerful scholars, and hopefully talkative ones.

He mixed the vodka with raspberry juice, making sure each Greek delegate received a large glass before moving on to the other group. The scholars in the new group all appeared human, with no extra eyes, forked tongues or extra digits, but all were absolutely silent during their meal. Perhaps their diet and silence were religious observances. In other circumstances, he might have been interested enough to ask. He served dessert and studied the group until it was time to collect the dirty dishes.

"May I ask you something?" Elliot said to the gray-skinned girl from the Greek delegation as he took her plate. He had noticed that she seemed reasonably friendly and was less prone to bickering than some of the other scholars. "Did the other kitchen servant, the woman named Imee, did she go with you into the marketplace?"

The girl looked up at him and blinked, perhaps shocked that a servant would speak to her. He knew that in ancient Greece slavery was common. But she was dressed in modern clothing.

"She did," said the girl. "Was she your friend?"

"She was. What happened to her?"

She set her hand on his, her skin feverishly hot, almost uncomfortable. "She cannot return."

"She's alive then? She isn't dead?"

"No, not dead. She is in a home for the insane in Thessaloniki."

CHAPTER 13

ASTRID DELETED THE VOICE MAIL from her boss, Mr. Augustus, and sighed. He wanted to see her before her shift began that day. Sometimes she wished she could join the Time Corps. As a psychopomp, she needed to stay in her own time and be available for a summons at any moment. If she was honest with herself, she didn't relish the thought of actually doing any of the dangerous work for the Corps, though sightseeing through history or the future might be fun. Mainly, she wanted the money.

Sure, the Corps helped take care of Sister and they let them both live in their house, but Astrid had to chip in for groceries and utilities. That meant she had to keep her cruddy job at Luna Park, at least until she left for art school at Columbia in early September. Time Corps members earned a salary, and could always make a nice fat bank deposit in the past and then collect it with interest.

A thought rose up in her mind. The Time Corps had plenty of money. There was no reason for them to insist on her keeping her job at Luna Park. Well, almost no reason. Either they wanted to keep her busy, or there was some advantage to her working there. On second thought, Julius owned the house, and it might not have even occurred to him that she didn't like her job. The Professor was the de facto leader of the Corps, but he was more focused on finding Elliot and getting Felicia home than on her employment preferences. Well, it didn't matter, because she was fairly sure that Mr. Augustus was going to fire her for abandoning her pretzel cart when she ran off with Gopan.

Once she arrived at Luna Park, she passed the game booths, rides and snack carts, noting that the ocean breeze was unusually strong and cool. She headed for Mr. Augustus's office and knocked. He called for her to enter, and when she did, she froze in shock. The man standing with Mr. Augustus was familiar to her, a tiny centaur with a white powdered wig, brass-buttoned navy jacket and a powdered face, complete with a false mole on his upper lip. His name was Gerard when he was in this form, and he had been both her captor and teacher when she had briefly lived in the Seelie world.

"First of all, you're fired," said Mr. Augustus. "That stunt with leaving your cart was unacceptable."

"I did leave the cash drawer with an employee," said Astrid. "No money was lost."

"And you also left your inventory sitting there."

She drew breath to argue, but it was none of Mr. Augustus's business that she had been on-duty as a psychopomp, nor did she care to allow Gerard to have that knowledge. Mr. Augustus's orange hair looked more streaked with gray than she remembered, and she wondered what toll his time with the Seelie had taken on him. Yukiko had told her that Augustus worked with the Seelie, doing their bidding, and was somehow enslaved to them. He had owned a music shop and had employed Hazel back in the nineteenth century in her home world. As one of the Twelve, she supposed he was as immortal as his siblings. No wonder he looked weary.

"Look, I'm only here a few more weeks," Astrid said. "Then I'm going to New York. Wouldn't it be easier to keep me than to train a replacement?"

"I've already hired someone else. I have your last paycheck."

Mr. Augustus handed her an envelope and Astrid had a sudden thought. Mr. Augustus might be firing her to help her. He was one of the Twelve, though that was no guarantee of ethical behavior. Some of the siblings were downright evil. But Mr. Augustus had been the one to assign her to the pretzel cart when she hired on, a place with salt and knots, things that repelled the sidhe, both Seelie and Unseelie. The only reason she had not been affected was that she had been raised in the human world. Perhaps he was once again attempting to assist her.

"It's good to see you again," said Gerard, stepping forward to kiss the back of her hand.

Astrid searched his expression for any sign of hostility or deception, but found none. Gerard, and his other form, Ghislaine, had been kind to her, even though they had been part of her imprisonment. They had done their best to help her learn to make Doors, and had never been cruel. Like so many other Seelie, they had to follow the orders of their higher-ups. The Seelie and Unseelie were both rigidly hierarchical.

"Sorry I can't say that I'm as glad to see you," she said. "I assume you are here about the first of my three tasks."

"I am," said Gerard and then reached for something on the desk.

From amid the papers and empty cups he lifted a wooden box the size of a thick book, ornately carved and tied closed with a black ribbon. Mr. Augustus kept his eyes on the box.

"What is it?" she asked.

"It's your task," said Gerard. "You are going to deliver this for us."

Mr. Augustus wasn't protecting her by firing her. He was freeing her up to do work for the Seelie. A low-paying, boring job suddenly had its appeal.

"Here," Gerard said. "Take it."

She obeyed and looked it over. "I suppose I'm not supposed to open it, right? Will it eat my soul or something?"

"Hardly. Be my guest and see what's inside," he said, raising a manicured hand, palm up.

Glancing at Mr. Augustus, who gave her a short nod, she pulled the ribbon loose and opened the box. Inside, a small glass sphere rested in a pile of Styrofoam packing peanuts. With the fancy exterior, she would have expected velvet or at least shredded parchment. The sphere was perfectly clear and without blemish or bubble.

"You are to take it to Yelbeghen, an individual who lives on an island in the Mediterranean," Gerard said.

"So you want me to make a Door, deliver this and come back? That's it?" It sounded too easy, deceptively so.

"It's an exchange. He has a Seelie woman who he is holding captive. If you give him this, he will free her."

"Does he accept this deal? Or am I going to have to convince him?"

"He has already agreed. You only have to deliver the orb."

"Then why send me? Why not go yourselves? Why waste one of my tasks on this? It's too simple."

Mr. Augustus looked pleased with her. He crossed his arms and looked at Gerard for a response.

"Yelbeghen does not care for the Seelie, as a rule. We need a human to go, and having chosen to be one of those kind of people," Gerard wrinkled his nose delicately, "you are our best choice. He will not harm you while you operate under the Seelie aegis."

"What is this Yelbeghen? What sort of being?"

Gerard straightened his jacket. "He won't harm you. He can't harm humans. Well, he can, but he won't. And being a Door, you're a rare being. He won't harm anything so precious."

"Tell me what he is."

Gerard sighed. "A drake."

"A drake? Like a dragon? Really? So is this a piece of some treasure?"

"If you want to put it that way, yes. It's very precious, and you cannot ever replace it should anything happen to it. Astrid, please understand, I know this is not a difficult task. It's merely one ideally suited to you."

He handed her a map, a modern one, with the exact location of the island noted. Astrid folded it and placed it into the box. As she did so, she felt a mixture of relief and apprehension. On the one hand, it was a simple delivery to a being who wouldn't harm her. The Seelie wouldn't send her into mortal danger and risk losing the two additional tasks she was bound to perform. On the other hand, if a Seelie wouldn't go, then this individual was dangerous. She might be human, but she was born Unseelie and was a psychopomp. Who knew how this Yelbeghen might behave?

"Before I go," she said, "I have a question. I want to know about the Library. How can I get Elliot out?"

"Oh, sweetling," said Gerard. "Please don't do anything stupid."

"So it's possible? It's possible to do it?"

"Well, theoretically, yes. You opened a Door once. It has to be possible to do it again, don't you think? But it's foolish."

"I don't care. Elliot is my cousin, and I'm bringing him back."

"Even if you could, even if you got him back alive, it wouldn't be to his benefit. He would leave half a person, mad and delusional. That's if he survived at all. Your doppelganger girl is a picture of mental health compared to someone who came from the Library. I know you don't like me, but you were my pupil once, and I do not wish to see harm come to you. If you love your cousin, leave him where he is, whole and sane."

CHAPTER 14

HUGINN SOARED OVER THE HOUSETOPS, stretching his wings and savoring the sensation of the air ruffling his feathers. From high up, this section of town seemed greener than from the ground. The trees in this area were older, as was the neighborhood, and the high trees concealed parts of the homes and streets. He thought of flying out toward the sea, but he had to stay close to home. Hazel had called the Professor and informed him that she was returning home.

He angled his wings and circled, looking down over swimming pools, sparkling pale blue against the yellow and brown yards and white cement patios. He soared over brown and gray rooftops and those made of red Spanish tile and past the silvery ribbons of the streets, crawling with cars gleaming in the sun.

It was a good day. He felt mentally sharp, as if his memory might not fail him as often as usual. His inability to retain information troubled him deeply, and often he felt as if Pangur Ban was more of a caretaker than a partner and friend. But then he remembered all of his thoughts and ideas, the intricate plans that had allowed them to infiltrate almost anywhere they chose, slipping in and out on wings and padded feet. They were the Time Corps's most proficient infiltration team, and he knew that if he were truly a liability, they would keep him confined to the house like the kittens or Sister instead of sending him on missions.

He flew back toward home, noting a white animal emerging from the house and disappearing under the tree. He landed in the backyard tree as Pangur Ban scaled it, settling in on a branch beside his.

"Something is wrong," she said. "The Professor is agitated."

"He's always agitated. Either that or miserable about something."

"It's different. He's different. I can tell."

The Professor was typically pleased when Hazel returned from one of her trips. He thought of her as a daughter and worried about her whenever she was away. But he also had a new wife.

"Did he and Felicia have a quarrel?" he asked.

"No."

Pangur Ban's hearing was sharp, and like most animals, she could sense human emotions.

"Something more serious then," he said. "Something bad with Hazel. If Hazel told the Professor what was wrong, he would either do something useful to help her or start swearing and drinking because he could not help. Since he is doing neither, I must conclude that something is wrong, but Hazel would not tell him over the phone."

"That is perceptive. Whose car is that?" asked Pangur Ban as a large SUV pulled into the long, narrow driveway that ran along the side of the house.

"It's Hazel and the car a rental. See the license plate frame?" Huginn said. "It says the name of the rental company."

The driver's side door opened and Hazel stepped out, followed by Mr. Escobar and five other members of her monkey crew. None of them noticed Huginn or Pangur Ban in the tree and the pair remained silent.

Hazel opened the back of the SUV and the crew unloaded a long covered crate which they then carried into the house. It looked heavy, but Huginn knew that the little primates who crewed Skidbladnir were unnaturally strong.

Pangur Ban climbed down the tree trunk and trotted to the cat door. If Huginn had been one of the humans, she would have said good-bye before she left him, but the two of them did not tend to waste time on meaningless words. Huginn flew into the house through the hatch in the upstairs window and navigated through the house, landing on the back of his favorite chair in the living room.

"Hazel!" the Professor pounded down the stairs and swept the small, freckled woman into an embrace, spinning her until he noticed the large box. He set her down. "What's this?"

"It's Neil."

Huginn hopped over to the top of a bookcase to get a better look as Hazel and the Professor lifted the lid off of the crate and pulled back the blanket that shrouded the body. On the bed of straw lay an earthen man.

"Dear Jesus," said the Professor. "What happened? What did this to him?"

Julius, Yukiko, Felicia, Astrid and Sister came in and Huginn watched as they looked over the edge of the crate and then pulled back.

"It was Mr. March," said Hazel. "He's alive, but he looks different now. Younger. He forced Neil to hold still and then he rubbed his thumb on the roof of his mouth. That's when he changed into this."

After glancing into the crate, Pangur Ban leapt up onto the bookcase beside Huginn.

"Any ideas?" she said under her breath.

"None. What could do this to him?"

Pangur Ban addressed Hazel. "Why did he rub the roof of Neil's mouth? Did he say?"

"Neil had letters there. I'll show you." Hazel pulled a pad from the writing desk and drew three shapes on it. Huginn, who had sharp eyesight, did not need to move closer to read them. The first two marks were arched and the last was similar to an X. All of them were in a script that looked like calligraphy.

"Hebrew," said Pangur Ban.

"Can you read it?" Huginn asked her.

"I can."

Julius picked up the paper and then handed it back to Hazel.

"It says 'Emet.' Truth," said Julius.

"But why would that be on the roof of his mouth?" said Hazel.

Julius rubbed his left temple and walked back to Neil's body. He sighed. "There is only one reason I can think of that makes sense with him in this state. It appears that Neil was some kind of golem. A man made from earth. And now he has returned to his original form."

"How can that be?" said Hazel. "He was a man. Flesh and blood."

"From what I can guess, he was March's creation. Now, March has corrected his mistake by destroying him. I wasn't present when my brother was returned to life, but it must have been part of the agreement to allow him to live again. He had to set things right."

"How can you say that? Set things right? He killed him!"

"Strictly speaking, no. If I am correct, Neil was an unnatural creature. He was never truly alive. March did a very wicked deed in making him. I am surprised the golem was allowed to live as long as he has."

Huginn watched as Hazel turned pink with rage. She looked like she was about to take a swing at Julius, who blinked at her serenely through his glasses.

"You knew, didn't you?" she cried. "You knew that your brother would come back from the dead. That's why you had no objections to killing March in the first place."

"Yes. And now that he's back, March is not killing humans anymore or having them killed by others."

"He killed Neil!"

"As I said."

"March is still a murderer, just as before."

"Not really. Creating Neil was a terrible deed. An unnatural deed. He created him to be an assassin, to do his ugly work of tampering with events by murdering certain key individuals. And now, in destroying his golem, he has set things back on their natural path. He is setting right his evil deeds."

"Neil was a good person and you know it. He refused to murder once he comprehended what he was doing. He was your friend. And he was killed. How could you say his death is a good thing?"

"I am not pleased, if that is what you are inferring."

Hazel looked like she was about to either burst into tears or punch Julius. Huginn placed about even odds on either. The Professor put a hand on Hazel's shoulder, seeing, as Huginn did, that Hazel was past her boiling point. Huginn saw her relax a fraction. The only person Hazel loved more than Neil was the Professor. She would control herself for his sake.

"I think perhaps you should give us a few minutes," the Professor said to Julius. The older man scratched his beard and climbed the stairs, presumably to return to his perpetual reading.

"Pangur Ban," said Huginn, having an idea. "In your travels, have you seen anything like this before?"

"I have not," she said. "Though I've heard the stories, of course."

"If Mr. March created Neil, could we not bring him back in a similar manner?"

Pangur Ban blinked at him. "I do not know how. The scholars with that knowledge would have died out long ago."

"We have a time machine."

"It cannot go back more than a few hundred years," said the cat.

"I've been working on a new device," said the Professor. "A dynamic temporal scanner and locking device. It might allow travel much farther than only a few hundred years. It's still in the developmental stages, unfortunately."

"But you could do it?" said Huginn.

"Given enough time, yes. I believe I could do it."

"There!" said Huginn.

"Even if we could," said Pangur Ban, "finding the scholars would be difficult. And I have the feeling that Mr. March, as one of the Twelve, did not bring Neil to life by the known means of creating a golem."

"But you do not know for sure," said Huginn.

"Correct."

"And these other people who knew, where could we find them?"

"The place where they gathered is inaccessible to us," Pangur Ban said.

"The Library."

"I believe so."

"That's it then," said Hazel. "Astrid will work on opening another Door to the Library." She turned to Astrid. "You've been practicing, correct?"

Astrid broke her silence, looking up from the floor where she knelt beside Sister who was weeping into her hands and rocking. In the commotion, no one but Astrid had noticed the girl's distress over Neil's death.

"Yes, but from what I understand, the Door I sent Elliot through was a fluke," said Astrid. "I can't repeat it."

"That may or may not be so," said Pangur Ban. "It's true that the Library is outside of time. And your Doors only open within your own time. So your creation of the Door must have occurred when our two points in time brushed together. You cannot control that or replicate it."

Huginn had another idea. "What if Astrid went through

one of her own Doors into the void. She can survive there indefinitely. Then she can get to the Library from there."

Pangur Ban considered it. "But Elliot cannot survive in the void. What if she needed longer than a few moments to escape through the void with him?"

"And there's another problem," said Astrid. "From what I understand, anyone who leaves the Library loses part of their mind. How could we get out with Elliot and the information for Neil without going insane?"

"Won't make any difference for me," Huginn said. "I'm half gone already."

"And even if I could get there," said Astrid, "Jeff, the head psychopomp, said I'm not allowed to bring the living through my Doors. I'd do it for Elliot though. And for Neil. And to hell with the psychopomps."

Hazel looked pleased with this notion. "Elliot passed through your Door before to get to the Library. And you weren't punished then. Also, when you and Yukiko went through your Doors, and then later when the sidhe used them, nothing happened. Maybe the psychopomps can't tell when you do it."

"Jeff said it destabilizes things."

"So does all of our time travel," said the Professor. "We destabilize, we restabilize, we fix time loops and make them into nice, orderly timelines with causes and effects. It's what we do."

CHAPTER 15

HAZEL SAT AT THE WRITING desk, copying the Hebrew letters from an open book onto a piece of unlined paper. Before, she had made the letters from memory, and though Pangur Ban and Julius had been able to read them, this time she wanted to get them exactly right. The clock struck two, but Hazel knew she wouldn't sleep.

She cut the scrap of paper into a neat rectangle and knelt beside Neil. His mouth was open enough to easily slip a piece of paper between his teeth. She put the paper in, and when nothing happened, she flipped it over so the letters faced up.

Nothing.

"Which word did you write?" asked a female voice from the shadows. Hazel jerked in surprise, and the white cat glided into the pool of light cast by the green-shaded lamp on the writing desk.

"Emet," said Hazel. "When Mr. March talked to Neil, he said, 'My Emmett.' I thought it was a name."

"An understandable mistake. Emet means 'truth,' but March must have rubbed off a letter, the last one, Aleph. Then it says, Met. 'Death.'"

"If we replace that letter, will he live?"

"I do not think so. But you can try it."

Hazel did, writing the single letter carefully. Pangur Ban jumped onto the desk and sat, tail curled around her paws, giving helpful suggestions. She could not write herself, but she was very old and had spent time with scholars and monks, studying their texts.

Placing the single letter in Neil's mouth did nothing.

"What else?" asked Hazel. "Can we paint it onto his mouth?"

Pangur Ban leapt onto Neil's chest and Hazel almost pulled her off. But the light animal could do no harm. The cat peered into Neil's mouth.

"There are no letters there now," she said.

"Maybe I should paint all three. Can you get one of Astrid's paint brushes? She won't mind you in her room. You won't wake her."

The cat agreed and Hazel waited until she returned with a fine paintbrush clamped in her mouth. Hazel then tried to paint the letters using an old bottle of ink from the desk drawer. It didn't work, and the letters were sloppy.

"Perhaps I should try again," said Hazel.

"If it were as simple as painting letters, anyone could do this," said Pangur Ban. Hazel felt like a fool for trying such a silly idea, but was grateful that the cat did not point out her folly.

"How did those ancient sorcerers do it? How did they bring a golem to life?" she asked the cat.

"A person had to be a very holy person to do it."

"Mr. March wasn't holy, that's for certain."

"Agreed. But that is how the stories go. Then they'd write a word, on a paper placed in the mouth. Then the golem would come to life and do its master's bidding. Of course, in all the stories, the golem goes bad and defies his master, just as Neil defied Mr. March. Perhaps it was in his nature."

"It was his nature to be decent and good. That's why he defied March. He was a free man."

"I suppose he was," said Pangur Ban.

"Do you have any other ideas?"

"Some of the stories have the holy man write the name of God on a piece of paper."

"So what's the Hebrew name for God?"

"El Echad, El Hanne'eman, El Emet, El Shadai, El Tsaddik. The One God, The Faithful God, The God of Truth, The All-Sufficient God, The Righteous God. Though those are more titles than names. There are more."

"Then let's get started."

Pangur Ban did not tire as Hazel wrote out each one carefully under her instructions. But the cat was nocturnal, and seemed intrigued with the puzzle. She sat patiently at the corner of the desk, occasionally licking a paw or swishing her tail.

Not one of the words worked. Hazel sighed and put her head in her hands. "Any others?"

"None I can think of. Perhaps Julius can help us in the morning."

"Hang Julius!"

"Don't be upset with him. He may help you. Just because one of the Twelve should not bring a golem to life does not mean he'd forbid you from doing it. Just know that every golem always turns on its creator."

CHAPTER 16

ASTRID SAT ON THE BED, certain she was about to vomit. There was no chance she was going to succeed at this and she knew it. The entire thing would be a giant disappointment and everyone in the Time Corps would be a witness to her failure and would blame her for being unable to reach Elliot.

"Are you ready?" asked Pangur Ban from the bedroom doorway. "Red Fawn is waiting downstairs."

"It's not going to work. I've tried over and over to make a Door to the Library. This will be no different."

"You didn't have Red Fawn to help you before."

"I'm not sure how much she can help. She's not a Door."

Astrid knew that Red Fawn's name had once been May and that as one of the Twelve, she was an observer and participant in the ordinary world. She had even helped Astrid when she was a child. But unlike her brother March, Red Fawn was not able to make warrens or Doors to other places.

Pangur Ban jumped onto Astrid's unmade bed and settled in beside her. "True, she is not a Door, but if she says she can help, perhaps she can. Julius will be there as well."

"Too bad the only one of the Twelve who can open Doors is March, and he's evil."

"He may not be the only one. But we work with the team we have."

Astrid glanced down at the cat who was looking across

the room, toward the window. Pangur Ban had been her pet cat since she was young, and at this moment, she felt the value of their old friendship.

"Whatever happens," said Astrid, "thank you for keeping watch over me when I was little."

"It was my pleasure. I'm only sorry I could not help you more."

Astrid's home life had been chaotic and violent, and Pangur Ban had only been able to silently watch. It had not only cost the cat emotionally, but had led to the death of one of her kittens.

"You paid a high price in protecting me," said Astrid.

"I did what was necessary. And that is what you must do now."

Astrid sighed and rose. Pangur Ban was correct. She needed to toughen up and do the job before her. Descending into hopelessness would never get Elliot back.

"Let's get this over with," said Astrid.

Downstairs, Julius and Red Fawn waited along with the Professor, Felicia, Hazel, Huginn, Pangur Ban and Yukiko. Even the kittens were sitting side by side on the coffee table. Sister and Santiago were nowhere in sight. Astrid was glad that Santiago wouldn't be there to smirk and tease her. As to Sister, she might be in the attic drawing or lying on her back in the yard, studying the blue of the sky. In the Unseelie world where Sister had lived, the sky was purple, and for some reason Sister found this difference fascinating.

Red Fawn gave Astrid a light hug, enveloping her in the scent of smoke and something tart, like lemon. She was the most racially ambiguous of the Twelve, who came in all of the colors, shapes and sizes that humanity did. Red Fawn usually tried to pass as Native American, running the Chumash Legends show at Luna Park and even claiming to be an Indian Princess when Astrid was young. When Red Fawn released her, the older woman looked her up and down, taking careful note of Astrid's fingernails and the state of her hair.

"You haven't been sleeping," Red Fawn said.

"Not well, no. I have a lot to worry about."

"I suppose you do."

Everyone watched Astrid, waiting for her to do something, so she turned toward the back corner of the room and made a Door to an empty lot near the house where she grew up.

"The hard part is making it go to the Library," she said by way of explanation.

She thought of the Library, the same one she had seen at Luna Park when she had sent Elliot through her Door. She pictured it in every detail, from the books to the quality of the light. The Door shifted, going black, then quivering with flashes of color.

From the corner of her eye, Astrid saw Red Fawn spit into her palm. And before she could react, Red Fawn gripped her hand, pressing the warm, wet spot against Astrid's skin.

It grew quiet in the room, almost as silent as the void between worlds, and the lights seemed to dim, making the image at the center of the Door clearer and sharper.

Library. The Library, Astrid thought. The colors continued to flash, but nothing materialized.

"Think of Elliot," said Red Fawn. "And how much you love him."

She thought of her cousin, of their times together as children, of their teen years, the times of poverty and difficulty, of his sunny optimism that buoyed up her own quiet darkness. He had always been sure their situation would improve. He had never doubted it. And he had sacrificed himself for her, sacrificed his safety. He would survive the Library, she knew. She had spoken with him when he was much older. But whether he spent a year or many years trapped in the Library was up to her.

The Door stabilized, and a library came into view. Then, just as suddenly, it was gone, replaced by streaking starlight, then darkness, then a flash of snowy hills, then of a flat rocky desert landscape, all of them flying by in a smear of blinding color. Astrid tried again. She used the void as a starting place, reaching out from there and willing her Door to move, not just in space in her current time, but through all times, all places, homing in on one location.

The Door quivered and solidified. Then, from behind Red Fawn, a shawl-draped figure darted forward and threw an armful of books through the Door. Sister backed away, her shawl hanging halfway off her shoulder, trailing on the floor behind her. She skittered back from the Door, backing into Yukiko who had leapt forward to pull her away.

The Door snapped shut and Red Fawn released Astrid's hand. The light in the room grew brighter and the sounds more distinct. People were talking, all at once, and Astrid had trouble separating the conversations in her mind. She sat on the chair at the writing desk, feeling disoriented and exhausted. Whatever Red Fawn had done to her, the colors in the room were painfully vivid now, and the sounds were sharp and uncomfortable.

Everyone was talking at once, but Astrid was thinking of the pile of books that Sister had tossed through the Door. Astrid knew them well. First was the Metallurgy book that Elliot had received long ago. Then there was a copy of her own fairy tale book. She had owned two duplicate copies of that one. And finally came her own sketchbook, the one she was working in now, half-filled with drawings. It was nothing special or valuable, but she was sad to lose it.

Elliot would one day give the fairy tale book to her when she was nine and then give her another copy on her eighteenth birthday. He would also deliver the metallurgy book to himself. In both cases, he had kept his identity a secret, posing as their grandfather through letters.

That meant one of two things. One, the Door she made was indeed to the Library, where Elliot would get the books and then deliver them when he was freed from the Library. Or two, Elliot got the books elsewhere and the ones Sister threw were the same ones, but older, and at the end of their lifespans.

Objects, like people, had timelines. An object like a book could not exist in a loop forever, going from Astrid to the Library to Elliot and back again to young Astrid. To avoid timeline instabilities, an object had to have an origin, a lifetime, and an end.

That meant that barring an unstable time loop, the books were now coming to the end of their lifecycles. Older Elliot would find the young versions of the books somewhere or other, give them to young Elliot and Astrid, and then after a few years they'd be thrown through this Door into who-knew-where by Sister. But if the time loop was unstable, these books would cycle through over and over, infinitely.

Maybe, Astrid thought, she wouldn't make such a shabby Time Corps member after all. They managed to keep not only their own personal timelines straight, but also fixed all sorts of complicated unstable time loops.

Sister signed something, making the same signs over and over.

"She says Elliot needed to return them," said Yukiko, translating for Sister for those who could not understand her personal sign language. When upset, Sister would revert to her old signs which were far different than those in American Sign Language. Yukiko, as a Kitsune, could understand all forms of communication. "She says they were due. There was a price to be paid. A fine."

"That was Elliot's Metallurgy book," said Astrid. "It had

something inside the cover about 'Library of A—' and a fine not to exceed 100 years."

"Yes!" signed Sister, going back to standard sign language. "He needs it. That's why he's trapped there. Because of the fine."

"I'm not even sure the Door was to his Library," Astrid said. "And he's trapped there because it's a terrible place, not because of a fine."

"It was his library. And he needed to return that book."

Astrid hesitated to tell Sister that she had only thrown perfectly good books into nowhere, but she didn't want to upset the girl. Her reaction to Neil's death had put the girl into a bad state and Astrid didn't want to push her into withdrawing further.

"You did it though," said Hazel to Astrid. "You made the Door!"

"Aside from one of us going through, there's no way to know it was the right one," said Astrid. "And then there's no guarantee we could get back."

"Try it again," said Hazel. "Let's see if there's any way the Professor can get a reading through the Door. If he can drop a sensor through, we can get readings."

"Astrid is too tired," said Red Fawn. "She needs some recovery time."

Sister slipped away upstairs followed by the kittens. She returned with the box with the orb that Astrid needed to deliver to the drake.

"The Professor should take readings on this," signed Sister.

"I have to deliver it," said Astrid. "As one of my three tasks to get the Seelie off my back, I have to take that to a drake on some island in the Mediterranean. His name is Yelbeghen."

At the word, Huginn raised his sleek black head, fixing her with one eye. "I think I know him. I remember something." He paused and clicked his beak. "He was old, even when I was young. He knew many secrets. Even long ago he knew things. And since you mentioned the Library, the Library of A—, it brings another thought to mind. It might be the library that vanished. The one in Alexandria."

"You mean burned," said Pangur Ban. "The Library of Alexandria burned."

"And then it was gone. Disappeared. Never to be seen again."

"Because it was burned," persisted Pangur Ban.

"There's more than that, old friend," said Huginn. "Yelbeghen might know. He'd know what happened to it, how to get to it."

"Are you sure that's the library Elliot is trapped in?" asked Astrid. "There could be lots of Libraries starting with an A."

"That have a fine of one hundred years for a book?" Huginn asked.

Yukiko held the glass sphere to the light, turning it this way and that. Then Red Fawn took it and sniffed it while Julius studied the box.

"Anything interesting?" asked Astrid.

"Just a glass ball," said Red Fawn. "But, they always are, right?" She winked at Astrid and her seashell earrings swung from side to side as she examined the ball, taking a moment to swipe the tip of her tongue over it and then squint in concentration.

"We'll take Skidbladnir to Yelbeghen's island," said Hazel. "Astrid will finish her delivery task and we can ask him about the Library of Alexandria. He may know about reviving golems as well. If he knows nothing, we then sail to Alexandria and travel back in time, take readings or just head straight in and see what we can see."

"I am not sure they are the same library," said Pangur Ban. "The Library that hosted scholars and mystics was not the ordinary one in Egypt."

"But it may have become that place once it left Egypt," said Huginn.

Sister nodded enthusiastically and reached up a hand to caress the feathers on the back of Huginn's neck. He lowered his head and closed his eyes in pleasure.

"It's settled then," said Hazel. "We set sail in the morning. Felicia and the Professor can stay here. They need to work on a machine that can take us that far back in time. So far, we've only managed a few hundred years in either direction from the 1860s, which was our point of origin. Once we're in Egypt, Astrid can make a Door back here and retrieve the improved time machine so we can use it to go back to the library before it burned. Astrid, will you sail with me on Skidbladnir?"

Astrid nodded. "I can make Doors if I need to travel anywhere for training with the other psychopomps."

"Huginn and Pangur Ban, will you come?"

"I would not miss it," said Huginn. "But can the kittens remain here?"

"They can," said Pangur Ban. "Sister and Julius can watch them."

"Yukiko?" said Hazel.

"I should stay with Sister," said Yukiko. "And I don't like the sea. There are strange things in the water."

"We could use your translating abilities," said Hazel. "Especially in Egypt. Felicia, Julius and the Professor can watch Sister. And you can set up a video conference if you ever want to talk to her yourself. The Professor installed a temporal uplink in my ship that will allow it."

Yukiko paused to think, and finally assented. "For Elliot's and Neil's sakes," she said.

Pangur Ban made eye contact with Astrid, and Astrid knew they were sharing the same thought. Sailing a ship full of time travelers and strange creatures to a drake's isolated island was folly. Besides, libraries could not detach from reality and become new places. Or could they?

CHAPTER 17

ELLIOT ADHERED TO HIS ROUTINE as time passed. Cooking, serving and cleaning filled his days, while his evenings were spent among the shelves, scrolls and electronic readers. He even used the reading chairs in the empty room and discovered that the shapes of words could be shot directly into the visual center of the brain via the optic pathways. It was uncomfortable at first, seeing words when his eyes were closed. But later, he discovered that he could accelerate the text, speeding through books far faster than his physical eyes could ever move over print. Unfortunately, the reading selection in that section of the Library was sparse and the older books contained more of the information he sought.

He learned that the Library was ancient, that it had once been a physical place, and that fire was its worst enemy. Well, no surprise there. True to the claims of the scholars and Malachy, those who left without permission went mad. And the only ones allowed to leave were those who had been invited into the Library in the first place, namely the scholars.

He learned the scholars' preferences and health needs, serving up mead, water, milk, and mulled wine, nectar or, on one occasion, chicken blood. He made pies and roasts, sliced raw meats into thin curls, baked spiced sweet bread and tart dinner rolls, tossed together salads of root vegetables and berries and simmered pots of savory soup.

Some beings, like the sidhe, both Seelie and Unseelie,

could eat no salt or meat. While Astrid could eat salt, she had never been able to abide eating meat. Others couldn't consume anything that grew underground or anything cooked. Most ate standard human food.

These scholars came and went, some returning multiple times, others only coming once. Some were intensely secretive about their research, while others discussed their findings loudly and with great animation. Most found what they needed on their own, but once in a while, someone asked for help.

Bennu was one of these.

The first time he saw her, he served her a bowl of white fish and buttered rice, per instructions that she preferred meats and fatty things without vegetables. She also loved desserts. She looked human, with brown skin, black eyes and hair. Her fingers were slender, and he noticed that every move was a little slower than it should have been, more deliberate and graceful.

When she spoke to him for the first time, his back was to her and he did not know who spoke, so low and soft was her voice. He turned from collecting the dishes in the empty dining hall.

"I require assistance," she said. "I am looking for information on a certain topic."

Elliot knew he ought to direct her to one of the librarians, the people like Malachy who could help her. But she looked at him with such clear, dark eyes, her hands clasped loosely in front of her, the light behind her silhouetting her form in the doorway, and he did not want to send her away.

"Sure," he said, and wiped his hands on his apron before tossing it onto the table. He had all night to clean, and if a beautiful girl wanted his help, who was he to refuse? He was supposed to make the scholars' lives comfortable, was he not?

"I need information on the people of the cold North,"

she said as they walked together along the tiled aisle that ran between high wooden shelves of books. Great stone columns reached to the ceiling two stories overhead with statues of giant scorpions perched at the corners of the room. They climbed a staircase to reach the second story, and for a moment, Elliot was disappointed that they would be so publicly visible. If even one of the librarians saw him, they'd send him back to the kitchens in an instant.

But then, Bennu led him through a doorway into a smaller reading room where one of the many directories waited. When Elliot had first arrived, he had not known what the empty white marble stands had been. But when he touched one, a computer screen had appeared and he had been able to use it to locate books on topics he wanted. When others touched the directories, they became the type of document that the person was accustomed to reading. For Bennu, it became a scroll, held open by two long wooden rollers with a cranking device to move through its text. Nearby sat a stack of other scrolls, no doubt ones Bennu had not found useful.

"You see?" she said, rolling the scroll a bit and indicating a few lines. "All they have are Iberian cultures. I need a place farther north."

"Which world?"

"The world of Men," she said, and it sounded sweetly old fashioned to his ears.

"That's my home world," he said.

"I thought it might be."

He knew from the Time Corps that his home world was a hub world, relatively easy to reach and easy to leave. That was why the Professor tended to stay there, as it was the best location for returning Felicia home. Her world seemed to be completely sealed from the hub world, though she had been able to come through, so travel had to be possible. Most of the Time Corps were born in the hub world, and Elliot had often wondered if some people there had a natural affinity for moving between worlds. His cousin, Astrid, certainly did.

Not only did the hub world open easily to other human worlds, but unlike the world of science and steam-power where the Professor and Hazel originated, Elliot's world also opened to the worlds of the sidhe, Seelie and Unseelie. There were other worlds too, where the scholars came from, all of them like little branches off of the larger tree of the hub world.

"Which specific northern area are you looking for? And in what time?"

"Scandinavia. I am not certain of the year according to your calendar. My people reckon time differently."

He touched the directory and the scroll slid away, changing into a computer screen. This was far more efficient, though Elliot decided not to mention it to Bennu, lest she take offense. Scrolls and smaller rolls of papyrus and skin had served humanity well for many centuries. They were simply slower than a computer.

He began entering the parameters of the search, but before he finished, he knew where she ought to go. The information came into his mind in an instant, like a bubble floating into view, and he found himself able to exactly picture the area that contained her information.

And in a moment he understood. He was becoming a librarian. That was how the people like Malachy could find whatever they required. The longer they stayed in the Library, the more connected to it they became. In time, he might be able to locate items as they did, by feeling them with his mind.

"This way," he said, and led her up staircases and through broad hallways lined with mounted tablets covered in jagged text and shimmering metal sheets that seemed to glow with their own inner illumination.

He entered a room filled with a segmented wall of scrolls and two shelves of thick books with heavy, rough pages.

These were the sort that were made by hand. He pulled down two of the books.

"Can I help you find anything specific?" he asked.

"I could probably use some assistance."

For the next two weeks, Bennu asked him for help after supper and he always agreed. It meant that cold food hardened onto the plates and pots, but it was nothing a little late-night scrubbing couldn't remedy. He simply gave up a little sleep and drank a little more coffee each morning. It was a fair trade for spending his evenings with Bennu.

She was from the desert, somewhere in the eastern Sahara that was tightly connected to the human world. She and her people appeared human, and her tribe had given up its nomadic way of life only two generations ago. Its permanent territory now included some farmland along one of the Nile tributaries, land good for grazing animals and farming. As an invited guest of the Library, she had been sent through the spot at the end of the marketplace stalls.

Bennu's mind was quick, and he occasionally doubted her need of him. But together, they pieced together the information she required. There were tribes far to the North, where the people were as light-skinned as Elliot, and she was to learn what she could to assist her people in forming trade agreements and alliances. She needed to learn their religion and the things they were likely to need, as well as things that might offend them.

"Why would you need to research for trade agreements with a group so far away?" Elliot asked one evening. "Surely they can't be coming regularly. And don't they clearly state what they want?"

"I'm not entirely sure," she said. "My uncle has asked me to get the information, and as the cleverest of my cousins, I was sent here to learn what I could. I do know that my uncle is wise and good and wants to spread worship of our goddess. Perhaps we can convert the people of the North."

She looked up at him, and the way the light caught her skin, he got the impression, only for an instant, of a silvery pattern at the corners of her eyes and along her collarbone. But the next moment, it was gone.

"What goddess is that?" he asked.

"Her name is Bast, and she is a beautiful black cat. She is kind, gentle and full of wisdom and compassion. She is unlike the brutal, bloodthirsty gods that demand sacrifice. She only wants voluntary self-sacrifice. Unbloody sacrifice. She abhors violence."

"I think the Norsemen already have their own gods. I'm not sure they'd adopt yours."

"Perhaps not at first. But once they learn of her, they will. At the very least, they will adopt her as one goddess among others. How can they not?"

"And if they do not?" he asked, uneasy. "You wouldn't go to war with them or anything?"

"I would not, though some of our young men are more zealous. And some of our priests interpret the words to mean that we must bring our goddess to others, even if they do not wish it. I do not agree with them, nor does my uncle. We agree that family, home, peace and stability are worthy of protection. We will defend them, but not launch an offensive campaign. It would be impractical anyway. Why travel a thousand miles to speak with barbarians?"

The days passed, and Elliot worked harder on learning the locations of things in the Library. He found that if he could clear his mind, the items in the Library would call out to him. Each floor, each room, had a different feel to it. All except one area, which felt like nothing at all.

During one evening of study, Bennu touched the end of her pencil to her lower lip, watching him.

"Tell me, Elliot. Why are you here?"

He was taken aback by the question, but decided to answer truthfully.

"It was an accident," he said. "And I'd like to return home."

"Why do you not leave? You can come with me through the marketplace."

"I can't. If I leave without permission, I'll lose my mind. I'm better off here, trying to find another way out. I've looked all over this place and haven't found anything to help me though. I think with time, I'll become enough a part of this place that I'll be able to find what I'm looking for. I'm not sure if it'll be too late by then."

"Do you think you are close to finding out how to escape?"

He sighed and found himself glancing up at the ceiling, to the one area of the Library he could not sense.

"I might be. There's an area far upstairs I might want to check."

"Back near the empty chairs? The ones that read into your mind?"

He thought about it. "Yes, but it's farther up than that."

"I thought it might be. There's a place I was told not to go. A forbidden area. It's a place not made for people, they said. I'm not sure what beings can go there, but I'm not among them."

"Do you know exactly where this place is?" He had a general idea of its location, but he couldn't be precise.

She frowned. "If I did, would you wish to go?"

"Wouldn't you?"

"Not unless I wanted to be thrown out of the Library, never to return."

"It would be terrible if you couldn't return," he said. "I would miss you."

Her cheeks colored and she looked down at her book. A minute later, he caught her watching him, but she looked away the moment their eyes met.

The next morning, she was gone. A week passed, and he wondered if she had been asked not to come back. Perhaps someone had overheard them discussing the forbidden area. Or maybe she had completed her research. Maybe her uncle had obtained the information he sought and had ordered her not to return.

One morning, he came downstairs to find Bennu sitting on a stool in the kitchen. She jumped up when she saw him.

"I didn't know where your quarters were," she said. "I never asked."

He noticed that her robes, usually crisp black with gold trim, were more shabby. The black was faded and some of the metallic beading was missing. Her brown leather sandals were more worn as well.

"I didn't prepare for this visit well," she said, noticing him studying her. "But I can come back again for a few weeks. I begged my uncle. He is upset with me."

"Why?"

"I learned that there was a secondary reason why he wanted information on the North. There will be an alliance. The Northerners are sending one of their young women to wed my cousin next month. And then, once the nuptial celebration is complete, I am to be sent North, to marry a chieftain."

Her voice caught and she put a hand to her mouth. Elliot did not know what to say.

"I refused, so my uncle was furious with me. But then, I agreed and he allowed me to return here. I don't want to go. But I have decided to make the best of it. I can bring knowledge of our goddess to the Northern people. I will be the wife of the chieftain, which places me in an influential place. I can bring her love to my new subjects." Her expression changed from one of determination to exhaustion. She sighed. "Can you tell me about the Northern men? Something that isn't in the books?"

"My ancestors were from Scandinavia," he said. "The Van Dorns. But I'm a distant descendant. I don't know much about them."

"I have heard they have long beards that hang down to their navels and are filled with crawling vermin."

Elliot laughed, and she looked up at him and smiled a little.

"And they're cold," she said. "Their skin is as cold as the snow."

"They're not cold. They're as warm as I am."

He put out his hand and when she touched it, he realized that up until then, she had never touched him before. Her skin was indeed warmer than his, but only slightly.

"I would rather stay with you," she whispered.

He pulled her close to him, and when she tilted her head back to look up at him, he kissed her. She let out a little purring sound and pressed herself into him, and for a minute, all his troubles vanished, and there was nothing but her, warm and soft in his arms.

"I want to help you get out," she said. "But I cannot be with you. I have to do my duty to my people."

He wasn't so sure. "Certainly you have other cousins who could marry this chieftain."

"You think I might avoid the match. But the decision is already made and I have given my consent. The letter is already traveling North. I can only hope he is a kind man."

"How long are you allowed to return here?" he asked.

"A few weeks."

He had an idea.

"I had a friend back home, a raven. He was Norse and came from the area you're going to. I may not be able to get out of the Library, but you could carry something for me. A message."

"But the time I live in is long before yours. How could any message survive that long?"

"He was alive in your time. The only problem is, his memory is shot and he might not be able to remember anything. Still, I have to try."

CHAPTER 18

ASTRID'S NIGHTSTAND CLOCK READ 3:12 a.m. Too early to get up and too late to get a good night's sleep. Sister breathed quietly in the dark on the floor beside her. She hadn't woken with any nightmares that night. Both kittens, Frieda and Diego, were curled up against Sister's body. Perhaps they were a comfort to her. They were learning to talk and would not be allowed out of the house until they learned to be silent in the presence of anyone outside the Time Corps.

The tree outside waved in the wind and the breeze blew in strong through the open window, rustling papers on the desk. Astrid left the window open for Pangur Ban to come and go, though she could also use the cat door downstairs.

When she woke again, the clock read 5:28, but it took a moment for the numbers to make sense. She blinked off the fog of sleep and noticed that the sun must be up, because things in the room were bright and clear. But no, the sky outside was still dark. The leaves on the trees, even ones across the street, appeared sharper than normal and she could even see the tiny details on the neighbor's mailbox. Odd.

Then she realized that she was standing up. On her bed. Her head was only a foot above the blankets and her legs were entangled in her empty pajama top. Terrified, she lost her balance, and when she threw her arms out to catch herself, they opened incorrectly, for the structure of them had completely changed.

They were wings.

The little cry of surprise she let out echoed through the silent room and Diego blinked up at her before his eyes widened in shock.

"It's okay," she whispered. "It's only me."

Well, she could still speak, which was odd considering the new shape of her mouth. This must be her aspect, the thing Jeff and the other psychopomps had told her about. But what kind of bird was she?

She hopped to the end of the bed, opening her wings for balance, wondering how difficult flight would be, and she studied herself in the vanity mirror. Two round, yellow eyes stared back at her from a brown and black face topped by two little tufts, like tiny horns. She was an owl. What species of owl, she could not guess. But she looked like an ordinary sort, the kind that could blend into the bark of a tree.

The wind blew again from the window and she turned. The sky was lovely and dark and the air was so cool and fresh that she could not resist. Opening her wings, she gave a few flaps, rising off the bed, testing her weight. Yes, she could manage.

She landed on the windowsill, her curved talons scratching at the paint, and Diego hopped up beside her. He looked at a nearby tree branch, the one his mother used to enter and exit the window. Astrid could tell he was gauging the distance.

"You stay here," she said as softly as she could, hoping not to wake Sister.

"Night," he whispered. "It's almost morning."

"Yes, but you have to stay inside. Your mother will be home soon."

"Soon."

She pushed off into the air, avoiding the tree and then

gaining altitude to reach the clear empty sky. Circling back, she spotted Diego watching her from the windowsill, his tiny face cocked slightly to one side. She soared over the housetop and into the night.

Ah, now this was the way things ought to be. Her eyesight was so keen, she could see the tiniest details below. And her wings were absolutely silent, making her feel like a part of the dark sky itself. The sounds of the night were more acute to her as well, the rustles of leaves, even the hissing swish of the vehicles on the roads. She was so light and agile, and as she got the hang of flight, she considered her situation.

If the owl was her aspect, what did that tell her? How could this ability prove useful?

But before she could give it much thought, she realized that she was not alone. A crow descended from above and she swerved sideways, so it only clipped her outstretched wing. She flapped to regain her balance and turned back to look behind her, for she was certain that was where the crow now was. He rose up behind her and darted toward her tail. She pulled up, but the thing struck her, hard enough to pull a few feathers out. They floated downward toward the earth.

Well, if this terrible creature thought it could intimidate her, it could think again. She was twice its size, and she had both a sharp beak and wicked talons at her disposal. She dove for the ground, an old human instinct perhaps, but she felt safer closer to the earth. Then, as the crow plunged down after her, she pulled up, letting it pass her. She dove for it, talons outstretched, but it darted away, veering off to one side and leaving her. For a moment, she thought she heard it whisper something, but that had to be a trick of the wind.

"Fine then, leave, you cowardly thing," she said.

The sky was growing lighter and she wanted to be indoors now, back where she was safe. She flew fast, scanning the rooftops and streets for familiar landmarks, but she was unused to viewing the area from this height. Ah, there was the park, so the Time Corps house was only a few blocks away.

She had almost reached the house when the crows came. There were four of them, and they cawed and shrieked as they flew at her. One tore at her right wing while another pecked her on the back of the head, hard. She barreled toward the ground, flapping frantically and twisting, trying to regain her equilibrium, but no sooner would she stabilize herself than another crow would tear at her.

"This is not your place, daughter of the grey-eyed one," one of them screamed, and Astrid turned her head so quickly she almost lost her balance.

The other crows took up a chorus of "dark-flyer," "silent-wing," and "night-hunter," as they pelted her.

She kept racing for home, dipping lower and lower, tearing at the crows with beak and talons whenever she got the chance.

Then, a fifth crow approached, but as it got closer, she noted its size. A raven.

"Out with you, vermin!" he shouted and flew over Astrid's back, colliding directly with one of the crows. She knew his voice. The others attacked him and Astrid spun around. Now things were more even. It was still four against two, but she and Huginn were larger and stronger birds.

After Huginn dipped and dive-bombed them twice and Astrid got two nice hunks of flesh in her talons, the crows flew away.

"Too many ravens," shouted one. "Two too many!" And then they flapped away and were gone.

"Better get inside," said Huginn.

She followed him to the house, memorizing the lay of the land, and they both flew in her bedroom window.

"How did you find me?" asked Astrid.

"I was out a little while ago and found Diego in the tree by your window. He mentioned that you were an owl. It didn't make any sense until I saw those crows after you."

She hopped across the bedroom floor, talons sticking in the carpet, and now Sister was up, eying her with curiosity and a little fear.

"It's me, Astrid," she said. "This is my aspect."

"Can you change back?" signed Sister.

Astrid hoped so. She thought of how she willed herself to open Doors and did the same for her physical form. A moment later, she was a woman again, albeit a nude one. She'd have to remember that little difficulty if she ever wanted to change form in front of others. She dressed and checked the time: 6:35.

That meant it would be 8:35 in Nebraska. She texted Jeff, "It's an owl," and set her phone down. She had no shyness about revealing her aspect. She needed all the help she could get, and she instinctively trusted Jeff.

A minute later, he texted back. "We can work with that. Shakespeare once wrote: 'They say the owl was a baker's daughter. Lord, we know what we are, but know not what we may be.'"

CHAPTER 19

After the excitement at dawn, Huginn needed a nap. But the birds outside made him uneasy and his mind was too filled with ideas for him to rest. In the past, the birds had given him no trouble. But he was not a psychopomp, and something about Astrid seemed to bring out the worst in them. The crows were typically decent neighbors though they were occasionally rude. But they had never turned violent before.

Frieda and Diego chased a lizard under the sofa, poking their little paws at it and then scampering around to the other side to reach for it again. They had already pulled the tail off the thing, and they paused from their hunt to bat it around the floor and chew on it. Sister crinkled up her nose in disgust, but Huginn understood the desire. The kittens had to learn to hunt somewhere, and until they learned not to talk in front of humans, they needed to hunt indoors or in the backyard.

"You look beautiful," signed Sister to Pangur Ban. "Like an Egyptian cat picture in my book." The white cat sat on the windowsill, her form tall and lean, paws neatly side by side, her tail curled elegantly around her feet.

Sister was referring to one of her history textbooks, and as Huginn had sat with her for many lessons, he saw the similarity to the image in the book. The photograph was of a statuette of a black cat, but that was the only difference.

Pangur Ban squeezed her eyes shut in pleasure, and Huginn wondered if he ought to compliment her more often. He had never thought of her as a vain creature, but he also knew that all beings liked being told they were beautiful. He would try to remember to do it more often.

And then another thought surfaced, another memory. He sat still, waiting for it to form, knowing he could not grasp at it without it vanishing like smoke. He had seen a white cat like Pangur Ban before, one seated in just that fashion. But it was not alive. Not dead either. No, it had been a sculpture like the one in the book. But he had seen this statue in person. In front of the figure had sat a wide, shallow, black marble bowl, carved around the edges with letters in his own Norse language, which he could read, and words in other scripts, ones that looked strange and unearthly. What had the words said? He could not recall.

"Godda snake!" cried Frieda, smashing the lizard down with her front paws. It wriggled free, and Diego tore off after it into the kitchen, closely followed by his sister. A few minutes later, Frieda returned to the living room in triumph, a limp lizard dangling from her jaws.

Huginn wondered how he had remembered the cat statue so clearly. He remembered so few things, but that memory and the memory of the couple walking through the village had been so clear. It troubled him.

That evening, he found Julius in the study, looking over the information on the cave painting that Hazel had brought back.

"Any progress?" asked Huginn.

"Sadly, none," said Julius.

Huginn hopped across the floor and flapped up onto the corner of the desk and then explained that a few memories had returned to him, bright and clear.

After a few moments of consideration, Julius said, "Your memories seem to be triggered by people you know, Sister and Santiago walking together and now Pangur Ban sitting." He rose to close the door.

"I suppose so," said Huginn.

"Have you had any other memories return?"

"Only a few, involving things of little consequence. Tiny things."

The chair creaked as Julius lowered himself into it. The man regarded Huginn with an odd look.

"Do you remember your brother?"

A little jolt of recognition went through Huginn, but then it was gone. "I think I had a brother. I feel like I did. But I can't remember him."

"I think he might have kept your memories," said Julius gently.

"Like Pangur Ban? She helps me remember so many things. I can come up with ideas, but I can't retain things."

Julius closed a few of the books that lay open on his desk, and then he stacked up his notes and put his pens and pencils into the desk drawer. Huginn sensed he was putting off saying something, and so he waited.

"I was never sure," said Julius. "I was never certain of who you were. I know that like Pangur Ban, you are long-lived, and your original name was probably Huginn. But I didn't know if you were one of the twin ravens, or if you simply had taken that name on your own. Someone might have given the name to you and you don't remember. Without your memory, we really can't know much about where you came from or who you are."

"But you said you think I had a brother."

"You might have. There were twin ravens, Huginn and Munnin. Thought and Memory. And you are very, very good at coming up with thoughts. Your ideas and plans have guaranteed many a successful mission."

"So you believe I may be one of the twin ravens?"

"Perhaps."

"Then where is my brother?"

"I haven't the faintest notion. For all I know, he might be dead."

But Huginn wondered. When the crows had attacked him and Astrid, one had said there were too many ravens. Two too many.

CHAPTER 20

Astrid had heard of the ship Skidbladnir, of course. It was legendary among the members of the Time Corps, many of whom had been passengers. But she had never seen it in person, nor had she seen Hazel, or Captain Dubois rather, unfold the thing and bring it to life.

It was two thirty in the morning, when the world was quiet and asleep, and they stood at the marina where the dark ships bobbed silently in their slips. Astrid supposed some of the boats could hold sleeping people, but Yukiko was with them, and though the Kitsune was now tailless in her fox form, her ability to create illusions was intact. She could conceal the group if needed, or at least confuse any witnesses.

Mr. Escobar, the capuchin first mate, handed Hazel a small folded brown cloth from within his vest pocket. Hazel walked to the end of the dock, knelt and unfolded it. Immediately, it grew into a miniature Viking ship. She dropped the small ship, no bigger than a toy, into the water, and within moments it expanded to full size. The thing was magnificent, not in a new and polished way, for the ship had seen battles and showed signs of its age, but beautiful in the way that elegant things of old were. They were made with care, and loved. This ship, in her way, might even love back, for the ship called Skidbladnir was alive.

"Please lower the gangplank," said Hazel, and the ship obeyed.

Hazel climbed aboard, followed by the few members of her monkey crew who had accompanied her to the Time Corps house. They carried the crate with Neil's dead body in it and took it below decks. The Professor had driven them to the marina, and the monkeys returned to the SUV to retrieve an extra time machine. One machine was built into Skidbladnir, but having an extra allowed flexibility. As unorganized as the Time Corps tended to be, Astrid had to admit that they did attempt to be prepared. Finally, Yukiko, Pangur Ban and Huginn climbed on board with Astrid bringing up the rear.

"The crew is on Santa Maria Island," said Huginn to Astrid, landing on the gunwale beside her. "We'll pick them up and then leave."

As one of the Channel Islands, Santa Maria Island was close to the coastline, not visible to the unaided eye except on exceptionally clear days, but easily accessible by boat. Some of the other islands were inhabited, but not Santa Maria. The place was strange, and people preferred not to go there. The Professor had once told Astrid that in some of the other worlds, the island did not exist at all.

The ship sailed slowly without its full crew, and they stopped at the island to gather them, ending their shore leave. Once on board, the crew took their places at the sails, as the wind was strong and there was no need for them at the oars. They picked up speed, heading south.

"Where are we going to sleep?" Astrid asked Huginn, setting her rucksack on the deck. "And where should I put my things? The ship isn't deep enough to have room for everyone."

"In the old days, we slept on deck. But this ship has room below, more room than it would seem. She's special."

Huginn and Astrid stayed at the front of the ship, next to the carved wooden dragon head, while the others went below decks to settle into their quarters or perhaps, in the case of Pangur Ban, to see if there were any mice in the cargo hold. Astrid leaned over the railing, watching the water strike the sharp point of the boat's prow, and break into white froth, churning past them.

"You've never been on a ship before, have you?" Huginn asked her.

"Not one like this."

"The best place to ride is up at the top of the mast," he said.

For a moment, she didn't understand the implication, and she thought he was merely making conversation. Then it occurred to her that he was sharing something important with her.

"The wind isn't too strong up there?"

"It is, but in a good way. Care to join me?"

She scanned the sky for gulls, and spotting some, pointed them out to Huginn.

"I don't think they will bother us," he said. "They're not as intelligent as crows, and they're only territorial if it affects their stomachs. Besides, they're far off and we're moving fast."

She took a few steps from the prow and changed into an owl, then pushed her clothing into a pile with her feet. She took off, and just as Huginn had told her, the wind was strong. But she was no fledgling sparrow, and she landed on the angled rigging at the very top of the mast. Huginn joined her.

"You're right," she said, taking in the flat line of the horizon, a darker line against a dark blue sky. The faint lights of humanity winked at her from the shore and a broad stripe of white moonlight undulated on the water. "It is lovely up here."

"You have a fine aspect," he said. "Better than the dull black dogs and horses and things that your kind typically take as aspects."

"You remember that information?"

"Swiss cheese has holes, but there are solid bits to it too. My memories seem to be improving a little lately. Once you get flying a bit more, I think you'll enjoy it. I think you will like hunting as well. Pangur Ban takes great pleasure in it."

"I can't eat meat, remember? I was born Unseelie."

"Ah yes," he said. "Well, it will be nice to have a fellow bird on the team."

"I'm not part of the Time Corps."

"Ah, of course not. I forgot."

"But you're sort of like me. We are both birds of death, in our own ways," said Astrid.

"Yeah, ravens and death. Pecking out eyes. Eating the corpses off the field of war. Desecrating the bodies. It's the way of my kind."

"Sounds like a blast," she said and eyed the seagulls in the distance. "Tell me, why did the crows call me those names?"

"I'm not certain. If I had to guess, I'd say they can sense that you're different from other owls. They don't want anything related to death near them. They might feel that you're out of place."

"Unnatural, you mean."

"In fact, you're quite the opposite. But still, no animal loves death."

"Can all animals talk?"

"No. Some, like Pangur Ban and me can speak with anyone. Some can only speak with other animals, some only with their own kind, some not at all. But they all will avoid death."

"I don't feel like death. Dark and evil."

"Death isn't evil. I mean, war and eye-pecking and corpse-eating aren't so pleasant for your kind. Humans, I mean. But death, that's not so bad. We're all part of the world in the capacity we're given. You can be what you are without too much angst, if you choose. You can find your place and be at peace with being a part of death. And you don't ever have to eat any corpses or peck out any eyes."

"I just—I thought I was just going to go to art school and have a regular existence. I thought my life would be different."

"So do you feel you are too big or too small in the grand scheme of things?" he asked.

It was a good question, but neither answer seemed accurate to her.

"It's just that this is not the life I would have chosen for myself," she said.

"It rarely is."

CHAPTER 21

ASTRID WAS ASLEEP BELOW DECKS when her phone dinged. She leaned over the edge of her rope hammock to grab the phone that rested on the shelf built into the wall and almost tipped herself onto the ground. Yukiko breathed quietly in her sleep in the hammock next to her. Astrid fumbled in the dark, squinting at the screen to make out the words. Before she could finish reading them, a man stood in the entry to their tiny shared quarters.

"You ready?" whispered Robin, glancing at Yukiko.

"We have a psychopomp job?" Astrid whispered back.

"Yes, and I'm supposed to train you. I sent a text, but these things are time-sensitive, so we have to hurry."

"What time is it?" she muttered, slipping on her sneakers and pulling a jacket over her pajamas.

"No idea," said Robin. "It's lunchtime at home. But this won't take too long."

Astrid shoved her phone into her jacket pocket and followed him through the Door he created. They stepped through into a shabby apartment smelling of cigarette smoke and stale air.

"Jeff told me that he already took you on a training job," said Robin.

"Yeah. This will be my second one."

"What did Jeff teach you?"

"How to pull on thought threads and convince the soul to go through willingly. He seemed to think I was a little clumsy with it."

"Well, it was your first time. And not all of us are as precise and delicate as Jeff."

"Are you going to teach me a different way?"

"In a sense. We all have our different methods. As long as the soul goes through, that's what matters."

They were in an apartment's living room and faint sunlight shone through the windows. Astrid pulled back the curtains to see outside. It was a city, but she could not tell which one.

"Sometimes it's amusing to try to guess where you are," said Robin. "You can check what side of the road they drive on, look at license plates and newspapers, or you can just check your phone and have the GPS locate you."

Astrid pulled out her phone and discovered they were in Bethesda, Maryland, and it was seven in the morning. Back on the ship, it had still been dark.

The apartment was small and cramped, with empty glasses and newspapers scattered about the living room. They found the bedroom drab, the tiny bathroom equally so. In the kitchen, a dead man lay on the floor, a coffee cup broken beside him, its dark contents splattered across the floor. He was in his seventies, with a beer belly and dark, sunken eyes.

The spirit of the dead man studied his empty body with a look of fear, and then he discovered that he was not alone.

"Oh, God," he said, backing away. "No. No, I wasn't that bad. I tried. I really did. You know that."

"We're not here to hurt you," said Astrid. "We're here to help you go home."

She made a Door beside him and he leaped away from it as if it were on fire.

"Please! Have mercy. You can't take me to hell. I tried."

"I know you did," said Astrid, approaching him. "It's going to be all right."

"Get back, you demon!" he yelled and darted into the living room.

"I'm not a demon," she called. Of course, she wasn't exactly angelic in appearance either. With her uncombed hair, black jacket, blue pajama bottoms and sneakers without socks, she must look strange, but she resembled a homeless woman more than any demon.

She heard the man weeping in the living room and turned to Robin for help. But instead of a man, a black terrier stood beside a pile of clothing. He trotted across the kitchen, his nails clicking on the floor and headed for the living room. Astrid watched as he stopped just in front of the man. He sat and cocked his ears forward, thumped his tail on the ground and gave a little yip.

The man regarded the little dog, and then reached tentatively to pet him. Robin licked his hand, then glanced back at Astrid.

She knew she was supposed to do something, as this was her training session, so she reached into the man's mind, just as Jeff had taught her.

His fear made some thoughts clearer than others. And in sorting through these thoughts, a picture of his life became clear. This man was not a good person. He had beaten his wife and children until one day, his wife had left him, taking his daughters with her. Then, he had spent the next decades alone, drinking and cursing them for his sorry condition. He had been a misery to work with, yelling at the other workers in the machine shop, reveling in his power as a mid-level supervisor. He pitted people against each other, undermined colleagues and took credit for their hard work. He was vicious, cruel and a liar.

But what could Astrid do with this knowledge? All of these thoughts were on the surface, there for her to read like blaring newspaper headlines. Deeper, there were other things, smaller cruelties, harsh words, ugly looks, a lifetime of bringing harm to others in ways both large and small.

She searched through the threads, looking for something useful. Somewhere, there had to be something that would ease his fear of punishment. But she found him cursing at his mother while she wept, hitting a girlfriend hard enough to knock her off her feet, stealing from the till at work and blaming a coworker who lost his job.

"The mother," said Robin, and Astrid wondered if the man had heard him. He continued to pet the dog. Perhaps Robin was using some power to keep the man calm.

She went back and studied the memory, the way his mother's worn cotton dress clung to her full figure, the way her gray hair curled, her bare feet and the tone of her voice. Then, Astrid moved the Door into the living room and pulled the thread, focusing her energy just in front of the Door.

The man looked up.

"She forgives you," said Astrid. "She knows you're sorry. She says you're her good boy."

She waited, hoping it was enough, and the man stood up. He didn't move toward the Door, and for a moment, Astrid considered running up behind him and shoving him through. She could do it, but she knew that was not the lesson Robin was trying to teach her.

Then, the little dog did something unexpected, he ran forward to the threshold of the door and sat. Astrid imagined the man's mother patting his head, and from the look on the man's face, he must have seen what she intended. She wished she could see it too, but her imagination would have to do.

He turned toward Astrid, tears in his eyes. "Promise me you're not sending me to hell?"

Astrid couldn't promise. By making the illusion, she was lying to him, no question. She had no idea if his mother forgave him. And she thought she'd rather physically throw him through the Door than tell him a comforting lie.

He watched his mother petting the dog, and Astrid glanced at the table beside the front door. A stack of mail waited, and she read his first name.

She imagined his mother saying his name, Joseph, and lifting her arms to embrace him. He stepped forward, and Robin hopped out of the way. The man went through the Door, and it contracted and vanished.

"If you'll pardon me," said Robin, and then trotted into the kitchen where his clothing still lay on the floor. Astrid waited until he returned a minute later.

"You did very well," he said and sat on the chair to put on his shoes and socks. "I always try to give comfort to the dead. They're frightened. Some fear hell and some are just afraid to let go."

"The dog trick seemed to work well."

"Most people like dogs. It sets them at ease and relaxes them."

"And then you pull threads in their minds?"

"More or less. I calm them, then search and find what's useful and then use it."

"I'm not sure my aspect will help as much. I'm an owl."

"Interesting," he said, standing and zipping up his jacket. "No, I don't suppose that would be very useful. Not the way Graciela and I have useful aspects."

"Is she a dog too?"

"Yes, and she told me that I was allowed to tell you that. The only one who's really secretive about his aspect is Jeff. I don't really care if you know mine."

"So Gopan is a cute little boy and you and Graciela are dogs. People like those things. They don't like owls."

"True. But no one ever promised your aspect would make your life easier. I wonder, though. Perhaps you have hidden wisdom."

"I doubt it."

"Yeah, me too," he said, smiling. "Well, you should make a Door back to that ship. I promise not to mention to Jeff that you're spending time with those Time Corps people."

"Thanks. But I have a good reason. I'm doing a task for the Seelie, which Jeff already knows about."

"Don't tell me," he said, putting up a hand. "All of the otherkind are nothing but trouble."

"But you're one of them. You're not a regular person."

"I'm a human being, just like you."

She decided not to mention that she was Unseelie-born. Jeff surely wouldn't give her away either. If Robin didn't like otherkind, she wouldn't give him any reason not to like her. She was about to make a Door when she thought of something.

"What do you think is beyond the Door? What if I just sent that man to hell or some kind of punishment?"

"Our job isn't to sort the dead. We're only delivery people. It's best not to trouble yourself. Whatever judgment waits, there's no way for us to know about it or to influence it."

He made a Door back to his home in Ghana, while Astrid made one to the deck of Skidbladnir. It was not yet dawn here and most of the crew was asleep in the rigging.

Robin was right. Her aspect might not be useful. But it was a part of who she was. She returned to her hammock, pulled her blanket over herself and lay there, thinking of flying.

CHAPTER 22

It took Elliot nearly an hour to climb the stairs and walk through endless corridors to the forbidden area of the Library. Bennu had gone home for the day, and he was glad. If she had been there, she might have attempted to convince him to abandon his investigation.

Instead of a blank area in the Library, he could now feel the draw of the place in his mind, faint, but present, pulsing like a tiny mouse heart, so fast it was almost a vibration. At each forking hallway or series of doors, he paused to choose, sometimes doubling back, but more often finding himself even closer to the place. Other parts of the Library pulled at him too, each in their own way, and he knew he was becoming more and more attached to this place as time passed. The sensation was benign, but he did not wish to deepen his connection. He feared that with time, his desire to leave might lessen. Perhaps, like Malachy, he might become passive and accept his fate.

He knew the place the moment he turned the corner. There was an unassuming wooden door, one among many, with a simple iron handle instead of a knob. It was neither locked nor latched. He pushed it open, expecting to find a dark room of aged books or rows of inhuman scholars, kept separate from the ordinary scholars for reasons of safety or secrecy. Instead, the room was a storage area, as jumbled as a child's toy box.

Shelves of books lined the walls, but there were also tables and boxes filled with reading materials of all kinds, electronic, stone, papyrus, skin and paper. Statues leaned together, some Victorian, others ancient, one was a knobby fluorescent green thing with a pulsing gelatinous covering. It looked vaguely humanoid.

There were doorways to either side, and he walked through the leftmost one into a room similar to the first. On shelves and in piles on the floor lay teapots of silver and earthenware, dishes, an oil painting of a boy in breeches, a pile of scarves and shoes and off to one side, a toy bird with real feathers.

The floor was covered in a mosaic picturing a Greek trireme, its sails full and its prow pointed slightly upward as it parted the water. The sea was all blues and violets with rows of identical curved white-capped waves, all rendered in bits of colored stone. An orange and red sun blazed just behind the ship, almost like a halo. The oddest part was the pigs. The animals swarmed aboard and leaped from the ship into the waves.

He paused and listened for anyone approaching. The place was silent. So far, so good. He let his mind wander through the nearby rooms, sensing each area's pull on him, hoping for a clue. Was the answer in one of the books in the first room? Or was it buried in one of the chaotic piles? Or perhaps there was no answer at all, and this place was off limits to scholars for another reason. Maybe it was just a storage area.

As he entered the next room, he stopped in his tracks. This room had four columns, one at each corner, each facing the center of the room. Columns were not at all unusual in the Library, but these were topped with faces. There was an elephant, the African sort with large, fan-like ears. The next was a lion, facing a zebra at the opposite corner. The one in the corner closest to him was a cobra. All four had their eyes and mouths closed, as if sleeping.

Tapestries hung on the walls here, some in an ancient style, though they looked brand new. Of course, they may be thousands of years old to him, but might have come to the library quite recently. A blank blue plastic sheet hung nearby, small lights and pulses of color appearing now and then. In front of it sat a low table with stacks of rough woolen blankets in reds and purples, a pink laptop computer, two matching marble bowls, as black as the void, a Victrola, pan pipes, a dish full of pet identification tags and a rice paper painting of a woman.

Then came the sound of rustling, like feathers, then something taking off, of flapping wings. He felt the thing, a malevolent thing, both intelligent and insane, half-dead and inflamed. If Elliot was becoming a part of the Library, then this thing embodied the Library in its very being. He knew two things. It was not kind and it would not be merciful.

Elliot ran, tearing through the rooms, past the treasures and detritus, his bare feet slapping the tiles and mosaics, his breath loud in his ears, his heartbeat louder. He sprinted past the mosaic of the pigs leaping off the ship with its green waves. Had they been that color before?

The flapping was drawing closer now, the sound of giant wings, the thing pursuing him, drawing closer. He shot into the hallway, not bothering to pull the door closed behind him. He darted down passageways, leapt down staircases and kept running until he found a quiet spot to catch his breath.

He listened. No sound. Nothing. He continued down the stairs, moving swiftly, until he reached the kitchen and then his quarters. He closed the door and pushed the crate up against it. It would be useless to keep anyone out, but the sound of the crate moving would wake him if anyone tried to enter.

Now he understood the warnings. The Librarian embodied this place, it was his as much as his own feathered body was. And he was not a benevolent being.

CHAPTER 23

"Mares' tails and mackerel scales make tall ships take in their sails," said Hazel to Mr. Escobar. He scratched behind his ear with his hind foot and then studied the sky.

The high cirrus clouds overhead were wispy, streaking across the sky like the tails of running horses. It meant the winds in the high atmosphere were shaping the clouds, possibly signaling the approach of a warm front. The clouds before a front could also coalesce into the thin lumpy blanket formation that resembled the scales of a fish. Either one could mean a storm was coming with high winds that necessitated them lowering their sail.

Of course, in this time she could check the web for a weather forecast, and she would. But she liked the old methods. They worked in any time and place and gave her a sense of continuity, of stability. She might love the sea and always being on the move, but sometimes it was nice to have a small sense of predictability. The stars were constant in their courses, allowing her to navigate when she didn't have more precise means. For those willing to learn the ways of the sea and sky, the water could be a lovely home, even if it could be dangerous. She verified her predictions with the onboard computer and told Mr. Escobar to prepare.

Mr. Escobar yipped out the order to lower the ship's striped sail, and the crew obeyed. They were in the Gulf of Mexico, and Yukiko was resting after creating the illusion of a modern-day ship for the workers of the Panama Canal. Now, they were in open water, heading for the tropical island nature preserve where the monkeys had their home. In the nineteenth century, when Mr. Escobar was born, it had not been a preserve. But the island had been declared off-limits to developers in the late twentieth century. Today, in the twenty-first century, the monkeys on the island thrived, safe from the threat of human interference.

"Good thing you'll be in another century," said Huginn, flapping down from his spot in the rigging. "Most likely there's no storm there."

"I hope not," said Hazel. "But there may be by the time we return. We made preparations. Are you sure you want to stay with Astrid in this time? I can ask some of the crew to stay with her."

"I lived through the 1880s once, and have visited it enough times. Besides, Astrid and I have some bird things to discuss."

They dropped Astrid and Huginn on the beach with the assurance that they'd return in an hour or so, according to Astrid's timeline. For Hazel and the crew, they'd be gone longer than that.

Hazel went below decks to her quarters, where the time machine attached to Skidbladnir was housed. The Professor had built it into a cabinet on the wall, and she flipped it open and set the coordinates. Then, after warning the crew, she turned on the machine.

In her personal past, the Time Corps required a synchronicity to travel. While running the time machine, events in the home world had to line up with those in the target world to create a rip in time. The synchronicity could be an earthquake, an animal stampede, even a person walking down a street. The easiest and safest event to replicate was a ship floating down a river. In most of the centuries before and after the mid-eighteen hundreds, Hazel and the Professor's point of origin, rivers were used for transportation. So they could sail along, activate the machine, and wait for a rip to occur, then travel through it, closing it before any other people were affected. Had they done such a thing on a busy street, people would easily have slipped into times not their own. Eventually, the Professor figured out a way to travel without synchronicities, which made travel easier, but no less dangerous once one got to one's destination.

Hazel was struck with a slight nausea and a touch of dizziness, but she did not allow it to trouble her. It was merely a side effect of traveling between times. She checked her time readings, verifying that they had arrived in 1885.

They disembarked, the crew buzzing with excitement, some of the youngest bouncing up and down, others tearing off into the rain forest. Not all of the crew were from this time originally, but many were. Some would be leaving the crew while new crew members joined. The crew of the Skidbladnir was fluid, and Hazel paid well, so the occupation was a popular one among the younger monkeys. A few years at sea earned them money and prestige. She knew that some of the monkeys worked on other ships, sometimes as advisers or navigators, often posing as pets. Hers was one of the very few ships where they could speak and work openly.

Hazel and Yukiko grabbed their packs and along with Pangur Ban, they followed the crew inland. An hour later, they arrived at the monkey village. It showed signs of human culture, from human-made ropes to an empty iron pot to one side. But it was unmistakably inhuman as well. The homes consisted of branch structures and canvas-covered platforms here and there high in the trees. Hazel knew from previous visits that most of the monkeys preferred to sleep out in the open, but a few had taken on some of the ways of humans. They traded with a few select ones, individuals who could be trusted not to reveal an island full of talking monkeys. Hazel knew that as the centuries passed, they would get the human governments to declare their island a nature preserve. But the nineteenth-century monkeys were far more concerned with getting gold for trade.

Hazel and Yukiko found a low log to sit on while some of the crew reunited with their families. Pangur Ban glided silently into the woods, presumably to enjoy hunting in a novel environment.

"They don't like me," said Yukiko after a few of the monkeys had approached and then fled when she looked at them.

"They don't like much of anyone," said Hazel and pulled off her boots. Her feet, like the Professor's and like everyone from her home world, had a large apelike big toe. It gave them good dexterity, but the difference was insignificant in terms of evolutionary differences with the humans from this world. Recently, she had seen the Professor using his feet to hold something while he worked on it, but a proper Southern lady would rather die than pick up anything with her feet.

On a practical level, it meant they had to wear boxy shoes and could never take off their shoes in front of anyone who didn't know their origins. It also meant that the monkeys from the hub world were fascinated by her and thought of her as somewhat inhuman. From them, that was a compliment.

"They're wary of strangers," she told Yukiko. "Humans have generally not been kind to them."

"I think they know I'm not human. Foxes are predators to monkeys."

Hazel glanced around, spotting pairs of simian eyes peering from the foliage, studying them. The faces were large and small, old and some very young. Some of them vanished when she made eye contact.

"They'll leave us alone for a while," said Hazel. "Then, they'll offer to make a fire to make us comfortable. I brought treats for everyone, and everyone's pay."

Later that evening, a cheery fire burned in the center of the clearing and Hazel concentrated on turning the stick in her hand so the roasting marshmallow would not fall into the fire. She handed off the toasted treat to Yukiko, who then gave it to the nearest monkey. The little fellow snatched it, bit into it and dropped it with a yelp as it burned his mouth. Another monkey grabbed it and ran off, followed by the first.

An old female monkey, the matriarch, settled quietly beside Hazel and waited until all of the marshmallows were distributed.

"I have heard about your mud man," she said. "I liked Mr. Neil Grey, though I only met him a few times. A quiet man. Not so much chatter like most humans."

"Yes," said Hazel, a stab of longing hitting her at the mention of Neil's name. "We're finding a way to bring him back. Have you ever heard of anything like this?"

The matriarch looked into the fire, the reflection of the flames dancing in her black eyes, and she sighed. "There are stories, but they are only that. Stories for our younglings."

"Stories of men turning to earth?"

"Not precisely. A monkey king born from a rock. He came from stone, you see. And he knew the name of God. Your first mate explained your golem story, and I noted the similarities. Also, the monkey king could turn each of the thousands of hairs on his body into copies of himself, like your Mr. Grey was able to make multiples of himself."

"He didn't clone himself. He only traveled to a certain time over and over so all the versions could meet up."

"My mistake," said the matriarch. "Well, the monkey king did not die and come back, as he was immortal. And he was a trickster, a master of clever words. Your Neil Grey was not like this."

"No, he wasn't. He said what he meant, or he didn't speak at all."

"An admirable trait. Would that more of your kind were like him."

Hazel could not disagree, and as the wood on the fire snapped and a breeze rustled the leaves, she missed him.

"What did you say about the name of God?" she asked the matriarch. "Perhaps the word can help us. I have used all the names I could find to revive him, but nothing worked."

"He is nameless," said the matriarch. "Or if he has a name, I have never heard it. I think the notion of the monkey king knowing the name was only a story. Like I said, I do not think it is any help. And I have other things I wish to discuss."

And then Hazel understood. The matriarch was working around to discussing payment for the next crew of Skidbladnir. This discussion of the monkey king was merely small talk to her. And Hazel had to admit that there could be little value in the story. It was too far removed from Neil's circumstances.

Hazel dug in her pack until she located the bag of gold that held the payment for the current crew. The matriarch set each gold nugget on the log beside her, counting them carefully. Hazel did not take offense. Unlike humans, the matriarch felt no embarrassment in ensuring that she had not been cheated.

"I want more next time," said the matriarch. "We are learning to set traps to capture ocelots and other predators that kill us. The humans have the materials we need, as we prefer the metal traps."

"How much more do you want?"

They negotiated a higher price, which Hazel didn't mind. What was money to a member of the Time Corps? With bank deposits spanning centuries, property and managed trusts, they could obtain money or gold easily enough. And the matriarch wisely insisted on always being paid in gold.

"Will you play for us?" the matriarch asked once they were finished with negotiations.

"I'd be happy to," Hazel said and pulled her violin case from her pack. She always brought it, as the monkeys loved music.

She tuned it and set it under her chin, noticing how the monkeys grew silent and still, some looking into the flames of the campfire, others reclining in the trees.

She began with a slow, soothing tune, followed by a few lively ones. Once the music picked up, the monkeys clapped and danced, whirling and leaping together in undulating groups that separated and reformed, only to break into smaller groups again. Her crew always enjoyed music, and though they had no interest in learning to play, they loved to dance.

Her heart wasn't in the happier tunes, though she knew she played them skillfully. Even Yukiko, who had been gloomy since the loss of her tail, tapped her foot and even smiled a little at the capering monkeys. But without Neil to listen, something was missing. He had always loved her music, and sometimes she suspected he loved it even more than she did, and creating music had always been second nature to her. Even as a homeless child on the streets of New Orleans, she had earned money from her playing and had drawn the attention of Mr. Augustus, an expert musician. She hadn't known then that he was one of the Twelve, but she had not earned her recognition at the music conservatory in Boston through the Twelve, but on her own merits.

Skill didn't matter though, not here in the humid jungle. Instinct mattered. Group loyalty mattered. Survival mattered.

Neil was dead, and as more time passed, she started to question if it was possible to bring him back. There was a man-shaped hunk of stone on Skidbladnir, but it was not Neil.

She glanced up at the sky. In the 1800s, the lights of modern cities didn't dim the stars, and she felt their uncountable multitudes, spinning in space, orbiting other bodies or being orbited by others. Billions of systems, pulling each other and being pulled in turn. She imagined that the stars were souls, together yet separate, dancing round one another like the monkeys, alive and pulsating.

The night sky always reminded her of her parents who had died in an influenza epidemic when she was young. She had always taken comfort in the fact that she would see them again someday in heaven. Neil had told her that he had no soul. If he was correct, then he was more than dead. She wouldn't meet him again on the other side of one of Astrid's Doors. If it were true, then Neil was worse than dead. He was erased from existence.

But giving in to hopelessness was not in her nature. If there was a way, she would find it, even if she had to tear apart time to do it.

CHAPTER 24

HUGINN WATCHED FROM THE BEACH as Skidbladnir sailed through a time rip into the eighteen hundreds, leaving him and Astrid in the twenty-first century.

"Sometimes I wish I could time travel," said Astrid. "Elliot told me about some of the things he had seen, and they sound marvelous."

"But you do travel through time," said Huginn. "Only you travel at one second per second, and always chronologically forward."

She walked up the beach toward the trees and Huginn followed, finding a perch on a large piece of driftwood. Astrid pulled out her phone and touched the screen here and there, scrolling through the screens to obtain whatever information it provided. Huginn did not see the value in such devices, but the modern humans did.

"The monkeys still live here," he told Astrid. "Even in this time. They're still around. Care to take a little flap about?"

It was good to have another bird as a friend, and he hadn't realized how lonely he had been on his flights until he had someone who could join him. He wondered how things had been with his brother. Had they always flown together? Was that why he longed for companionship?

He watched Astrid as she considered his offer. "I can't. Graciela texted me a little while ago and told me it was going to be a busy day. Lots of sticky souls. She's going to take me for training later. I can't be away from my phone."

"Can't she find you without your phone?"

"Yes, but if I'm flying, she won't have an easy time catching me."

That seemed like an advantage to Huginn, but he was not the one responsible for escorting the dead.

"Could you do me a favor?" asked Huginn. "I'd like you to ask the other psychopomps a question. Is there any way they can check to see if someone has died?"

"I don't think there is a list or anything, but I'll ask. Who do you want to know about?"

"A brother. I think I had a brother once, and I want to know where he is. His name would be Munnin, and he would look just like me. We were twins."

"And you think he's dead? How long since you last saw him?"

"I can't remember."

"Do you have a general idea? A year, a century?"

"No. I don't know."

She looked up at him with pity, and Huginn hated it. He despised his inability to remember anything and he wished others didn't feel sorry for him. His existence was not a constant misery, and unlike the humans who seemed to have existential crises over the littlest things, he felt sure of who he was, most of the time anyway. Even without his memories, he still had his keen mind.

"I'll ask them about your brother," she said. "But if you can remember one place or time when you were with him, couldn't you travel back in time and see him again?"

"I can't travel within ten miles of myself. And I have the feeling we were inseparable. Wherever he was, I think I was with him."

"But Pangur Ban could do it, or Hazel or one of the other Time Corps members," she said.

"Perhaps, but that would not tell me where he is now."

"Aside from Pangur Ban, is there anyone else old enough to remember your brother?"

He thought about it. Santiago, the Coyote, was old, but he had always stayed in the southwestern part of North America. He would not have known a Norse raven. There were other ancient beings, surely. Who else was still alive who was old enough and might remember? Mongolia and Dubai were home to some old dragons, but then so was Wall Street. There were a few others though. They tended to be reclusive.

"Perhaps Yelbeghen," he said. "He's old. Do you think you could ask him?"

"Sure. Did you know him when you were young?"

"I have never met him before."

"Which means he never met your brother either, right?"

"Probably true."

"It's still worth asking," said Astrid. "You never know." But her tone indicated that she didn't think asking the drake would be helpful. Well, what did she know? She was wasn't even two decades old. She hadn't seen the things that the old ones had.

Astrid's phone gave a little chime and she scrolled through it. "I'll be back soon," she said. "If the ship gets back, go ahead without me. I can make a Door and catch up."

Huginn had a terrible moment when he wondered if he would remember that information. What if he forgot and no one knew what had happened to Astrid? Oh, but these modern people had phones. Hazel would call her on the phone. He had forgotten about that.

A woman appeared down the beach, stepping through one of the shimmering Doors that psychopomps created. Astrid raised her hand in greeting.

"I just thought of something," Astrid said, turning back to Huginn. "What about Skidbladnir? She's Norse and old. Wouldn't she know something about your brother?"

He watched Astrid greet the other woman and both of them stepped through another Door. In the trees behind him, a bird screamed. For the first time in his regrettably erratic memory, he was alone.

The ship called Skidbladnir had carried the Aesir, the old gods, and all their armor. They were all dead and gone now, relegated to memory and stories. All of the old gods around the world were gone, as far as he knew. Even the god Yukiko had served, the Japanese rice god named Innari, who had survived into modern times, had died in World War II. Huginn and Yukiko were among the orphaned beings left behind. He supposed Skidbladnir was as well.

He did not know how much time passed before Skidbladnir sailed back into view, but the sun was still up. He flew out to it, not wanting the ship to go to the trouble of coming to shore if Astrid wasn't there. He wondered why she hadn't simply changed into an owl to leave the ship earlier, but then she would have to carry a bag of clothing with her if she wished to become human. It was so much trouble to cover a furless, featherless body.

Later that evening he perched on the gunwale to one side of the wooden dragon head at the prow of the ship.

"May I speak with you?" he asked.

"It would be my pleasure," said the ship. "It is good to have a fellow countryman on board. So many skraelings walk my decks."

The ship tolerated but did not like the people from North America. She called them by the old term, skraelings, and thought them a savage and barbaric people, whether they were monkey, human or otherkind. Skidbladnir obeyed her captain Hazel, but it was more out of duty than affection.

"How much do you remember about the old days?" he asked.

"I remember much, my brother."

"Can you tell me? I remember little."

"I remember the battles, the conquests, the mighty warriors who walked my decks. I saw them leap from me onto beaches and destroy villages, taking what they wished. I watched them drink and feast on shore afterward. I watched the villages burn and knew the fear of being burnt myself. I rammed ships and was wounded over and over again, but I was repaired."

She told him of a few particularly brutal battles and Huginn listened, remembering bits and snatches of things. But he did not take the pleasure in it that she did. Oh, certainly there was glory and honor, the pitting of strength against strength, but there was also the stench of smoke, the screams of terrorized people and the feeling that something was wrong. Perhaps that was merely his twenty-first-century self thinking that way. He had been Guntram, a war raven. He had feasted on the dead with no qualms. It all seemed so long ago now.

Skidbladnir continued, "And then there was the god we served, Odin. He was a wanderer as well as an occasional escort for the dead. He had but one eye, but with you and your brother, he had five eyes. It made him wise. Oh, and he was clever. Having you made him more clever. Having me made him stronger."

"How did he die?"

"I did not witness it, and for a few centuries, there was talk that he would return. He never did."

"Have any of the other old ones survived?"

"Only us," she said. "Though I have not seen the entire world. It is large."

"Have you heard anything recent about my brother, Munnin?"

"I have not, but I remember him. He was just like you. But you worked forwards while he worked backwards."

"I don't understand."

"He held the past in his mind, all the things that had already come to pass. You thought of possibilities, the endless open space that is the future."

"We were better together. It is hard to live without him."

"Well, if you die, then you can thank the gods that your suffering will end soon and you can join him."

"I don't want to die. I simply said it was difficult without my brother. I think if I had him, I would feel whole."

"Now I am the one who does not understand," said the ship.

He attempted to explain it to her, but the ship was a different sort of being. She did not feel incomplete or sorrowful. Even the thoughts of losing her various captains and crews did not bother her too much.

"We are both relics of a dead age," said Skidbladnir. "But I still hunger for the sea. I am not ready to travel to the hall where the mead flows just yet."

"And neither am I," Huginn admitted. Broken as he was, he did indeed have his eye to the future and the endless possibilities that waited for those who survived.

CHAPTER 25

ASTRID FINISHED SENDING AN OLD Polish woman through her Door into death and turned to Graciela who stood to one side of the hospital room, her arms crossed as she observed.

"Not bad," Graciela said. "Now let's get out of here. I hate the smell of hospitals."

She made a door and Astrid followed her to a rocky hillside somewhere windy and mountainous.

"From what I understand from Jeff, you're an artist," Graciela said.

"Yeah. I'll be starting at Columbia for art school in the fall."

"Then this should be easy for you. Making Doors is all in the visualization. Jeff asked me to help you make Doors to all different places, even ones you haven't been."

For the next hour, they practiced opening doors to the Australian outback, a Miami pizzeria, a dreary Russian apartment complex and the deck of a cruise ship.

"This will do for a while," said Graciela. "Come on."

Astrid studied the people on the cruise ship, and noted that yes, they could see the two of them. Graciela found the buffet and grabbed a mimosa for herself and an orange juice for Astrid, telling her that she was underage. Graciela found a seat and dug around in her purse.

"I got you a little something."

She handed Astrid a small velvet box which Astrid opened. Inside lay a gold heart pendant on a chain.

"As the only other woman on the team, I thought I'd get you something as a welcome gift," said Graciela. Astrid thanked her and Graciela motioned for her to turn around so she could fasten the clasp. "It's to remind you of two things. First, is don't listen to your heart. It lies."

Astrid started to mention the contradiction, but Graciela shushed her.

"Let me finish. The heart lies, but it tells the truth too. See, in this job, it's hard to keep from feeling terrible sometimes. You send children through the Doors, babies too. Some people are afraid or angry, some will call you names."

"One man called me a demon," said Astrid.

"See what I mean? So you can't get too emotionally affected or it'll make you crazy. You do your job, you herd those people through, and you move on. Got it?"

Astrid turned around and Graciela nodded approval at the look of the pendant. She herself wore a necklace of bright green and gold beads with matching earrings, high heels and a bulky but fashionable sweater over tight black slacks. As always, she looked like a fashion model.

"My aspect is a sheepdog," said Graciela. "A Belgian sheepdog, specifically. Longish hair, all black. I'd show you, but getting dressed again is a pain. I know what I do, and it's a job. I get the souls where they need to go, and that's enough for me. Now, Robin is all cuddly with his souls and Gopan cares about their emotional well-being, but they don't get attached. For us women, it's harder."

Astrid thought the idea was a little old fashioned, but didn't say so.

"As women, we bring life. But you and I also bring death. We love the babies we bring into the world, but we also can become too emotional about the souls we send out of the world. Just remember to let your head rule."

"I suppose you should have gotten me a gold brain on a chain."

"That wouldn't look fashionable at all," said Graciela. "This looks much better."

"Are you the best at making Doors?" Astrid asked. "Is that why Jeff wanted you to train me?"

"Yes, I am. But the others are competent enough. They'll get you into the house of the dying. I'll get you to the bedside. It hardly matters, as they get the souls through just as well as I do. Don't worry about it. You're doing very well for a beginner."

Astrid hadn't been concerned about how well she was doing. Her Doors were accurate enough.

"I have a question. A friend of mine has a brother who might have died. Is there any way to check on who is alive or dead? Is there a list?"

"No. No list. No record. We don't attend most deaths, so keeping records wouldn't help much anyway."

Astrid took a sip of her orange juice and asked, as casually as she could, "Have you ever heard of opening Doors outside of time?"

Graciela gave her a knowing look. "I heard about you making Doors into the void before you met any of us. And yes, we can go to the void if we wish. But outside of time? No. We are beings grounded in the here and now, in the very solid things of life and death. What could be more immediate and time-bound than death?"

"What about into other times? Like into the past?"

"Look," said Graciela, setting her hand on top of Astrid's. "We're family, in a sense. And family looks out for one another. Those Time Corps people are dangerous. They're this collection of crazy people doing crazy things. I know your cousin was involved with them, and I'd hate to see anything bad happen to you because of them. Just be careful."

"I will," she said, but she had no intention of abandoning hope for Elliot. Just because Graciela said they couldn't make Doors to other times didn't mean it wasn't possible, just that she hadn't personally done it, or didn't know how. After all, the Professor had made doors through time. And what was the difference, when one got down to it, between a person making a Door on their own or using a machine to make one?

CHAPTER 26

There weren't many mirrors in the Library, but Elliot was now on a mission to locate them all. He found them on walls, on remote tables, there were even a few in the rooms of the Library that housed statues and pieces of art. He remembered that Astrid found making Doors out of mirrors was easier than making Doors out of thin air. He also knew that she had once used two sides of a clamshell mirror as a pair of related Doors.

If he couldn't do anything to help the Professor to find him using science, then he would see what he could do for Astrid. One way or another, he needed to let them get a lock on his place and time, even if it was ever-changing.

He now knew why the forbidden area of the Library was off-limits. It wasn't because it held secret knowledge. Rather, it was the living quarters of the Librarian. Learning this had been a disappointment, but thinking of all the junk in those rooms had led him to the epiphany about the mirrors. His trip had not been a complete loss.

Bennu was still requesting his assistance after dinner each night, and he gladly obliged her. They discovered that her future husband lived in Norway, and focused their reading on that area. Sometimes they researched, sometimes they took walks through areas of the Library where nobody cared to go. Other times they found secluded places for extended time alone.

"If only I could find a pair of mirrors," he said to Bennu one evening as they walked. "A connected pair. Then you could take one and somehow get it to Astrid while I kept the other. Then she could use it to get a lock on me."

"Why a pair?"

"Maybe it's a stupid idea, but if they're connected, then that connection might just be enough of a thread for her to use one to find the other. She's done something like that before."

"A mirror would not survive a thousand years," said Bennu. "Not even if we took good care of it. Glass breaks. Metal tarnishes. And there is no way to make sure it gets to her. Aside from surviving, it would have to travel halfway around the world."

He led her down another corridor, opening a few doors to see what was within, hoping to discover mirrors or anything else of use. He found only rooms of reading materials or occasional storage areas.

"I have an idea," said Bennu. "You said your friends were time travelers. Did any of them come to my time?"

"No. The machines only work a few hundred years before and after the 1800s."

"That is unfortunate."

"No, wait. Two of them were alive at that time. They didn't time travel there, they lived through those years in the ordinary way. Pangur Ban was in Ireland and Huginn was hanging around Norway and Sweden, though I know both of them traveled extensively."

"So they will be alive when I return home."

"Yes, but it's not like I can send them a letter. Besides, if they had talked to you, then they'd already know where I was and would be able to find me." He thought about it for a minute. "Perhaps one of them could pose as a scholar. Pangur Ban studied with monks. She could do it."

"But she hasn't, which means she won't. Correct?"

"Yeah," Elliot sighed. "There has to be something else."

Late that night, as he washed dishes and scrubbed down the kitchen counters, the idea came to him.

"I thought of something," he said to Bennu the moment she came into the Library the next day. He pulled her aside, ignoring the looks from the other scholars who were horrified at the bold conduct of a kitchen servant.

"Huginn's memory is a wreck," he said. "But Pangur Ban's has always been sharp. We could make something that would draw her attention. Something she'd remember and be able to put somewhere and then be able to retrieve in the twenty-first century."

"Something indestructible," said Bennu, considering. "Metal or stone."

"That's what I was thinking. You have stone-workers in your city, right?"

"Yes, but it would be difficult—"

"So we only need to think of what would draw Pangur Ban's attention," Elliot said.

"It would have to be something simple—"

"And something that would last a long time."

"Elliot, listen." She had stopped in her tracks. "You don't understand. I don't have time for anything elaborate. I can only return here once more. Next week, I can come again. Then, they are sending me to the North."

Her voice broke, and Elliot pulled her close, kissing her.

"I'll find a way," he said, his cheek pressed against the top of her head.

He felt her shake her head. "They're making a statue for me to bring North," she said. "A version of the goddess Bast. We could not obtain black marble, but we did have white. And the Northerners will not know the difference. It will be a gift for my husband."

He hated the word, and as unreasonable as he knew it was, he hated the man. Some hairy barbarian would have his Bennu, and short of kidnapping her, he could do nothing about it. Even if he got out of the Library, the time machines couldn't go back far enough for him to find her.

"I wonder if we could use the white Bast," he said. "Pangur Ban is white too, but I doubt a cat statue would draw her attention. We'd have to carve some words on it. Words she could read."

"In your language?"

"Maybe. But she won't speak modern English in your time. I'm not really sure what language she'd speak. Ancient Irish?"

"We only have a week. Is that enough time for you to learn to write in this ancient language?"

"I don't know. I wish there was a way I could do something to the statue so the Time Corps had a way to find me. I wish I could attach a mirror, one of a set, to help Astrid."

"Would any reflective thing do?"

"I suppose so, but it has to be indestructible. Like you said, metal will tarnish."

"What about water? A bowl of water serves as a mirror. And a stone or metal bowl could last a thousand years. It could tarnish or be chipped and not affect the reflective surface."

"That could work," he said.

"But how to connect the two bowls so they act like two connected mirrors?"

He thought about it, and the moment he remembered something, his stomach lurched and his heart beat harder.

"I know what I need," he said. "But it's back in the Librarian's quarters."

CHAPTER 27

"YOU COULD SWOOP DOWN ON their heads, screaming," said Gopan to Astrid. "That would scare them through the Door."

"I don't think Jeff would approve of that method," said Astrid, taking a bite of her egg salad sandwich. They were downstairs in a hospital cafeteria, and Astrid was treating Gopan to lunch after an emotionally grueling training session involving twin baby boys. One twin had died and refused to leave the other. The living one had simply screamed.

"And I thought you cared about the emotional well-being of the souls," said Astrid. "Scaring them with a screaming owl is hardly good for them."

"I do care. But I'm trying to think of how your aspect could be useful to you."

Astrid didn't think her owl aspect was helpful at all, not the way Robin's was, or even Gopan's. Both of them could comfort the dead, while Graciela could too, if she chose. Once again, she wondered about Jeff's aspect.

"I think aside from flying around and seeing in the dark, it's useless," she said. "Just a nice perk of being part of death. I guess it's compensation for stuff like today with the babies."

Gopan, she had learned, always appeared in his aspect of an eight-year-old boy. He became serious. "I know we're joking around, but this job can take a toll on you."

"I know. Graciela said not to let it get to me."

"She's right. But honestly, if it didn't get to you, I think that would be worse. Can you imagine doing what we just did and feeling perfectly good afterward?"

She thought of the twins, the way the dead twin had reached his ghostly little arms toward his brother and how she had been forced to carry him to the Door and push him through. The other one had screamed, the body of his dead brother still warm in the incubator beside him.

"See, here's how it is," said Gopan, taking a sip of his soda. "One day, you'll turn seventy and you'll retire. Then hopefully many years later, you'll die and you will walk through that Door and you will see exactly what waits on the other side. How you prepare for that time is what you're doing here. What you are now, owl aspect and all, is important. But not as important as that person that you will become. That's why I'm so interested in your aspect."

"I don't even know why I ended up with it. The only thing I can think of is a little metal owl bell I've had since I was a baby. It's been on my nightstand all my life."

"Tell me about the owl," said Gopan. "What does it mean to you?"

"You sound like a psychologist."

He shrugged one shoulder and Astrid took a deep breath.

"It's just a metal bell in the shape of an owl."

She didn't tell him that it had traveled through time with Elliot, was made of cold iron which caused pain to the sidhe, or that she was immune to it because it had been on her nightstand from her infancy onward, causing her pain but forcing her to develop immunity. It had also been instrumental in saving the world once.

"Is it the same species of owl you are?" Gopan asked.

"A great horned owl. That's the kind I am and I suppose that's what the bell is. It's stylized."

"And how do you think of this owl bell? Is it friendly?"

"My God, you are a psychologist. Is that your day job?"

"Nope. But I'm old enough to know a few things about human nature."

"Well, it has round eyes and it seems to always be watching everything, taking everything in. It's a little sentinel, standing guard."

Gopan spread his hands. "And there you are!"

"A guard?"

"And an observer. You're an artist, looking at everything, taking it in. Noticing details that others might not. You are a thing of seeing, a pair of round eyes, taking in the world and processing it into art. You stand watch, like a guardian."

Astrid wasn't sure what she thought of that. Yes, she observed things, and as a naturally shy person, she tended toward the edges of gatherings while her cousin Elliot liked to be in the thick of things. Quiet observation came naturally to her.

"See, knowing that about yourself might make you a better psychopomp," said Gopan.

"I don't know how helpful that is on a practical level. How does it make me do a better job?"

He took another sip of his soda. "I'm not sure. The souls go through the Doors either way, but maybe it affects you differently than the rest of us. Graciela sees this as a duty. Do it and don't get sentimental. Robin genuinely loves his souls, which helps him to cope with the emotional damage from jobs like today's twins. Jeff sees things in a more complex way, all interweaving pieces making up a whole."

"And you?"

"Me? I just want to know the meaning behind it all."

"Oh, is that all?" she said jokingly. "I thought with a child for an aspect, you'd be carefree and happy."

"Oh, I suppose I am. I do like a good laugh."

"How come you always show up in your aspect?" Astrid asked. "Everyone else stays in their ordinary form."

"I like this one."

“You aren’t horribly deformed or some hairy otherkind monster?”

“Nope. Just a man.”

“A man who isn’t a psychologist, right?”

“Actually, I’m a bartender.”

CHAPTER 28

HAZEL PUSHED BACK FROM HER desk, closing her ship's log and setting it on the shelf overhead.

Both Yukiko and Astrid were in her quarters, Astrid on her stomach on the floor, drawing, her box with the glass sphere beside her. Yukiko was curled up in a chair, reading. Their own shared quarters were cramped and damp, though they had hammocks, blankets and enough storage for their belongings. The captain's quarters boasted a sturdy table, comfortable chairs and a rug on the floor. The crew didn't care much for human comforts, and though Neil hadn't cared about a drab, tiny space below decks, Yukiko and Astrid had.

"If you don't like your quarters, I can tie up another hammock in here, maybe two," said Hazel, surveying the space.

"That's all right," said Astrid. "I can sleep in there. It's just that there's not enough light for drawing and it's a little cold."

Yukiko didn't say a word, which Hazel thought intolerably rude. She had never much cared for the Kitsune, but their paths hadn't crossed too often, so her personal feelings were of little consequence. Elliot had been fond of her, but he liked almost anything pretty and female. Sister adored Yukiko, but she also adored Santiago, so her taste in companions was questionable.

Yukiko was disgraced among her people by the loss of her tail, which might explain why she stayed with the

Time Corps. She had a reputation for being quiet and standoffish, but basically decent. Perhaps she stayed in Los Angeles because she had nowhere else to go.

"Will you grow another tail?" asked Hazel.

Yukiko looked up at her in surprise. It had been an indelicate question, but Hazel wondered about the strange woman who appeared human but was really a fox spirit.

"A century, maybe less." Yukiko's voice was soft. "I can earn another through service, though that's rare."

"Is that why you're helping us?"

"No. I owe Neil and Elliot a favor. I met them long ago in San Francisco, when I was young."

"Wait," said Astrid. "Does that mean that Neil will come back? He still needs to see you in your past."

"He might have already done it," said Hazel. "How old was he when you met him?"

Yukiko looked like she was thinking about it. "In his thirties or forties, I'd guess. Hard to tell."

Well, that was no help at all, thought Hazel. If only she knew that Neil would live beyond his forties, then she'd know he would return from his stone form. It would give her hope.

"How old are you, anyway?" Hazel asked Yukiko. "Were you born in Japan?"

"I was. And I'm not that old, not for a Kitsune."

The ship lurched hard, and Hazel popped her head out the door to consult with Mr. Escobar.

"Rough seas tonight, ladies," she said, turning back. "I hope you don't get seasick."

Astrid grabbed at her pencil as it rolled away and then continued her sketch. It was a drawing of a monkey, one of the crew perhaps, but it had no background or scenery yet, just the rough shape of its body and head.

"How did you end up in San Francisco?" Hazel asked Yukiko.

"You're full of questions tonight," said Yukiko.

"We're stuck on a ship. Might as well swap some tales."

"I came to San Francisco as a bride, a mail-order bride. I didn't have much choice."

"What was your husband like? Did you grow to love him?"

"He died," Yukiko said flatly.

Astrid glanced up but then went back to her drawing.

"I'm going to go up and study the monkeys' hands," said Astrid. "I can't get this one detail right."

She closed the door behind her and the ship tilted, sending Astrid's box with the orb sliding across the floor. It banged into the wall hard and Hazel grabbed it and opened it. The simple glass sphere lay on its bed of Styrofoam packing material, unbroken and whole.

"It's fine," she said.

"Here, let me see it," said Yukiko.

Hazel handed over the box. "Can you use your magic on it?"

Yukiko took the ball and studied it. "I already tried. I tried seeing through any illusions put on it, but I didn't find anything."

"Do you think it's made of some rare material? Is that why it's valuable?" asked Hazel.

"It looks like glass to me, but I suppose that's possible," said Yukiko, eying the ball. "After all, if a dragon wants it, it must be worth a lot."

The ship heaved and Hazel grabbed onto her desk to keep her balance. A sharp bang came from the cargo hold, and she was glad that Neil's body was in her quarters, safe. She listened as crew members headed down to tie up the cargo more securely. Any loose items might damage the hull, and though Skidbladnir was strong, she was not unsinkable.

She loved the ship, as grouchy and disagreeable as she could be at times. But if Hazel had been imprisoned in a tiny glass bottle, as Skidbladnir had, she might be grouchy too. She wondered what it had been like for the ship and crew, all those years, trapped in glass.

Trapped in glass.

Son of a gun.

"There's something in it!" she cried, startling Yukiko. "It's not the glass ball that's valuable. It's the thing inside it!"

"There's nothing in it. It's glass all the way through," said Yukiko.

"Skidbladnir looked like a model ship when she was in her bottle. It wasn't until she got to her own home world, the hub world, that she returned to her normal living state and her monkeys became visible. Perhaps this glass ball is similar."

Hazel took the ball from Yukiko, but the Kitsune was correct, the thing was just glass. But perhaps the thing was not from this world.

"Astrid!" she called up the steps, and the girl joined them.

"This sphere, we think it might be like the bottle that Skidbladnir was in. It might be a container."

"It's possible," said Astrid. "I've considered it. But I wouldn't know how to open it, short of breaking it."

"Not to open it, just to see what's in it. If it's from a different world, then taking it to that home world would reveal what's inside."

Astrid looked at her, eyes widening as the idea sunk in. "It's from the Seelie, so it probably originated in their world."

Hazel handed the ball to her. "Can you open a Door to Seelie?"

"I can, but I'd rather not go back there if I can avoid it. We're not on good terms." She glanced around Hazel's quarters, then ordered Yukiko and Hazel to stand back.

A cloud of mist appeared in front of Astrid, dilating open to reveal an empty beach. The sky was pale orange.

It wasn't the orange of a sunset, but was the differently colored sky of another world.

Astrid held the sphere through the Door, and Hazel pressed close to see. Once the ball was in Seelie, something became visible inside. At first, it looked like a pile of cloth, but then she saw that it was three women, all asleep.

"Slaves," said Yukiko. "They're being sent as slaves."

Astrid pulled her arm back and closed the Door. "How can you be sure? Is it possible they're going willingly?"

"As willingly as I did," said Yukiko. "There might be a trade, a deal or some kind of threat. Whatever it is, they're trapped in there."

Hazel grabbed the ball over Astrid's cry of protest. The interior was empty and it looked like a simple glass ball once more. But if there were people inside, they weren't going to stay there for long. She had aided the Underground Railroad during the Civil War and she had helped free Neil from his master. She had no tolerance for the buying and trading of human beings, even if they weren't really humans, but Seelie.

"What if they're willing?" asked Astrid. "What if they asked to go?"

"Then why put them in this if they can travel normally?" said Hazel.

"Some of the Seelie can't travel in our world."

Hazel held up the ball. "Honestly, do you think those girls are in there of their own free will?"

"There's no way to know without asking them," said Astrid. She did not try to reclaim the ball.

"Then let's ask them," said Hazel and hurled the ball at the bare floor where it shattered with a lovely musical sound. For a moment, nothing happened and the shards lay exploded on the wooden floorboards. Then, Hazel leapt back as three full-sized women materialized on the floor, curled together like a pile of puppies. They roused quickly and huddled with their arms around each other. All three were identical, from their pale skin and violet eyes to their black hair that they wore tied back. Even their robes were identical.

"Where is our master?" asked the one in the center.

"Do you mean the drake?" asked Hazel.

"We were meant for Yelbeghen. Where is he? Has something changed?"

"You could say that," said Hazel. "We're days away from him. And you're free people."

Her words did not have the expected effect. One of the women burst into tears. Another comforted her, saying words that Hazel could not understand. The third stood up and approached Hazel.

"If we're free, then we'd be better off dead."

CHAPTER 29

ELLIOT DID NOT HAVE TIME to ponder the irony of a time traveler being short on time. Bennu would only be back once more, and then his opportunity to smuggle anything out of the Library would be lost. He had to hurry.

The thought of never seeing Bennu again twisted like a serpent in his stomach. Yet, through all their time together, nothing he had said convinced her to abandon her duty to her people. Her entire life, she had been groomed for the possibility of being traded in marriage, and though she had never anticipated being so far from her desert home, she had tried to accept the idea with grace. He admired her fortitude, her courage and her devotion to her people. He even admired her desire to bring her peaceful goddess to the warlike Northerners. But none of that would keep her with him. Unless he found a way out, she would be lost to him forever.

He stood at the end of the hallway where the door to the Librarian's quarters waited, one in a row of doors, unmarked and unremarkable. He wished this place had a standard day and night, then he could perhaps predict when the Librarian would be in his quarters, asleep or out.

Though he had asked the librarians a few discreet questions, no one seemed to know if the Librarian held to any set schedule. The Library seemed to function without him, staffed by the trapped and the willing and maintained by the same. But it stood to reason that the Librarian left his quarters at some point. The creature had to eat and do something other than rattle around in the mad chaos of his maze of rooms.

The twin black marble bowls waited inside, in the room of the animal-faced pillars, the room where he had first heard the Librarian's wings. He opened the door, listening. Nothing. He pushed it open, wide enough so he could make a fast escape, and then headed for the room with the bowls.

He passed the piles of jumbled objects, stacks of reading material and hanging tapestries, pausing for a moment at the mosaic where a Greek trireme had sailed while pigs dove off its deck. It had changed. Now, the mosaic showed a pastoral scene of green and brown fields dotted with white sheep. On the horizon were gray shapes, wolves, cresting the hill. Behind them the sun burned red, but it could have been either a sunset or a great fire. He couldn't tell.

It didn't matter, because Elliot knew precisely what this signified. This was a time slip, an anomaly where small details, and sometimes larger ones, changed. Most people were oblivious to them, adjusting their reality to the changes and never knowing the difference. But he was one of the rare people who could detect such time anomalies. His partner, Neil Grey, had told him that the ability would come in handy one day. Perhaps this was that day. He kept moving, heading to the chamber with the columns.

When he arrived, he was actually relieved to find that the animal heads at the tops of the columns were watching him, carved eyes wide open. It made him uneasy, certainly, but it meant that this area of the Library was definitely part of a time anomaly. Technically, this was a time anomaly within a place that existed outside of time. And he himself was a being out of his own time standing at the center of this time anomaly. So was the Librarian, he supposed. Were these rooms of the Library the locus of the anomaly, or was it the Librarian himself?

He would have sworn the twin bowls had been sitting on the table with the stack of woolen rugs. He moved a few things, but they weren't there. Pulling everything off that table, then the one beside it, he found nothing.

Searching the piles of objects in every corner, he considered the implications of the time anomaly. An anomaly was an instability, and instabilities, both real, like physical objects, and symbolic, like shorelines, could be dangerous. They could also be useful. Any objects from the time anomaly couldn't help but be connected to the anomaly.

He swore silently, turning in place, searching. The ears on the elephant head were smaller now, elegant and trim, those of an Indian Elephant. The cobra's mouth had opened, six-inch fangs exposed and forked tongue curling upward at the tip.

Had the Librarian moved the bowls? What if he knew that Elliot wanted them? Had he somehow heard Elliot and Bennu discussing the bowls? Was the Librarian so connected to this place that he knew everything that went on here? That had to be it. After a good five minutes in the room, he knew with certainty that the bowls weren't there.

They had to be farther in. He walked through other rooms, moving silently on his bare feet, listening and reaching out with his mind, trying to detect what was up ahead. Now that he was inside the forbidden area, he could feel the additional rooms to either side and chose a path through them.

The deeper he went, the more tidy the rooms became until he came to a chamber of neat curios in glass-fronted cabinets, two plush chairs and a fireplace. The fire was out, but the embers still glowed. He looked through the cabinets, but the bowls were nowhere to be found. They had to be farther in, and if the Librarian knew Elliot wanted them, they'd be with the man himself.

Now was the time, he supposed. The time to face the Librarian. What could the thing do to him anyway? Peck him to death? He supposed a great winged thing could very well do that. Or he could have vicious talons to shred his flesh. But what if the Librarian was something else? A griffin, a winged man or just a person who could make illusions, like the wizard in the Emerald City? Whatever he was, it was time to meet him.

He crept into the next room, a place filled with low couches and cushions, so much more welcoming than the exterior rooms. Perhaps the other rooms were meant to keep others out, to distract them with intriguing items so they would not reach the interior. But no, that made no sense. If the Librarian wanted to keep people out, he could simply lock the door.

The adjoining room held a long wooden table set with a gold runner with twin candlesticks at its center. They were lit. There were only two chairs, one at each end of the table, and each place was set. Identical black marble bowls sat at each place, one filled with an assortment of fruit and the other nearly empty. The uneaten fruit was accompanied by a full wineglass and folded napkin, while the other place setting had clearly been used.

Why would the Librarian set two places? Had he been expecting him? Or was this set for someone else? And if it had been set for a guest, why had the Librarian eaten without the person?

It didn't matter, because he wasn't staying. Any being who kept people trapped in the Library for a lifetime and drove them insane if they escaped wasn't someone who was going to help him. Elliot knew what he wanted.

Elliot grabbed the bowls, dumping the fruit out on the table. Grapes rolled across the table and an apple thudded to the floor. The pointed flames on the candles dipped sideways, flickering and then righting themselves, and Elliot spun around, but no one was there.

Silence.

He was more careful as he left this time, unsure if the Librarian might be around any corner, blocking his exit. Creeping around corners, clutching the bowls to his chest, he finally made it to the room with the columns.

When he saw the things watching him from the top of each column, he ran. Each one was topped with a human face, all with eyes open, each one's mouth curved into a smile.

CHAPTER 30

ASTRID ATTEMPTED TO OFFER FOOD to the three women, but they insisted they were not hungry. Hazel muttered something about it being crowded in her quarters and headed up on deck. After some tea, the crying girl eventually calmed down. Once Astrid reassured them that the ship was on its way to Yelbeghen's island, they relaxed and told her their names were Isadora, Briar and Opal.

"Why did you say all would be lost if you were freed? Did you want to be in that glass ball?" Astrid asked. Opal's lower lip trembled and Briar put her arm around her.

"We slept inside, so it wasn't frightening," said the one named Isadora. "We were meant for Yelbeghen. He was supposed to be the one to release us."

"Why does it matter how you get out?"

"He wants his gifts intact. He prefers to open them himself."

"And you three are 'gifts' for him."

"Yes, and I want to make sure that my sisters and I reach him soon."

Though she pressed them, they continued to insist that they wanted to be delivered to Yelbeghen, and that they should travel with all haste. The three girls insisted on sleeping together, so Astrid and Mr. Escobar tied up three hammocks in the cargo bay, as it was the only space large enough.

"Women on a ship are bad luck," said Mr. Escobar. "They bring trouble."

"The captain is a woman," said Astrid.

"She doesn't count. She's the captain."

"And Yukiko and I are too."

"Yes, but now there are just too many of you. And now there's crying and sniveling. I suppose we'll be rid of those three soon enough."

The next day, they came to shore on a small Mediterranean island between Sicily and Tunisia. They left the ship near enough to the closest town to take on supplies, but far enough away to avoid detection. Yukiko, who didn't enjoy the sea, said she was glad to get off the ship to purchase supplies. She went alone, and Hazel asked Astrid if she would take the girls off the ship for a while. Astrid agreed and the four of them walked into town with Pangur Ban trailing behind.

When they were halfway there, Astrid suddenly felt a pulling sensation inside herself. She knew exactly what it was, a psychopomp job.

"Pangur Ban," she said, "could you look after the girls? I have to do a job."

"Certainly," said the cat.

Astrid made a Door, just as Graciela had taught her, arriving on the side of the road next to a demolished car. After she had sent the young dead man through her Door, she returned to the road she had left. It did not take long for her to find her charges, as they were wandering down a street, looking in shop windows. Opal clung to Isadora, while Briar trailed behind, glancing often at the sky.

"This island is so unlike our home. And the sky is a strange color," she said to Astrid. "I'm not sure I like it. It looks so cold."

Compared to the pale orange of the Seelie sky, Astrid supposed it did. "I know someone else from the Unseelie world who now likes the color. She's always looking at the sky. She was a slave there, but then she got free."

"How did this person get free?" asked Briar.

"Someone took her place," said Astrid.

"I don't think that will happen for us. Triplets are rare. There are none to take our place."

"What did Yelbeghen pay for you?"

"It wasn't a sale, not like human exchanges. Our village is small, an island, and the drake helped us. Long ago, he had a dear friend among our people. The friend is dead now, but the drake occasionally visits the island. A generation ago, our birth rates were too low, and the few babies born often died. Some were born deformed. The village was poor, and even if they had money, they would never have lived on the mainland. So they stayed and suffered."

"They didn't like the other Seelie?"

"On their island, they were largely free of the queen's interference."

"How did the drake help you?"

"He gave us his special blessing and cured the land. They offered him payment, but he said he'd claim payment another time. When my sisters and I were born, healthy and strong, he said he wanted us when we came of age. Our parents wanted to refuse, and they petitioned the royal court for assistance. The court offered none, even insisting that we be given to the drake sooner than our father wished."

"I thought they hated the drake. I thought they feared him."

"They do. He helped our island, but he would never have helped those aligned with the royal court. It's the ruling class he hates, though the members of the court were the only ones who could get us into the human world to deliver us to him. The court does not want the drake upset with them. He can be ferocious. But he can also be kind."

"It doesn't sound like kindness if he asked for people as payment," said Astrid.

"Still, the price was fair," said Briar. "Many babies have been born, and they're fat and healthy. Our crops are good, and the village has entered an age of prosperity. He has taught our people the ways of commerce and trade, so we are better than before. Our people thrive, and we must be content with that, whatever happens to us."

"I could return you home right now if you wanted to. I'm a Door, and I think I can open a Door into Seelie fairly easily. You and your sisters could go home."

Briar sighed. "I would like to, but it's impossible."

"Would the drake curse your land?"

"No, nothing like that. The blessing, once given, cannot be removed."

"Then what's the problem?"

Briar did not answer, but joined her sisters to look in shop windows. Astrid hung back and Pangur Ban stepped up beside her.

"Well?" said Astrid, too soft for humans, but knowing the cat would hear.

"Their ways are not your ways, nor mine," said Pangur Ban. "And technically, they go willingly."

"They go under duress."

"All hard decisions are made under duress. Many such trades have happened with women agreeing to exchanges like this for the sake of others. Women have long been a form of currency."

"I suppose you consider yourself lucky that you aren't one of us."

"I do, yes."

They paused their talk until a group of people had passed.

"You've seen a lot in your life, haven't you?" Astrid said.

"Sometimes I think too much. In a way, Huginn is fortunate not to remember his long, long life. I see how that girl, Briar, is afraid, though she does not say so. I also think that she fears for her life."

CHAPTER 31

Hazel watched as a Door opened in her quarters, dilating open until she could see straight into it. On the other side stood Astrid holding a cardboard box in the kitchen of the Time Corps house in Los Angeles. Astrid hugged Sister good-bye then stepped through the Door which then closed.

"The Professor told me to give this to you," said Astrid. "He can walk you through the installation over the phone."

Hazel called him on her mobile phone and set it on speakerphone. How wonderful that a man born in 1832 and a woman born in 1846 could speak to each other across the world. The other Time Corps members were born in later centuries, and didn't appreciate things like television, airplanes and anesthesia. Well, Felicia did, but that was only because she was a doctor who had lived in both the nineteenth and twenty-first centuries and had done unanesthesized surgery on Civil War soldiers. But the others would never see the world as she and the Professor did. Even driving in a car was wondrous in its fashion.

"Hey, Professor," she said when he answered. "Tell me what this thing does."

"It allows the machine to develop a dynamic time lock using a predictive algorithm that lets it fix onto times normally outside the vicinity of our origin point."

"How far from our origin point?" The machine had first come to exist in the mid-nineteenth century, but little by little, the Professor had expanded its abilities to reach farther times.

"A few thousand years, though I'd certainly not recommend it. You won't speak the language or know the customs."

"Yukiko is with us. She can communicate with any human alive."

"I know. But I want you to take care. I worry about you."

"I know. Now tell me how to attach this thing to my ship."

They spent the next hour going through the installation, and when they were finished, Hazel wanted to give it a try. But with everyone on shore, including Yukiko, she knew she should not. Besides, they had no idea exactly where they needed to go, and she was wise enough not to fool with time unnecessarily.

"You be careful," said the Professor. "Oh, and Felicia sends her love."

"Wait, Professor? Now that you're married, what are you going to do once you find a way to get Felicia home? Her world is so hard to reach and you might not be able to come back. Will you stay with her?"

He was silent for so long that she wondered if he was going to answer or if he had been distracted by something in his laboratory.

"I'm not going to leave you. I'll find a way to travel between the two worlds."

"But if you had to choose?"

"I won't. Now get that thing working, and may God watch over you."

They hung up and Hazel closed the cabinet that contained the time machine, now upgraded with this dynamic time lock device. She glanced at Neil's crate and said a little prayer for him, wherever he was. If the Professor left for Felicia's home world and could not get back, she'd still have her ship and crew. Of course, she would be welcome to go with them, but in Felicia's world, things like talking monkeys and living ships could not exist. She could leave the ship to Mr. Escobar, but hated the thought of it. Either way, she'd lose someone.

But the Professor was stubborn if he was anything, and he'd find a way. He always did.

For now, she enjoyed her solitude. With everyone on shore and the ship docked, she had some time on her hands. She had not realized what a solitary life she normally led, but with Astrid, Yukiko, Pangur Ban, Huginn and the triplets on board, the ship felt crowded. Of course, the monkey crew far outnumbered them, but they never troubled Hazel in her quarters or asked for special meals or sulked like Briar or cried like Opal. Even Neil, who often joined her on Skidbladnir, sometimes as bosun and other times as a guest, was so quiet and unobtrusive that she hardly noticed him.

She took out her violin and looked over its familiar curves and glossy reddish finish. It even smelled good, of rosin and polished wood. The instrument had been a gift from Neil when she was eleven and he was in his forties. Her first violin, the one from her father, had been destroyed by her cruel uncle and the mysterious Mr. Grey had given her a new one before he had left her century.

She tuned it and then played, slipping into the familiar state where she was unaware of the passage of time, cold or hunger, where only the sound and the sensation of the music enveloped her. She played some Irish songs that the Professor had taught her, then a few Baroque pieces, which Neil had always loved. She slipped out of her reverie at the feeling of being watched.

"Please don't stop," said Neil.

She almost cried out at the sight of the man leaning against the door frame, his hands in the pockets of his black duster. He was younger than she had last seen him, perhaps in his late twenties or early thirties.

"It's you," she breathed, then forced herself to act rationally. This was a younger version of Neil, crossing her personal timeline. She couldn't very well run to him or tell him that his own corpse was lying in a crate against the wall.

"Of course it's me. I was in this time and I saw from your archived logs that you were here on this date. Please, don't let me stop you from playing. It's half of why I came."

It was all she could do to keep from throwing her arms around him. Tears stung her eyes as she played for him. When she was finished, she set the violin in its case.

"I wish I could play like that," said Neil.

"I've offered to teach you."

He looked down and shook his head. "It won't be the same. How old are you now, anyway?"

That would have been a much odder question if they hadn't known each other asynchronously for so long.

"Twenty-three."

He seemed to brighten. "And how many months?"

She counted them up. "Five. Why? Is something going to happen to me before I turn twenty-four?"

"No, I was just curious. What are you doing and where are you headed?"

"A Greek island. A delivery. Nothing interesting."

"I doubt that, but if you don't want to tell me, then don't."

He sat down and lifted the little toy jackal off her shelf. It had long ago stopped working, but she had kept it all these years, another gift from the older version of Neil.

"Did the Professor make this for you?" he asked.

"No, I got it during Mardi Gras when I was young."

Hazel knew he had seen it on her shelf before and perhaps wondered why she had kept it. When he was older, he would see it being sold by a New Orleans street vendor and would purchase it for her. She closed the violin case and set it aside. She was almost afraid to turn back to him, as if he'd vanish like a ghost. She found him sitting there as solid and real as ever. She bit her lip to keep from crying, both from joy at seeing him and sorrow that it was the last time.

"God, Hazel. What's wrong?" He came to her.

She studied his face, the set of his jaw, the brown of his eyes. How many people wished that they could see their dead loved one once more? And here he was. But she had to be strong. No blubbering and weeping.

"Oh, nothing," she said. "I just have a full ship and I needed some time alone."

"I can go if you want."

"No, you don't bother me. Not like everyone else."

"High praise indeed. Well, Elliot is waiting for me back at our hotel. We're leaving tonight for the nineteen twenties. I don't suppose you'd care to join us?"

"I have to complete this job."

"You could complete it, then travel back in time and come meet us in a few hours at our hotel."

"The island isn't ten miles across. I couldn't." She wasn't able to time travel within ten miles of herself, and Skidbladnir would be docked in her current place until morning.

"Ah, no. But we could meet you farther out."

She thought about it. She could do just that, if she wanted to. Neil was around forty when he died, which meant she had years and years to find him, travel with him, do whatever she liked. She and Neil and Elliot could have adventures, years and years worth.

"What's in the crate?" Neil asked, noticing the box holding his body.

"Just supplies. The cargo hold is being used as a bunk by a few people, so I had some items moved in here."

She hated lying to him, even about a small thing, even to save him from the pain of facing his own death.

“You can’t tell me, can you?” he asked. He knew she was lying.

She shook her head.

“I should go.”

“Wait. Did you ever find out anything about the letters in your mouth?”

He glanced at the open door, rightfully cautious about anyone overhearing.

“No,” he said, and then left.

But she wondered if he too was keeping a secret.

CHAPTER 32

"SOMETHING HAS ARRIVED," SAID MALACHY to Elliot one morning in the kitchen.

"Things are always arriving here, aren't they?"

"People, yes. But things, more seldom."

Elliot dried his hands on the dishtowel tucked into his belt and then took down a large bowl and started cracking eggs into it. The scholars would be having scrambled eggs, toast, fruit and coffee this morning. He wasn't in the mood to do anything more elaborate.

"They were your books," said Malachy.

He stopped. "Which books?"

"I found them among the stacks, spread out as if someone had tossed them onto the floor. I checked the records, and they had been taken by you."

"I've never checked out any books," said Elliot. "I borrow them, but I never take them out of the Library. I couldn't if I wanted to."

"I did not say you checked them out. I said you took them."

And then Elliot understood, or he thought he did.

"Let me see these books."

There were four items: a Metallurgy book, two identical fairy tale books and a black, half-empty sketch book with Astrid's name written on the inside front cover. He had seen all but the sketch book before.

"Why did you say I took them?" he asked Malachy.

"It's what our records showed. You owe a large fine on all but the black one."

"A fine not to exceed one hundred years? Like it says here inside the cover?" He opened the Metallurgy book, where the label was half torn out, but partially readable.

"Yes, but it looks like you never paid the fine."

"I haven't taken the books either, so your records are wrong."

But he knew they were perfectly correct, or he hoped they were. Because these were books that he would give to a younger Astrid when he was older. When she was nine, and again at eighteen, she would receive the fairy tale books as gifts. He supposed he would give both of them to her to make sure she knew how important the content was. If it weren't for her knowledge of the stories, she would never know that salt and knots repel the sidhe. So much of what she needed to know was contained in those books. He would also give her mythology books and others, scattered through her birthdays, all as part of her education.

As for him, he would deliver the metallurgy book to a younger Elliot, who would then have a metal owl bell forged. It would help Astrid to save the world.

"The records are correct," said Malachy. "And your fine is fair and just. You have begun to pay it."

"I won't live a hundred more years. Maybe eighty more, if I'm lucky."

"Then that is all you can pay. We cannot ask for more."

"How generous," he said, but Malachy did not seem to understand the sarcasm. "It's not a fair fine," Elliot explained. "A lifetime of service for one book is too much."

"Three books."

"Fine, three books. It's still a ridiculous fine. And besides, they're here now. They're returned."

"The Librarian sets these rules, not me."

Elliot was close to saying what the Librarian could do

with his rules, but Malachy excused himself. As soon as he was gone, Elliot flipped through Astrid's sketch book.

Despite Elliot telling her otherwise, she had never believed that she had any real talent. He knew that she was only her repeating what her mother said. No matter how good Astrid was, his aunt always told her it was a useless ability.

It may not be useful in the traditional sense, but no one with any sense could deny that Astrid was talented. She had been one of a very select few to be offered an art scholarship at Columbia. She captured movement and stillness, curves and distance just right, but with her own style that was detailed and, he had to admit, a little dark. He paged through drawings of her room, the inside of the commuter train, parts of Luna Park, a shark-tailed mermaid, a woman with a ram's head, a bipedal raccoon person in some kind of monk's robe and oddly, a number of pictures of mirrors and doors.

Mirrors. Doors and mirrors.

He had seen mirrors become Doors before, with Astrid there to open them. But could she create a portable Door, one made of pencil on paper? Was that why she sent the book to him?

"Astrid?" he said, peering into one of the mirror drawings. "Are you there?"

He watched. The pencil shading inside the mirror frame did not move. Of course it hadn't. That was a stupid idea. He was standing in a kitchen, talking to a sketch book. He slapped it shut.

Elliot continued his breakfast preparations. As he cooked, he pondered, occasionally glancing at the pile of books on the kitchen counter.

These books could form an unstable time loop. Not the sketch book, as that was clearly Astrid's and he hadn't given it to her. But the other three, the Metallurgy and two fairy tale books, originated in the Library. If he took these books from the kitchen counter and got them out of the Library and into his world, then they'd have no stable origin. They'd endlessly loop, from today, to being taken from the Library, to Astrid and his own past, to whatever event led them to be dropped back into the Library, and then back to this kitchen counter.

That would not do. It formed an instability, and though some instabilities could be useful, an object with no origin created an instability. Even the black marble bowls had a stable origin, though he didn't know what it was. They also had a future. He hoped their future involved traveling with Bennu to the North and signaling Pangur Ban and Huginn.

That meant that the books in front of him had to go back into the stacks, but they also had to come with him.

After breakfast, he consulted one of the Library computers and found the location of the shelves for his books. He found the Metallurgy book first, pulling the newer version from the shelf and replacing it with the older version. The time loop was now resolved. The thing would go from Library to young Astrid and Elliot, to being dropped back into the Library, and back to its shelf, where it would sit and rot for all he cared.

He opened the younger book and tore out part of the inner front cover where it said "Library of Alexandria." Now it just said "Library of A—."

He found one copy of the fairy tale book, but could not find another. For a few minutes, he was afraid that the thing would have to remain an unstable time loop with two versions existing side by side. But when he consulted the computer again, he found another copy three floors down.

He went to his room, set the new books beside his bed, and then picked up Astrid's sketch book again. Aside from the clothes he had arrived with, it was the only object from home. He flipped past the strange animal people and studied the other drawings more carefully. There was the front of the Time Corps house, a picture of Sister sitting on the floor, looking up at the sky through a window and a picture of Pangur Ban sleeping. Like all cats, she was sweet looking when she was asleep, but Elliot had never petted her once he knew she was sentient. Astrid was the only one who did that.

He stopped short when he turned the page to the picture of the mirror. On the mirror's surface, in Astrid's writing, was one word: Elliot. It was written backwards.

It hadn't been there before. He knew it hadn't. Did that mean that this book was part of a time instability? Was this one of those minor detail changes that only he could detect?

Perhaps. But perhaps it was something else.

He dug a pencil stub out from under the edge of his bed and he wrote six words on the center of the mirror:

White Bast

Bowl

Norway

Time Lock

CHAPTER 33

ASTRID KNEW SHE HAD SEEN something, and it was no trick of the light. She sat on the ship's deck and held the page of her sketch book down as the ocean wind tried to whip it closed. The day was overcast and chilly, but aside from Hazel's desk, being out on deck allowed her the best light for drawing.

Something in the drawing had moved.

The thought that she might be imagining things did not cross her mind. Six months ago, she would have shut the book and thought that she had an overactive imagination. But today, she lifted her paper up to better catch the light.

This sketch book was one of her newer ones, as Sister had tossed her old one through the Door. This one was only about a third full, and she had drawn things she had seen, taking an opportunity to draw a few members of the crew as well as some practice sketches. She often drew whatever was in front of her, but interspersed throughout the book were drawings of various types of mirrors. She had sketched many before, simply because she liked them and enjoyed working at portraying the reflection of a room. Getting the distance and perspective correct was an entertaining challenge.

One of the drawings near the end was still blank in the center, but she was certain she had seen a face in it. Now, it was simply empty. She knew it was possible for her to make a Door with a drawing, but the only time she had done it, she had only needed to travel a few feet, through a cold iron barrier. Now she wondered if she could do more.

She waited, watching the image for movement or anything at all. Nothing happened, and after a few minutes, she filled in the empty mirror frame with shelves of books, trying to replicate the brief image of the Library she had seen when she had sent Elliot through, and again when Sister had thrown the books.

Huginn landed just behind her. “You should put that away and come do something fun,” he said.

“Does that look like the Library to you?” she asked, holding up the book.

“It looks like any library. But since the Library looks much like any other library, yes, it looks like the Library.”

“Be serious. I’m trying to help Elliot.”

“By making a drawing?”

“By trying an alternative method of Door-making.”

Huginn sat silent for a while, and she wondered if he had any ideas. She asked him.

“Nope. But I’m waiting to see if it works.”

“I don’t think I can do it while being watched,” said Astrid. “It’s a tricky thing.”

“Fine, fine. But if you change your mind, let me know.” He flapped away.

Astrid knew that Huginn wanted to go flying with her. They were half a day from the drake’s island, but being stuck on the ship was difficult for those of the group who weren’t sailors. Even a short flight over the endless water was a pleasant diversion. At least she could leave when she wanted to.

She stared at the drawing, concentrating, imagining that the picture was real, like a little portal through which she could stick her finger. She waited, the minutes ticking by. Nothing occurred.

Frustrated, she erased the interior section of the

mirror, leaving the frame empty once again. Then she sat and tried concentrating. It remained blank.

She looked up at Huginn, a black dot circling overhead, and decided she might as well join him. As she went to close the book, the erasure lines twitched, then became moving lines, forming into a thousand streaking points, like comets. The picture was moving, too fast to form into a single image. Then, it went blank.

She continued to watch, but nothing more happened. Huginn returned to her side and she told him what had happened.

"Could you read it?"

"I don't think it was words. It was just a bunch of lines moving really fast."

"Unfortunate. Pictures or words would be so much more useful."

"You're right."

She took her pencil and wrote her cousin's name on the mirror, and she and Huginn watched as it sat there, as ordinary as could be. Then, she felt the pulling of a psychopomp job within herself.

She shut the book, set it aside and made a Door to a room in South Africa where a woman was dying. When she returned, a member of the crew was sitting on his haunches, paging through her sketch book. She suppressed the urge to tell him to get away from it, reminding herself that he wasn't a child or curious animal, but an intelligent being.

"Why do you do this?" he asked, examining the pictures. "Why do you make images on paper? It serves no purpose."

She wasn't sure how to answer. "Well, I enjoy it, for one. And people like looking at other people's drawings."

The monkey looked up at her quizzically, his black eyes narrowed in thought. "Why is that enjoyable?"

"I don't know. I suppose we like to look at the world the way other people see it. To see what they see."

"Why not look with your own eyes?"

"We do that too. But it's sometimes—"

One of the crew members called the monkey over, and he bounded away. Astrid picked up her book and flipped through.

The drawing had changed.

Under Elliot's name was a bunch of jagged script. They were letters, but they were misshapen and unreadable. Then, after a moment, she understood that they were backwards. That, and the person who wrote them had terrible handwriting.

There were six words, and she read them carefully to herself.

"Hey, Huginn!" she called, and he flapped down from the rigging.

"Take a look at this."

It took him only a moment to read it.

"I used to live in Norway. But white Bast ..." He glanced over at Pangur Ban, who was sitting inside a coil of rope, eyes closed. "I've seen a statue like that before."

Pangur Ban must have overheard their conversation and decided it was more interesting than lying out on deck. She slid over.

"Did you see the statue in Norway?" Astrid asked Huginn.

"I don't remember, but it's possible. The thing that confuses me is how I remembered it. I mentioned it to Julius, and neither of us knew why."

"Don't you remember random things sometimes?"

"I do. And it wouldn't concern me, but I have so few memories from that time, and I've only remembered them very recently."

"This is true," said Pangur Ban. "You had not mentioned these memories before. It has only been in the last few weeks that you've remembered them."

Astrid thought about it. "Do you think maybe a future

Elliot came and reminded you a few weeks ago so you'd remember now?"

"I would have noticed," said Pangur Ban, "even if Huginn forgot."

"We need to figure this out," said Astrid. "If this is all Elliot wrote, then he picked every word for a reason.

"I'll ask Hazel if I can use her computer," said Pangur Ban. At Astrid's look, she explained, "I can type a key at a time. And I can read."

"Of course, I'm sorry."

"Huginn," said Pangur Ban. "You should join me soon. We will see what else you remember."

The cat left them.

Again, Astrid felt the pulling sensation. She sighed. "I have to go do another job."

"Very well. But be proud of yourself. You did make a new kind of Door, in a way."

Before she went, Astrid grabbed her pencil and wrote, "We're coming."

CHAPTER 34

"Mr. Escobar, you're acting captain," said Hazel as she pulled her pack onto her back and took one last look around the ship. "Take good care of her."

"Of course," he said.

Hazel, Astrid and the three sisters walked down the gangplank, and Hazel turned to watch the crew pull it back up, then turn the ship and sail out into deeper waters.

Yukiko, not relishing the idea of meeting a drake, had chosen to remain on the ship. She, Pangur Ban and Huginn were headed to Norway, where they had a few places they wished to look for this white Bast statue. How it could be useful in finding Elliot, Hazel did not know. But it was the only idea they had, and if Elliot had deemed it important enough to communicate, they'd follow his lead. Skidbladnir herself had also proved useful, as she remembered many of the cities that Huginn might have visited in his early years.

Hazel knew they would take good care of Neil's body and the ship, but it was hard for her to watch the ship go. She had her phone, and Yukiko kept hers on her person at all times, so they were not out of touch until the ship traveled in time, which it would do shortly. It would return within a day, but she hated to be separated from her ship, even for a short while.

"You ready?" asked Astrid gently.

"I'm not afraid, if that's what you mean," said Hazel.

"Dragon or no, I'm going to ask him what he knows about golems. Anyone that old has to know something about them."

Opal sniffled and wiped her eyes with her sleeve, and Hazel had to keep herself from ordering the girl to grow a spine and toughen up. At least Briar and Isadora weren't so easily frightened.

"Stop it. You'll be fine," she said to Opal. "You don't have to stay if you don't want to."

"No," said Isadora. "We're going."

Astrid gave Hazel a look, and Hazel decided to leave management of the Seelie girls to Astrid. Hazel headed up the beach to search for a footpath or some way inland that didn't involve hiking through thorny, waist-high plant life.

From where they stood on the beach, the island appeared uninhabited. But they knew better. Whatever the drake did to the place, he managed to keep it from being detected by human equipment. Hazel had tried to find it with her navigational systems, but to no avail. The only way they knew its location was from the map Astrid had received from the Seelie.

"I think we should go this way," said Astrid, pointing in the opposite direction from the one Hazel was taking.

Hazel didn't feel like asking about the mystical force or feeling that compelled Astrid, so she followed behind.

"I think I see some stairs," said Astrid. She pointed, and sure enough, a set of wooden stairs, made of pieces of ocean-smoothed driftwood, scaled the side of a low hill.

A pebbled footpath led them farther inland, and Hazel noticed that some of the plants didn't look like native coastal types. Evergreens with bluish needles sat side by side with plants with large, waxy burgundy leaves, like those in a tropical forest. Groupings of mushrooms clustered in shady spots beneath wild spiky plants and immaculately maintained topiaries.

They crested a low hill and came to the house. It wasn't

quite a mansion, but the section she could see was as large as one of the plantation houses outside of the New Orleans of her youth. The architecture was different, as it seemed to consist of a series of connected structures and its exterior surface resembled white sand or smoothed stucco. The roof gleamed in the sunlight, mostly black, but occasionally glinting the bluish silver and purple of mother of pearl.

"It's beautiful," said Isadora. "I think we will be content here."

Opal gaped at the house while Briar trailed behind, more interested in the immediate surroundings and only occasionally glancing at the building.

As they drew closer, Hazel noted low walls surrounding small yards and gardens, each wall inlaid with smooth round stones or bits of seashell. They passed a pond, and paused to admire the fish, but Hazel drew back in horror when she saw that among the gold and white koi swam snaking eels, each with the sharp-beaked face of a featherless bird.

"He is wealthy," breathed Opal. "I wonder if he will come out to greet us or send a servant."

But no one came. Paths crisscrossed the area around the buildings, all of them curving and serpentine, many with decorative wooden or stone borders. They followed the main one up to a high arched tunnel, the only visible entrance. At the end glowed a sunny interior garden. They paused just inside the archway.

"I can go in alone," said Astrid. "He's expecting me and the Seelie said he wouldn't hurt me."

"We go in together," said Hazel. She had no interest in being left behind, especially since she was the only one in the group who was uninvited. Besides, if there was trouble, she was armed. The three girls would be useless. Opal would probably cry. And though Astrid could make

Doors or turn into an owl, that didn't seem as tactically promising as a nice loaded pistol.

Isadora followed Astrid through the tunnel followed by Opal. Hazel brought up the rear, noting that Briar looked terrified.

A man appeared at the end of the tunnel and stood waiting for them. Hazel had met many servants, from slaves to paid staff, but she knew this was no servant. It must be Yelbeghen. He was tall, but not extraordinarily so, and dressed in a fine tailored suit jacket, slacks and black leather loafers. Hazel did not follow men's fashions, but she was certain the clothing was expensive. As they drew closer and the drake shook Astrid's hand, Hazel noted that he looked decidedly unhappy.

He was not particularly handsome to Hazel's way of thinking. His coloring was normal, with dark hair and grayish eyes, but his mouth was too wide, his eyes too far apart. His nose was too flat, and when he looked the three girls up and down, she thought she saw his nostrils twitch in an inhuman manner.

Like all the strange beings in the hub world, he was a variation on a theme. Most of the inhuman beings, the otherkind, seemed to be modifications on the human pattern. Most operated with a good imitation of human appearance, but with some variation unique to them. Yukiko looked totally human, as did Santiago, but both could change into canines. A few beings, like the Seelie, might be more beautiful or strange than an ordinary human, but they were known for this. Even her monkey crew, as purely animal in appearance as they were, spoke in human tongues.

"Come inside," Yelbeghen said, frowning.

He led them into the house, floored with dark Spanish tile and decorated with pieces of artwork ranging from a set of ancient orange and black Greek vases to a large modern sculpture made of jagged pieces of colored metal that rotated on glittering stems.

"I have prepared a room for you," he said to the three girls and gave them directions to it. They climbed the stairs, with Briar glancing back at Hazel and Astrid before following her sisters.

He turned and looked at each of them in turn, from Astrid to Hazel and back again, his face expressionless. Hazel felt a stab of fear for an instant when he looked into her face, perhaps an ancient reflex at being in the presence of a predator. She thought of the pistol at her hip, of the man's size relative to her own, of the likelihood that Astrid could do some creative Door-making to get them out if necessary.

"You are the Door?" he asked.

"I am," said Astrid.

"And you? What are you?" he asked Hazel.

"I'm Captain Hazel Dubois."

"A human then."

He turned away, uninterested, and studied Astrid. Hazel was horrified when she noticed that Astrid was looking at him as if he was an ordinary person, not a monster in human skin. She looked almost comfortable in his presence.

"You may stay a few days, if you like," he said to Astrid, and Hazel wondered if she was included in the invitation. She had no desire to stay. "I have never met a Door before."

And there it was. That was why he liked Astrid. She was an uncommon type of being, and as a drake, he couldn't resist a rare thing. Well, Hazel wasn't too common either. She was a woman from another world. She wasn't the only person from her home world here in the hub world. The Professor came from that time and place also, though she'd die before betraying him to the drake. But let Yelbeghen think she was a simple human. The last thing she wanted was any extra attention from the creature.

He invited them to a sitting room where an older man placed a tea set on the table between them. Yelbeghen poured and offered them each a cup.

“A luncheon is being prepared,” he said. “But why don’t you tell me about your trip.”

“The glass globe broke,” said Astrid.

“I can see that the glass globe broke,” he said, his tone changing from genteel to hard. “It was supposed to be carefully transported.”

“And it was. It’s just that there was a storm—” said Astrid.

“I broke it,” said Hazel. “I saw that there were people inside, and I broke it.”

He turned his inhuman eyes on her and her blood ran cold. She didn’t look away, but sat up straighter. If he was trying to intimidate her, he would not succeed.

“I have no truck with the buying and trading of human beings,” she said.

“So you decided to destroy something that wasn’t yours.”

“That’s right. Those girls aren’t yours either. I brought them here, but one word from them and I’ll take them with me again.”

“On your ship.”

“Well it won’t be on my broomstick.”

He smiled then, revealing ordinary human teeth. His eyes sparkled with cold merriment.

“I don’t like you, little freckled woman,” he said “but I might find some respect for you.”

“I’m delighted.”

“You don’t like me either,” he said.

“No, I don’t. Because I know your kind. Wealthy with power over others. You can harm or help, and you use the power for personal gain to the detriment of others.”

“Is that so?”

“How can it be otherwise? You helped the Seelie on the

girls' home island, but demanded payment in people. You could help for free. You don't seem to lack for anything."

"I lack all sorts of things. Many things."

"Like triplets for slaves?"

"Not slaves. They will not serve me. They are guests," he said.

"Guests who can't leave."

"They came willingly. I did not notice them trying to run away."

"Because they'd be dishonored if they returned home," said Hazel. "You'd go attack the Seelie or something. Fly through the air and burn their cities to the ground."

"I have no interest in that. And you read too many stories."

"Pardon me, but I think I need some fresh air," she said and rose. She was furious at her inability to do anything about the girls. If they didn't want to be freed, it was only because they didn't understand their situation and were ruled by fear. But without their consent to leave, she couldn't force them off the island. Astrid was just as constrained as she was, perhaps even more so because of her indebtedness to the Seelie.

"Wait a moment, if you please. Tell me why you came," said Yelbeghen. "Astrid had a delivery to make to me. Did you come merely to tell me that I'm a terrible human being?"

"You're not a human being at all."

"And now you understand."

CHAPTER 35

After lunch, Astrid stood in the marble-floored hallway outside the closed pair of tall doors as Yelbeghen spoke with the triplets alone. She tried again and again to get the picture of the mirror in her sketch book to allow her to contact Elliot, but it never worked again. Perhaps, once again, the Library had come closer to her time and place and allowed the message to travel. Or maybe the fluke had been with her, and her ability to recreate it was gone. She slapped the sketch book closed and shoved it into her bag.

Hazel had gone off in a huff, disgusted with the whole business with the triplets. Astrid understood her frustration, but she wasn't quite as single-minded on the issue. Sure, forcing the girls to come was wrong. But they hadn't truly been forced. They had been asked and convinced. It wasn't an ideal situation, but as Astrid studied the drake's home, she saw that they'd live a life of comfort and luxury. She had seen the world of the Seelie, and Hazel had not. The place was beautiful, sure, but the royal court made life a misery for many. The entire species was rigidly hierarchical, and the court brooked no deviation from its orders. She wouldn't live there for anything. Escaping from such a place and living on a lovely island wasn't the worst thing that could happen.

She would have to speak with the girls later to see if they still wanted to stay. She thought she knew the answer already. Unless the drake was terribly cruel, they'd rather stay than go home. Astrid would then return to the Seelie, the first of her three tasks complete.

Yelbeghen didn't seem like such a bad companion either. It was strange how she felt drawn to him while also being a little repelled. He was foreign, alien even, but still she felt a little tug of attraction inside, pulling her to him.

Oh, but she was a stupid girl. She only felt that way because she was flattered by his attention. She wasn't much to look at and though she was already eighteen, she had never had a boyfriend. Her mother had tormented her over it, saying how she was too ugly and strange to get a man. Perhaps that was true. The drake was only fascinated with her because she was a Door. He was handsome, in an unusual way, but it was only her sense of loneliness that made her feel anything toward him. He was a dragon, for heaven's sake.

The double doors flew open and Yelbeghen stormed into the hallway.

"They're flawed!" he shouted, turning on Astrid. "First, you break open the package, and then you deliver an unmatched set."

"What's not matching about them? They're identical."

She glanced in towards the girls. Briar knelt on the floor with her sisters on either side of her.

"That one!" he pointed at Briar, "is no virgin. She confessed it. Tell the Seelie that the deal is off."

"I was supposed to deliver them, and I did. I wasn't told anything about virgins."

"Nor should you have been. It's none of your business. You are a delivery girl, and you have delivered faulty goods. Now deliver this message to your masters: The deal is off."

He spun on his heel, but Astrid grabbed his arm. He yanked his arm away and looked at her like she had spat in his face.

"Now you wait a minute," she said. "You brought these girls here as sex slaves?"

"Of course not. Why would I want to ruin them?"

"So you wanted virgins, but not to have sex with."

He exhaled heavily through his nose, and when he spoke, he did so in a tightly controlled tone.

"I am not a human being, as your friend Captain Hazel Dubois has so astutely noticed. Why would I want three girls for sex?"

"You look like a man to me. But fine. You're not using them as prostitutes. Why do you care one way or the other?"

"Because they're Seelie triplets."

He seemed to think this explained it. A moment later, she understood. The dragon wanted young maidens. Of course he did.

"Then the girls are free?" she asked. "They can go home?"

"No! They will stay here. The middle one can scrub floors on her knees, since she seems to prefer that position."

All three girls were weeping, and Astrid noticed Isadora and Opal were now holding each other while Briar cried alone. No wonder she had been so afraid to come. Pangur Ban was right about that. But she was wrong that the drake would kill the girls. Astrid would make a Door to Seelie and throw them through herself before she allowed that to happen.

"She'll do no such thing," Astrid said. "It's not her fault you didn't specify what you wanted. And even if you had, she can do whatever she wants."

"What do you know about it? I can tell you are human but not human born. A Door to the silent void, but so full of words. Talking and talking."

"Damn right I'll keep talking."

"Then you can talk to the Seelie, those stupid, flighty, lying, conniving little beasts and ask them why exactly they sent me an unmatched set."

"Maybe they didn't know."

He considered this, and then stalked down the hallway and outside, spouting a string of profanities aimed at the Seelie. She followed.

"All right, that's enough," she said and he paused.

"You are not nearly as frightened of me as you should be," he said.

"Why? Are you going to change forms and eat me? Burn me to a crisp?"

"Among other things."

"But you won't. The Seelie said you wouldn't harm me if I came. Why is that? Is it because I'm a Door?"

"I would never destroy something so rare. There is that part. But you—you really have no idea, do you? You do not know how much we are the same."

CHAPTER 36

"WHY TWO RAVENS?" BENNU ASKED Elliot.

She set one bowl on the kitchen counter and lifted the other to examine it. At the top of the wide, flat rim Elliot had carved two ravens standing beak to beak, wings folded.

"Symmetry, for one," he said. "Also, as I was reading up on ancient Norse so I could write a few words that Huginn might be able to read. I kept finding things about Huginn's twin brother. I don't know if our Time Corps Huginn is the same raven or a namesake, but it hardly matters. The Northerners will interpret it as a representation of their own twin ravens. It might ensure the thing's survival."

He had not been able to write anything in old Irish for Pangur Ban, but he hoped he had done enough. All around the rim he had carved Norse and English, along with some of Bennu's desert language, which she had written on a paper for him to copy. In each language he had written four words:

Bowls are mirrors

Astrid

By necessity, he had been forced to render her name phonetically in both Norse and the desert language, but it would have to do.

"My stone carvers created a long rectangular base for the Bast statue," said Bennu. "I had them leave room in front to place the bowl. They will attach it securely."

"And then you'll take it North."

"I have to. It's the only way to get you out."

In one of the cruel turns of time travel, every available option forced him to lose Bennu. If he stayed in the Library, she would leave. But if she traveled North and took the bowl that would hopefully free him, then he lost her to marriage that way as well.

"It's good work," continued Bennu. "How did you carve it?"

"Slowly with an old kitchen knife. It took hours. I could only carve one of the bowls. The blank one will be staying with me."

"The carved one with the statue will be a good wedding gift for my husband. Combining the statue of my cat goddess with his twin birds is a good representation of my marriage to the Northern chieftain. It merges our worlds."

"It's just a bowl and a cat statue. It doesn't mean anything."

"I know you dislike the idea." She touched his hand for a moment, then wrapped the carved bowl in a piece of heavy burlap for safekeeping. It would return with her to the desert in nine and a half hours. Too little time, Elliot thought.

"Have you asked about having one of your cousins or sisters marry this guy?" he asked. "She could bring the bowl."

"I've told you. It has to be me. My sisters and cousins are already promised to others or are too low-ranking or high-ranking to be a good match."

"I could try to come for you after you deliver the bowl, but before you marry."

"No. You must not think that way. My destiny is set. If I were to flee or vanish before my wedding, it would be disastrous for my people. Don't fear for me. I will be minor royalty and will be well treated."

"And after the wedding?"

"You would kidnap another man's wife?"

"It wouldn't be kidnapping if you came willingly."

"Wars are fought for such acts," Bennu said. "Besides, I will be expected to provide heirs."

"You might reconsider. My home time and place is beautiful. I lived on the coast of another continent, on the beach. It's sunny there most of the time and we have an ocean. Plenty of sand, if you like that sort of thing."

"I do love the sand and sun. But I love my people more."

"And me?"

"And you. Do not worry about my comfort. I will have plenty of furs to keep me warm. But I would rather you warm me. There's still time. My research is complete, and we have the length of a night."

Well, that was forward. But he knew they had no time for coy games.

"But what about your husband?" he asked, forcing himself to something resembling rationality. "He'll be able to ... you know. Won't he be able to tell that you've been with someone else? That he's not the first?"

"He's human, and their religions do place a high value on this in a female. But my people do not. He will not reject me for it. If he did, it would put diplomatic relations in jeopardy. Also, who is to say you are the first either?"

She gave him a sidelong smile and then slipped her arms around his neck. "Time is short, my love."

Later that night, Elliot sat up in bed. He did not sleep. He didn't want to. Bennu made tiny sounds in her sleep, little sighs and murmurs. He studied the faint silvery markings around her eyes and collarbone and wondered where she came from and exactly what she was. It made no difference to him, but when he had asked her, she simply repeated that she was one of the desert people. That was all she knew. It was what they were and what they always had been.

His tiny quarters were shabby, but with Bennu here, naked and warm beneath the covers, her black hair fanned across his pillow, the place was perfect. He was old enough to know of the ephemeral nature of happiness like this. But he was also young enough to bring her here anyway. He would pay for it later, but it would be worth it.

He flipped to the page in Astrid's old sketch book, hoping once again that new words would appear. But after seeing "We're coming" in Astrid's writing, the drawing had not changed at all. He could only hope that the information he had provided would be enough for them to find the white Bast and the bowl.

Not long before Bennu was due to leave, he woke her and she dressed. He walked her out of the Library and to the end of the marketplace row. As she wept, he kissed her good-bye, not caring if every soul in the marketplace saw them. Let them look. They were free to come and go. If it bothered them that others suffered because of the Librarian, so much the better.

That evening, as he cleared dishes from the tables, he heard the soft swish of Malachy's leathery feet on the floor behind him.

"My human friend had a wife in the outside world," said Malachy.

"So you said."

He knew Malachy meant well, but he was in no mood to talk with the tortoise. It took all his willpower not to crash into the Librarian's quarters with a kitchen knife. Only the message from Astrid in the mirror saying "we're coming" and his faith in the Time Corps kept him from doing it.

"My friend wanted to leave because of this wife," said the tortoise.

"Well imagine that. Someone meant something to him. He wasn't content just helping researchers and serving up food. How ungrateful of him."

"You are clearly upset."

"I'm not upset," he said. "Okay, yes. I am upset. This

place is a prison. It's cruel and it's inhumane, and everyone just goes along with it."

"Some of us know when things are beyond our control and are unchangeable."

"Yeah, I get it. The Librarian does not change. He's this big scary thing and no one can talk to him."

"He has killed people before. Or driven them mad. The death of his wife in the fire drove him mad."

"Lovely. Death, insanity and enslavement."

"I am here as your friend," said Malachy, rearing up on his hind legs in that disconcerting way of his. "I want to help you find contentment."

"Only freedom will make me content."

"But when Bennu was here, you were happy."

"She made the prison bearable."

"Perhaps one of the other librarians might interest you."

"I'm not looking for a bedmate," said Elliot. "I wasn't looking for anyone at all."

"If you did not want anyone, why did you allow yourself to grow attached to the desert woman? You knew it would cause you pain."

"Because she was special."

"There are many rare and special things here too."

"No. There's not. It's beautiful and I could spend a lifetime reading and learning, but there's a whole world out there. Multiple worlds, and I've seen them. I've watched the Wild Hunt pour through the sky, screaming. I've danced with heiresses and wandered deserts, surfed waves high enough to make me feel like a grain of sand. I've seen things so beautiful they would change you. If you had seen them and then you became trapped here, it would burn you inside."

The tortoise blinked at him, uncomprehending. Elliot carried the dishes into the kitchen and Malachy followed.

"Where did you come from?" Elliot asked Malachy. "Don't you miss it?"

"An island. There was not much to do. And here, I have plenty to do."

"It's still a prison."

"A beautiful prison. A fair and lovely one."

"But still a prison. Being trapped here has cost me. And it has cost Bennu. If I could get out now, I could take her to whatever time she liked. Her people would figure out another bride for the chieftain. If diplomatic relations are so critical, they would be forced to. Now, she's trapped with a man she doesn't want because of this place. And I'm trapped too."

"Your heart will be at peace if you accept what is and is not possible," said Malachy. "I do not like seeing you in pain like this."

And that was where he and Malachy differed. It wasn't that Malachy was a tortoise and Elliot a man. It was in their acceptance of what was and their ideas on what could be.

"Perhaps after a good night's sleep, you will feel better," said Malachy.

"Yeah, I'm sure that'll help," Elliot said, and wondered if Malachy could perceive the sarcasm. The tortoise left him and he finished his work. He brought the marble bowl to the kitchen and filled it with water, keeping it nearby so he could see if Astrid was using it to communicate.

At first, he had thought the Library wasn't such a bad place to be trapped. But the place had grown hateful to him. It had hurt him. More importantly, it had hurt Bennu and his friend Imee.

Damn the books and the scholars. He wanted to see it burn.

CHAPTER 37

ASTRID FOUND A QUIET CORNER of the garden to make her Door and stepped from Yelbeghen's island to Mr. Augustus's office. He was the owner of Luna Park, one of the Twelve, and though he must have seen plenty of strange things in his long, long life, he leapt from his chair when she appeared.

"Christ, Astrid!"

"I need to talk with the Seelie."

"Fine," he said, his hand on his chest. He took a deep breath. "Fine. Just don't do that again."

He picked up the phone and Astrid took a seat. The radio played a jazz station, something with a heavy brass section. For a moment, she was tempted to ask Mr. Augustus about it. Had he been there when jazz music was born? He loved music, and Hazel said he was an expert musician. Though enslaved by the Seelie in some way Astrid did not understand, he had some freedoms. He ran his park and seemed to keep a low profile. Perhaps he even managed to find some enjoyment in life.

A few minutes later, Gerard knocked on the door. Astrid wasn't shocked when he appeared as an ordinary man outside, and then changed to his half-equine form as the door closed. Such illusions were necessary to travel in the human world. He glanced around briefly, as if expecting to see someone in addition to Astrid and Mr. Augustus.

"Good to see you, sweetheart," he said, and he seemed genuinely pleased to see her again. He kissed the back of her hand, and she didn't pull away, but tolerated it as best she could. Gerard had never been cruel to her, and she had to learn some kind of diplomacy if she were to survive all three of her tasks and not antagonize the Seelie further.

"Good to see you too," she said.

"How comes your Door making?"

"It's fine. That's not the problem. Yelbeghen said to tell you the deal is off."

"What? Didn't you deliver the orb?"

"Yes, but it broke on the way, and he's unhappy because one of the girls isn't a virgin. He wanted a matched set."

"Well, that does make things more difficult. You were supposed to bring back a Seelie girl that he has on his island. That was the task."

"No, my task was to deliver the orb. I delivered it. Task complete. I'm heading back there soon to get my friend and then we're leaving. I just wanted to deliver his message and be done with it."

"That won't do, sweet pea. You have to bring back the girl."

"I was there when you gave her the orb," said Mr. Augustus from behind his desk. "You told her to deliver it, not to strike any additional deals. You said the deal had already been made. I'm an unbiased witness."

Astrid shot Mr. Augustus a grateful look. With a tight smile, he crossed his arms and waited for Gerard's reply. Astrid supposed any small act of defiance toward his masters must be gratifying.

"The task was complete according to what you told me," Astrid said. "There's no getting around it."

Gerard rubbed the bridge of his nose. "I'm going to catch hell for this, but I'm going to have to make this your second task. You bring back the Seelie girl and you're finished."

"What, you want me to kidnap her? The drake would

notice and be upset. Isn't there some kind of mystical deal that makes her belong to him or something? You people have all sorts of rules about that."

"You can't kidnap her, no," said Gerard. "You have to get Yelbeghen to agree to release her."

"And how to do you propose I do that? Why would he give up one of his treasures?"

"That's up to you to figure out. You managed to outsmart both the Seelie and Unseelie in the past. I'm sure this will pose no problem. Now, I need to be going."

"No," said Astrid.

"Pardon me?"

"No. I won't do it. It's impossible and there's no way I can succeed. What am I going to give him in return? Sing him a song? I have nothing to offer him in exchange."

Gerard sighed. "Let me put it this way. The father of this girl did not give her up willingly. He has been part of the court for years, but as long as he was the only one pressing for her return, he could accomplish little. Now two of her cousins and her sister are also on the court, and it has taken years to get them there. The family has power, and they want the girl back."

"I don't particularly care for your court members and their intrigues," she said.

"I don't expect you to. But I do want you to understand that I'm not assigning you this task lightly. We truly are without any recourse. You have to bring her back."

"And if I don't?"

"Astrid, I know you don't believe me, but I do like you. You were one of my favorite students."

"You helped imprison me in the Seelie world, you lied to me about my parentage and tried to teach me Doormaking so the Seelie could use me for their own purposes."

"And the alternative?" he said. "Let you go to the Unseelie? How much of a pleasant sightseeing trip was that for you? From what I understand, with me you were provided food, a lovely house, room and materials to create art and you were treated kindly. The Unseelie beat you, hurt you and cut out your duplicate's tongue."

"You could have left me in the human world."

"With your mother? Who hurt you and was cruel to you? Ah, my Astrid. I have known many people in my life, human and otherkind. And I know that your human mother harmed you far worse than your biological Unseelie mother. With the Seelie, you were better off."

This conversation had turned in an unpleasant direction. She wasn't here to discuss her abusive human mother, her evil Unseelie mother or anyone else in her life. She simply wanted to get the task over with, get information from Yelbeghen about the Library and start art school.

"That's all in the past," she said. "It has no bearing on this task."

"But it does! You see, I am authorized to alter our deal, if necessary. And as I am forced to assign you a second task, I am also forced to assign a penalty if you do not complete it. Please understand, I don't do it out of any personal malice."

"I'm sure you are only doing as you're told," she said dryly. "Only following orders, right?"

"I'm glad you understand. Now, if you do not return the Seelie girl from Yelbeghen, the Seelie will do something dreadful to you."

"Like imprison me?"

"Yes, somewhere you can't escape."

"That might be interesting to see. I have four psychopomps for friends who can make Doors, multiple time agents who can go through time and some very strange near-immortal friends who might not be okay with that. The Seelie world attaches to the human world easily. It's not too hard to get there from here."

She wouldn't say it, but the psychopomps could very

well give her up, as they weren't supposed to make Doors to other worlds aside from death. She didn't know if they'd break the rules to recover her. And the Time Corps had no way to get to the Seelie world yet, but the Professor might develop one. After all, this was the hub world, and many worlds branched off from it. She was pretty sure the Time Corps valued her enough to go to the trouble. And if they didn't, then the older Elliot, the one who would get out of the Library, certainly would. She just had to get him out of the Library first.

"We could imprison you in cold iron, make you suffer."

"And what good would that do? What fun is having a Door without using her? And in using me, you take your chances that I won't make a Door straight into the void and kill you all.

"You might die with us."

"A price I'd happily pay."

She knew she wouldn't die in the void, that she could remain there quite happily for some time. That was assuming that the resident void wyrms didn't devour her.

"We can also harm your family," said Gerard.

"I don't have family," she said.

It was only partly the truth. She had never known her father, her mother had hurt and disowned her and had not spoken to her in months and Elliot was in the Library. Aside from Elliot's mother, her aunt, who was there to hurt?"

"You care for your duplicate? The human you were made to replace? We know you took her place in Unseelie to free her. You sacrificed yourself for her then because you cared about her, correct?"

Her heart began to pound. Not Sister. The girl had been beaten, burned, mutilated and driven half mad.

"What would you do to her?"

"I'm not sure. Take her for a hundred years. Make her

bear half-human children to be cup bearers in the court. Any number of things."

"And what's to stop me from making a Door and getting her?"

"A Door through time? You can't. Time passes differently in various parts of the Seelie world. We could take her to a place where she'd age a day while a century passed here. You'd never find her."

"I'd find her or die trying. Then you'd be without your Door."

"How interesting," said Gerard. "If we threaten your safety, you don't mind too much. But go after the girl and it matters to you."

"That's because she's not like you lot," said Augustus. "You didn't count on that, did you?"

"You should not talk," said Gerard. "It was not your bravery and fearlessness that landed you in your current position."

"You're both equally badly off," said Astrid. "What I want to know is why you two don't do anything about it? Surely there are enough people angry with the Seelie to fight back."

"It's not so easy," said Gerard. "You have your sister, your cousin, and even your mother. We have loved ones too. We do as we're told."

"It's like the Mafia," said Mr. Augustus. "But some of the dons have animal heads."

CHAPTER 38

For three weeks, Huginn, Yukiko and Pangur Ban sailed up and down the fjords of the icy Norwegian coast. More than once, Yukiko asked Huginn if he could remember anything more. Each time, he saw her disappointment when he said that he had told her everything he could. He remembered the white Bast statue and could even remember the strange, unreadable script on the bowl as well as the words he could understand but not recall. But he had no other information on where the thing might be.

Even Pangur Ban was losing patience with him.

"You're certain it was on the coast?" said Pangur Ban one afternoon.

"Yes. Men were carrying things from a village to a ship. So it had to be on the coast."

"We need more," said Pangur Ban. "We are wasting too much time."

"We're time travelers, we can return to the moment we left Hazel and Astrid, and the three of us will live centuries more," he said. "We have time."

"You do not understand my meaning," she said. "We are not making progress. We are wandering."

"If I knew more, I would tell you," he said.

"I know you would. I had only hoped that perhaps you had another memory come to you. Do you remember anything more about the ship?"

He thought back. "I know it was my ship. I had been

on it, because I knew that there was a tear in the sail that had been patched. I remember flying over it and landing on it."

"Was it Skidbladnir?"

"No. I don't think so. But I suppose it could have been."

He knew that was no help. And so they continued on up the jagged, irregular coastline, stopping at various towns along the way, the Asian woman taking the appearance of a Northerner walking beside a cat with a raven flying overhead, going through the Norse towns, searching and asking questions about the white Bast and about a bowl. Even so, they were no closer to finding the statue than they had been when they started.

"Bast was an Egyptian goddess," said Huginn one evening after another day of fruitless seeking. "Was she ever worshiped in the North? If we can narrow that down, we might have better luck."

"We've considered that possibility already," said Pangur Ban. "Bast wasn't worshiped anywhere in this region, not by any city, people or tribe. We discussed this weeks ago."

"Sorry," he said, ashamed that he had not remembered.

"But why would Elliot say 'Bast' instead of just 'cat,'" said Huginn. "He must have meant for us to know the Egyptian connection. He wants us to look for something Egyptian."

Yukiko got up and left for the captain's quarters, where she was staying. No doubt she too was weary of Huginn's inability to remember their conversations.

"It wasn't only the Egyptians that worshiped her," said Pangur Ban. "Her cult spread throughout the Middle East and even to the Roman Empire."

"Yeah, but the Romans would worship a tortoise shell if it was shined to a nice polish," he said. "No, it's Egyptian, or at least North African."

"Very well," said the cat. "How does that help us? We've

already been looking for any people who honor the deity. We've found none."

"Instead of looking for a whole tribe or people who worshiped her, maybe the statue was the possession of an individual. Maybe Elliot himself. He's a time traveler. Maybe he already owned or made this statue and put it somewhere for us to find."

"He'd have given us a more detailed location than just 'Norway' if that were the case."

"True. He would have. He definitely would have. That means he himself doesn't know where in Norway it is. That means he didn't see it himself in a certain year, or he'd have told us the year. So it must be that he knows the area, but not the time and not the exact place."

The cat waited, giving him the silence he required when his brain was functioning well and he was birthing an idea.

"If he didn't know the time, then that's important," he said. "A Time Corps member always knows where in time they are. If he doesn't, then he's either lost, or outside of time."

"He sent the message from within the Library. So he was outside of time."

"Yes. But the bowl had to make it into the ordinary world. He had to get it out. But he didn't just toss the thing into the void, hoping it would wash up somewhere useful. He knew, from his place within the Library, that it was going to Norway."

"Do you think the Library brushed up against Norway and he got it out somehow?"

"Or he knew someone who could take it for him. You said the Library was filled with scholars. They'd come and go. Why couldn't one carry something out?"

"A possibility, but it puts us no closer to a location."

Huginn had to admit that she was correct. And he had lived so long, that pinpointing a date within his youth was impossible as well. He flew up to the top of the sail, taking his favorite perch and studied the coastline, distant patches of deep green cut by jagged slate-colored rocks, thrusting upwards. The land was so much emptier in this time than the twenty-first century, so much wilder. The people were as well.

A gust of wind buffeted him, but he held on, turning into the bracing, frigid wind, relishing the sensation of being near his ancestral home. A moment later, something struck him so hard that he fell, the sky and sea spinning wildly in his vision until he flapped and righted himself. The ship was sailing on without him, and he flew after it. As he got closer, the thing hit him again, or rather he hit it. It was like flying into a wall, or a large glass window. Not that he had ever done such a foolish thing before.

He tried another angle, and again, he could not approach the ship.

"I can't reach you!" he cried, "Tell Mr. Escobar to turn around!"

A monkey near the top of the mast lifted his paw to show that he heard, and the little creatures scrambled to turn the ship. Once they were near, he landed on top of the dragon head.

"It's me!" he cried as Yukiko and Pangur Ban joined him. "I'm close to myself. That's why I can't go any closer to shore. We can't go within ten miles of ourselves, which means I'm here!"

Yukiko perked up at that. "All we need to do is find you and ask you about that statue. Oh, but what if you don't remember where you saw the statue?"

"I may not. But my brother will."

Yukiko walked into town, Pangur Ban beside her, and it didn't take her sensitive sense of smell or keen eye to know that this place was a war zone. The stench of burning was everywhere, and even the icy ocean wind did not carry it away. She pulled her coat tighter around herself and adjusted her appearance to be an average-looking Northern European woman of about thirty, unremarkable and hopefully undesirable.

Ships sailed away, one by one, vanishing into the distant fog, carrying away spoils and possibly people. This town had been sacked, and though there were still residents here, they moved quickly, heads down, as if wishing to become invisible. Music and song came from the largest building, toward the center of the settlement.

"I would not go in there if I were you," said Pangur Ban. "To be a female here is dangerous."

"I know. I just want to find the ravens and leave."

They searched the town, keeping to the edges of things, slipping silently between buildings and avoiding anyone who didn't look terrified. Eyes watched them from slitted windows and peeped at them from shadows. Not a soul spoke to them.

"The ravens are in the big building," said Yukiko. "They have to be."

"Then I will go inside. You should not."

Yukiko agreed. Even if she changed into her fox form, she would draw attention. These were hunters, and the pelt of a snow-white fox might be too tempting for them to resist. No one would care about a little cat.

But Yukiko would not be idle while Pangur Ban looked for the ravens. She studied the passersby, finding a woman in her fifties, one of the oldest people in the settlement. She used a little of her magic to make herself seem small and nonthreatening.

"I am looking for two ravens," said Yukiko. "Have you seen them?"

"No. I apologize, but I must be going."

"Wait. Please."

Yukiko watched as the woman almost stopped, but

then her sense of fear and wariness must have taken over and she continued on. Yukiko fell into step beside her.

"Have you ever seen a statue of a white cat?"

The woman did not answer, but instead looked up overhead. Two black birds flapped into the sky from the top of one of the nearby buildings. Side by side they rose, then turned toward the sea, flying out toward the ships in the distance.

Yukiko cursed. The ravens had not been in the main hall and now they were gone for good. Before she could question the woman again, she slipped away and into one of the houses. Yukiko had to find Pangur Ban, and quickly. Perhaps they could catch the other ship and still speak with the ravens.

The door of the house where the woman had gone opened and a younger man appeared.

"You're not from here."

"I'm not. I'm looking for a statue."

"So my mother said. What do you want with it?"

"Do you know where it is?"

"I've seen it. Why do you want it?"

She wasn't sure how to answer, but she used a little magic to make herself appear harmless and small.

"It's important to me. Could you tell me where it is?"

He looked her up and down. "Why, so you can take that too?" He glanced toward the main hall and Yukiko heard the sounds of a baby wailing from within his house.

"I'm not with the invaders. I am seeking to avoid them, in fact. But tell me, is the statue here in town?" she asked, watching him closely in case he gave away its location with a look.

"It's half a day's travel south. In the next village. They were attacked too, and it might have been taken. Now get out of here before they do something to you. You shouldn't be out alone."

The older woman appeared behind him, bouncing the

fussy baby on her hip. Of the voices inside, she had only heard children and the man's mother.

"Did they take your wife?" Yukiko asked the man.

"Her and others," said the old woman, now with a gleam of hatred in her eye that Yukiko hadn't seen when she was in the streets. "The filthy animals."

"Is she still here in town?" asked Yukiko.

Perhaps, if she used her ingenuity, she could trick the invaders into abandoning their captives. A few choice illusions, a little cooperation with Pangur Ban and Huginn, and she just might be able to save a few.

"No. All the captives were already taken by ship," said the man.

Fury burned inside her, both at the invaders and at her own inability to stop them. Even with Skidbladnir, they were no warrior crew. They'd be killed quickly if they pursued the attackers.

"I'm sorry," said Yukiko. "Will you stay here?"

"We don't know yet," said the man. "But I'm not raising my girls where those men can get them."

She wished she had brought some money, gold or gems or anything valuable. Instead, she took off her earrings, simple gold studs, and gave them to the man.

"I hope your gods bless you," she said, and meant it. Once, long ago, she had been a servant of mankind, but also a servant of a kind and compassionate god. He was dead now, but it did not relieve her of her duty. She needed to remember that. Tailless and dishonored, she could still find purpose.

She located Pangur Ban, explained about the ravens flying away and headed back to the ship. Huginn was disappointed when he learned about his brother, but they had a location, at long last. They headed south, finding the next town. It was slightly inland, and they never would have known about it had the man not mentioned it.

This place had not been attacked recently, but on the

way into of town they found a few burned-out buildings, empty and picked-over. They got a few suspicious looks, but Yukiko concealed all three of them with enough magic to cause people to pass them by without trouble.

Near the center of town they found a small temple, one story high with a wood-beam roof and rough stone walls. The interior of the place was dedicated to various Norse gods that Yukiko could not identify. Huginn took a particular interest in a crude statue of a man with one eye open, round and staring, and the other socket empty. The thing looked bizarre, like a winking elf, with a slightly pointed head. It had no real detail and wore no clothing other than a crude kilt-like garment.

Yukiko recognized him. She also knew what it was like to lose the god one served, and she did not disturb Huginn as he sat in silence, but looked around outside instead. She asked a young man where she might find the white cat statue. He told her it was just outside of town to the east.

They arrived to find the statue almost enveloped into the huge roots of an overhanging tree. The cat faced south, and it did resemble Pangur Ban, or any white cat for that matter, though it was slightly smaller. The cat shared a rectangular base with a shallow black stone bowl. A stone marker leaned up against the tree, obviously many years old as the base was partially sunken into the earth. There were other markers around the area, scattered here and there. Some of the stones were set into large elaborate patterns while other stood alone.

"Graves," said Huginn, hopping up to the cat statue.

"I thought the Norse burned their dead," said Yukiko. "I thought they launched them out to sea on flaming boats."

"Most did burn them," said Huginn. "But only a high-ranking person warranted burning up a perfectly good boat. The rest were burned on land."

"Then why this grave?"

"They'd bury the remaining parts and ashes, usually with a few personal possessions." Huginn paused to read the words carved into the stone. "This was the wife of a chieftain. Foreign born. From the far south."

Yukiko studied the black marble bowl with the two ravens carved into it, beak to beak. There was writing along the rim, some in what she knew was Norse, some in another language, and some in English. It said, "Bowls are mirrors. Astrid."

"It says the same thing in Norse and a very old language from northern Africa, said Pangur Ban. "It's rather crude, if I may say so."

"At least the English is readable," said Yukiko.

"The language doesn't exist in this time," Pangur Ban said. "We're the only ones alive who can read it."

"That's why I couldn't read the English the first time I saw it," said Huginn. "Only the Norse."

Yukiko picked up the heavy thing by its rectangular base and turned to go.

"That's odd," said Huginn, and Yukiko turned back. His head was cocked to one side. "This isn't a grave after all. It's only a memorial marker."

"Did they launch her out in a boat?" asked Yukiko.

"Perhaps. All I can say with certainty is that there's no body here."

CHAPTER 39

HAZEL HAD TO CONCEDE THAT Yelbeghen's island was not a bad place to stay. It boasted all sorts of gardens, from spare desert landscapes where rough red lizards basked on rocks to tropical areas teeming with scurrying furry creatures that peeped at her from the undergrowth, only to disappear when she drew closer.

There were birds too, and Hazel felt sorry for them, as the nearest land was over a hundred miles away and they could not fly to freedom. Ordinary brown ducks paddled around a murky green pond, but there were more colorful animals as well. Bright blue and gold storks waded through a marshy area along with smaller silvery bitterns. She also spotted a flock of ordinary brown sparrows and a solitary black and white hawk, which she only saw once, passing overhead.

The topiaries frightened her. At first, they had seemed like ordinary sculpted bushes, carefully tended and decorative in a staid, traditional sort of way. Most were geometric, but a few depicted living things, large rodents and serpents, birds with wings outstretched, an elephant and a rearing horse. To the far southwest of the house, a row of topiary people stood, including children, a woman with a folded parasol and a man touching his hat. She found them charming. Then one turned its head to watch her pass and she rushed away down the path.

After a long walk toward the center of the island, she found a fenced pasture with a few drowsy-looking sheep and some lop-eared goats grazing. A big creature, perhaps a bull, munched on grass in the distance. Spying her, it headed over and she could see it more clearly. It was an ox, a mammoth example of its species, with so many horns she couldn't count them. There were perhaps a hundred. The thing's head must have weighed a ton, but the animal managed to maneuver the horns well, raising its chin over the fence to gaze at her with soft, brown eyes in the hopes of a treat. She scratched its ears and it grunted, low and guttural and blew warm breath from its nostrils. The goats and sheep noticed Hazel and trotted over. One had nine eyes, all of them blinking at different times and another had triple cloven hooves instead of the typical split ones. Most were ordinary, as far as she could see.

Hazel checked her pocket watch. Finally, her appointed time with Yelbeghen drew close. At first, she had thought he lived alone. But along with servants, he also had other people living there. Some were temporary guests, while others lived there permanently.

She found the drake in a sitting room upstairs, one that provided a view all the way out to the ocean. He was alone, sitting in one of two matching apple green chairs that faced each other across an empty table. She noted that he had not served refreshments, which among her people in the South would have been a conscious insult. She was not certain what it meant to drakes.

"If this discussion is regarding your raven friend's brother, I already told Astrid that I don't know. And if it's about Astrid's desire to take my Seelie friend from me, then I must tell you that your efforts will be wasted," he said.

"I have a different problem. A man who was turned to earth."

"In what way?"

"He's a golem. His master came and removed one of the letters from his mouth, and now he's dead. His body turned to stone. Have you encountered anything like this? Do you know how to help him?"

"I have never heard of a golem returning to life, no. They are created, obey their masters for a time, then rebel and become destructive. In the end, they must be destroyed."

"But this golem wasn't bad. It was created for bad purposes, to kill people. But then he stopped and became good."

"Whether the creature had a bad or good purpose is all in your point of view."

"It's objective reality, however much you may wish to characterize it otherwise. He was created to kill. He refused. His master destroyed him. And I want to bring him back."

"And you thought I would know how?" He seemed genuinely mystified by this idea.

"Well, you're very, very old, correct?"

"Yes."

"And we had to come here for Astrid to deliver that ball to you, so I thought you might know something about golems."

"I know nothing of bringing them back to life," he said.

"Do other people know? One of our friends said there might be information on golems in the Library, the Alexandrian one that burned. Is that true?"

"I haven't been there myself, so I can't say what that place holds. It just might have what you're looking for. From what I know, no one ever wanted to revive a dead golem before."

"Well I do. He means a lot to me."

"I know the Librarian assisted the late Isis when she had troubles with her husband. Perhaps, if he could regain his sanity, he could do the same for yours."

"He's not my husband."

"My mistake."

"Who is this Librarian?" she asked. "Would he know how to help Neil?"

"Thoth. The ibis. Or, he used to be. Now he's just insane. But long ago, when Isis's husband had been turned to earth, he helped her. He won't help you, however. You are no deity. Your deceased friend was not a god or demigod, and you are as insignificant a person as could be, living ship or no."

"You're such a flatterer."

"I simply state a fact," he said. "Some people are valued differently than others."

"Yes, I've heard. I lived through that era already. It seems you never left it."

"And value is in the eye of the beholder," he said and uncrossed his legs. Leaning forward. "But far more interesting to me is this notion that you want to go to this Library to revive your friend."

She decided to tell him about Elliot. If Yelbeghen hadn't been to the Library in all this time, then he wasn't likely to notify anyone that the Time Corps was trying to infiltrate the place. There was no telling what he might know.

"We have another friend trapped inside the Library," she said. "We want to get him out."

"I see," he said, and rose. He walked to the end of the room and back again. In a way, it reminded her of the Professor. Whenever he got busy thinking, he paced. Yelbeghen was more graceful, less animated, and unlike the Professor, he was unlikely to come up with some kind of wild, time-tearing idea.

"You have a Door who can move between worlds," Yelbeghen said. "But she can only travel within her own time. But you also have time machines, but the Library is outside of time. An intriguing problem."

"The Library wasn't always outside of time. It was in Egypt."

"Correct. But it was only an ordinary library then. An extraordinary one, I should say. But not like it is now."

"How did it burn? And how did it end up in the void?"

"Well, this was long after Isis and her troubles with her husband, you understand. Thoth was the god of knowledge and scribes and so forth. Seshat was the goddess of wisdom and writing. She was his daughter. She was his wife. It's best not to think too closely about those things when it comes to the Egyptians. But they were like peas in a pod, to use one of your human phrases.

"Being what they were, they loved the private document collections and the homes and places where scholars met. When the humans built the library in Alexandria, some of the priests asked for Seshat's blessing. Naturally, she gave it. She was, in a sense, the librarian of the place. She knew every jot and curve of every word of every scroll. But then there was the fire and the place burned."

He took his seat again, and Hazel waited for him to continue.

"I don't know what started the fire, but Seshat wouldn't leave her beloved library. Presumably, she tried to extinguish the flames. Thoth went in to get her out, but she died. Her loss drove him mad."

"How did the Library end up in the void?"

"I don't know. But somehow it did. On this side, the place was destroyed, but in the void, the Library still existed. With time, I suppose they've added onto it. I know people visit there still."

"How do I get inside?"

"You have to be a renowned scholar with various recorded accomplishments, an impeccable reputation and the necessary personal connections."

"But what about someone like me? Or Astrid? What about ordinary people?"

"No. Not even Astrid, rare as she is, would be admitted."

"We have a friend, a cat, who studied with monks in Ireland. She's a scholar."

"If she had the ability to go to the Library, she would know. It would never be something unexpected to her," said Yelbeghen.

"I see. How do the scholars get in? Where's the entrance?"

"Planning on storming the gates? The entrance moves, and I have no idea who guards it or who determines where it appears. For all I know, it's the Librarian himself. Though how he manages it in his insane state, I could not guess."

"With the time machine and a Door, we might be able to get inside."

"Unlikely," said Yelbeghen. "And if you did, you couldn't get back out. And if you did manage to escape with your lives, you'd be as mad as the Librarian himself."

"What about when it was on this side? When it was still part of this world? There had to be a moment, when it was still burning, but not in the void yet. We could use our time machine, get there, go inside the ordinary human library, then ride it into the void and find Elliot. Maybe we could even find whatever we need to help Neil."

"An interesting idea."

"How would the gods look, if I met them?"

"Just as you and I do. Well, perhaps they'd be a little more beautiful than we two are. You were not gifted with beauty, and I do not look quite as human as I might."

"All right," she said, choosing not to respond to his insult. "So Thoth was an ibis or human, and what was Seshat?"

"Just a woman, but I don't know. As far as I know, she's dead. Even if she survived, I wouldn't seek her out if I were you. Wherever she is, Thoth will be also. You want to avoid him."

"Why aren't you trying to talk me out of this?"

"Because I hope you go," he said.

"And Astrid?"

"I'd like her to stay, naturally."

"Why do you care if I go or not? Would my death and the death of my companions amuse you?"

"Not at all. You seem to misunderstand me. I do not love death and destruction. Those of my kind who were brutal and violent are no longer in this world. You do not like my collections, but I know you have toured the grounds. You have seen rare things, animals and other beings who would be out of place in the ordinary world. They have no other place to go. This place is as much a sanctuary as a home."

"Right. And slave owners used to tell the abolitionists how happy their charges were."

"If you insist on misunderstanding me, then I cannot say anything to convince you."

"You haven't answered my question. Why would you want us to go?"

"I have learned about the ship you captain. If you die, you leave Skidbladnir behind."

"In the event of my death, the ship goes to Mr. Escobar. I've made arrangements."

"Still, he's a monkey. They all are."

"How do you know about my crew?"

"I make it my business to know about any interesting items I may wish to acquire."

"Well, the ship would belong to him, and there's nothing you could do to take it."

"He has family and there are islands that his people might like. Lush, remote ones with more fruit than their little fuzzy bellies could hold."

"Well, we're not intending on dying. So you'll have to resign yourself to disappointment. If we can get into the Library right when it burns, we could get Elliot and get out."

"And what about your friend who is not your husband?"

"We have a good number of people, some who are very good at infiltrating difficult places and finding lost things."

"You speak of the raven and the cat."

"Don't tell me you know about them because you want to acquire them."

"I would not object if they wanted to live here, but from what I understand, they are happy out in the ordinary world. I would not take them unless they were willing. Now, tell me more about your ship."

CHAPTER 40

"HAVE YOU INFORMED YOUR MASTERS that the deal is off?" Yelbeghen asked Astrid over dinner. They were the only two eating, as everyone else had opted to eat in their rooms. Astrid didn't blame them. Hazel simply wanted to leave and was looking forward to the return of Skidbladnir while the triplets were keeping to themselves.

"The Seelie aren't my masters," Astrid said.

"They force you do to what you do not wish to do."

"Most of life is doing what you don't wish to do," said Astrid. "School, work, supernatural bargains. You might get a bad hand, but you play the hand you're dealt."

"An interesting way of seeing it. You know, if you were under my protection, they could not ask anything of you."

"And if I was under your protection, I'd have to live here as a captive, like the Seelie girl they're trying to get back."

"Did the Seelie make any counteroffer?" he asked.

"No," she said. "They just said that I was supposed to negotiate with you. But unless you can think of something you want, something I could provide, then I have nothing to offer."

"You underestimate yourself, Astrid. You have much to offer."

His look made her stomach flutter, but it also made her interior alarm bells go off.

"Just tell me what you would take in exchange for

freeing the Seelie girl," she said. "Then I'll talk to the Seelie and see if they can provide it."

"You."

He touched her hand and she jerked it away.

"You mean for me to take her place?"

"Ideally, yes."

She had been through something similar before. She had taken Sister's place to allow the girl to be freed. And now, she could take the Seelie girl's place to ensure Sister's safety from the Seelie. On one hand, it would work and Sister would be safe. On the other, what else could they threaten her with? If she was willing to give herself up every time someone threatened a person she cared about, she'd never have a free day or even a free moment. Every being who knew what she was could threaten to harm Sister, Elliot or her other family or even the members of the Time Corps. And then they could have her do whatever they wished. She'd be a puppet on a string forever.

"No deal," she said. "I'm not for sale."

"I don't mean for sale. Merely a choice, a free choice on your part."

"I don't understand why you're fascinated with me. I'm not the only psychopomp in the world."

"No, but an Unseelie born psychopomp, and a virgin to boot?"

She was horrified that he knew this detail of her life. How had he figured it out? Was it a look, a scent, some other indefinable thing that only beings like him could detect?

He had touched her hand. That must be it. It was the only way. He had not known about Briar before he had taken the three girls to that room. He must have touched each of them and figured it out.

"This obsession with virginity is strange," she said. "You know that, right?"

He shrugged. "Your inability to place value on it is just as perplexing to me."

"And I suppose if I agreed, you wouldn't be interested in changing my virginal state, right?"

"Not unless you wanted to. I would not object."

"That's terrible. Why do that with me, but not to the Seelie triplets?"

"It's different with you. You're a Door."

As if that explained anything. What, did he think she'd perform some Door magic during sex? Maybe she could send them both into the void. She wondered if drakes could survive there.

"I can't," she said. "For one, I have psychopomp duties to perform. I'd have to leave at a moment's notice. And secondly, I am starting art school soon."

How simple and human that sounded. Art school. New York. Scholarships and an apartment. Drinking coffee and studying. Here she was, a being who could travel between worlds, and she was clinging onto a life of a mundane human woman.

"You could still do those things, as long as you returned to me."

The dining room was empty, and he was surrounded only by beings that either needed him for a safe place to live, like the strange wildlife, or were forced here, like the Seelie girl and the triplets. She studied him as he poured himself more wine, and again she felt that little tug inside. What was it he had said about them being alike?

"I can't," she said. "I won't be anyone's property again. If you had ever experienced it, you wouldn't ask it of anyone."

"Tell me."

She did. She told him about her time in the Unseelie world as a servant, but unlike other servants with no chance of escape, she had always maintained hope.

"It was only because I was a Door that I knew I'd get out some day."

Her phone dinged, and she glanced at it. Gerard had sent her a text.

"They have Sister!" she said. "The Seelie took her, as insurance for me to get the Seelie girl back."

Her phone rang. It was Gerard.

"If you harm a hair on her head, so help me, you will pay," Astrid said before the little centaur could say a word.

"She's fine! She hasn't been harmed. She's safe in your old house in the Seelie world."

"And you better not be giving her anything to eat. She's human born."

Though Sister had eaten in the Unseelie world and escaped, she had never been in the Seelie lands. Eating anything might trap her there.

"Nothing, not a bite," said Gerard.

"How do you know? You're calling me from the human world. You can't be with her."

"Iolanthe is with her."

"Oh, that makes it all better. She's worse than you are. You send Sister back right now, or I'm coming there myself and anyone who tries to stop me will find themselves standing on a Door that drops into the void."

She could only imagine how frightened Sister was. After enslavement and years of torment, the poor thing was probably having an emotional breakdown. All her progress, all her struggle to fit into the human world, were now up in smoke.

"Listen to me. Astrid," said Gerard. "She's only being held as insurance that you'll finish your task."

"I was working on the task, I'll have you know."

"Yes, but they wanted me to inform you of the extra incentive."

"You want to talk about incentive? How about this for incentive? Yelbeghen is right next to me, and if you don't send Sister home this instant, he and I are both going to show up and the Seelie will find what it's like to choose between freezing in the void or burning alive."

She glanced at Yelbeghen, who took the napkin from his lap and tossed it onto the table. He tipped his head toward the door, indicating he was ready to go.

"I can't do anything," said Gerard. "I'm under orders."

"Then get your orders changed. You have one hour. Make that half an hour. Human time, not that crazy Seelie time."

She hung up the phone and found Yelbeghen smiling at her.

"Do we have to wait the entire half hour?" he asked with a gleam of mischief in his eye.

"I wasn't intending to. I'm going to Seelie right now to get her."

"I'll go with you," he said. "In case you need someone to burn anyone to a cinder."

"I didn't mean that. But if they hurt her, you can do what you like. Oh, but you have to stay here. I can't take anyone through my Doors. It's not allowed."

"I can get there myself. But even if I do, how do you plan on getting Sister out without making a Door?"

He was right, but it didn't matter. Let the psychopomps cry about it. Let the worlds be destabilized.

She made a Door to Luna Park, stepped through, then made another Door, making very, very sure it led to the proper place in the Seelie world.

Her old home was unchanged. The rooms were bright and comfortable and the building was still surrounded by cold iron. It was fortunate that Sister could not speak, as she might have said something when Astrid appeared out of nowhere. Instead she gave a little cry, and then leapt up from her spot nestled in among a pile of cushions on the floor.

"Where's Iolanthe?" Astrid whispered, and Sister

pointed to the next room. Astrid motioned silently for Sister to take her hand, and a moment later, they were in the living room of the Time Corps house.

"Professor!" yelled Astrid.

The man appeared at the top of the stairs, black hair wild and shirt sleeves rolled up.

"Ah, you're back!" He headed down the stairs.

"Did you know that Sister was taken by the Seelie?"

"What? No. When was that?"

Sister signed, "It has not been long. Only fifteen or twenty minutes."

"You need to take her somewhere safe," said Astrid. "Another time maybe. In the past. The Seelie could eventually live long enough to find her in the future. But they can't go back in time."

"No!" signed Sister. "I can't see you there either. I would be alone."

"If you stay here, the Seelie will use you to get to me. They'll do it again, and next time, they might not just let you sit in a nice room. Time can pass strangely there, and I might not be able to find you."

"Hazel has a house in our home world," said the Professor. "She lives there when she's older. In the late 1950s, early 1960s. I could take her there."

"Hazel would be there with you," said Astrid to Sister. "And you can use the machines to come back to see me whenever you liked."

Sister looked unsure, but there was no time for delay. Right now, the Seelie were discovering her absence. They could arrive at the house at any moment.

"Go now," she said to the Professor.

Sister squeezed Astrid in a tight embrace and kissed her cheek.

"I'll see you again soon," said Astrid. "This isn't forever."

She hoped it was true.

"Come upstairs," said the Professor. "I already have the coordinates."

Astrid waited until they were gone. Ten minutes later, the Professor returned in different clothing and with a few days' worth of beard.

"Hazel is looking after her. Older Hazel, once she retires. Sister is settling in, and though they won't have the computers and cell phones that you young people like, she'll be all right."

"Thank you."

She knew she ought to go to Mr. Augustus's office to summon Gerard and inform him in person of what she had done, but if the Seelie wanted her, they knew where she'd be. Besides, she had a feeling that Yelbeghen would take her side if the Seelie decided to punish her. No sense in staying here with vulnerable people when an angry drake was available.

She returned to Yelbeghen's island, stepping through the Door into the dining room where their food still sat, now cold. The drake ate meat, but had kindly provided her a vegetarian dish. A little breeze blew in from the adjoining room, and Yelbeghen appeared.

"I've dealt with the Seelie," he said. "They will not seek out Sister again and the queen has sent her apologies."

"The queen? You had an audience with the queen?" Even Astrid had never seen the queen or even the higher court members. She had only dealt with lower-level bureaucrats and errand runners.

"Well, a surprise audience," said Yelbeghen. "She couldn't very well refuse me when I showed up in the middle of her throne room."

"How did you get there? Do you have a secret portal or something here on the island?"

"Something like that."

Then it hit her, and she felt like a fool. That was why

she had felt the strange draw to him. That was why he had said they were alike.

"You're a Door," she said.

"I find it far superior to spending thousands on hiring ships and paying for airfare," he said.

"Are you a psychopomp too? Are you the retired old one that Jeff talks about?"

"No. I'm just a Door."

"Are all drakes like you?" she asked.

"You're highly unlikely to meet any others of my kind. Now, let's discuss your task for the Seelie."

"You didn't get the queen to relieve me of my tasks?"

"It was all I could do to get them to promise to not come after you for taking their captive without completing your task."

"That's the thing. They can still get to other people I care about."

"Loving anything makes you vulnerable to losing it. It's the nature of attachment."

"And here you are, attached to all your collections."

"Now you understand the tragedy of my circumstances," he said, but with a touch of humor in his expression.

"And you understand mine. Without you giving up one of your possessions, I can't complete my task."

"Offer me something in return."

"What? A drawing? I can draw pretty well. I can make a piece of art for you. An original drawing from a psychopomp. You can frame it."

He thought it over. "Come, let's go outside. I have a lovely garden that only blooms at night."

She allowed him to take her outside to a small garden where a fountain bubbled, moonlight glittering on the water. Pale flowers drooped on their stems, open in the night air. Their fragrance was faint but sweet and mixed with the tang of the salty ocean air.

"This is all very romantic," she said. "But I want to talk about freeing the Seelie girl."

"I thought we were," he said.

"Look, just tell me what you think you want in exchange. No slavery. No sex. Got it?"

"How about dinner."

"What do you mean? Me have dinner with you?"

"Every night."

"For how long?"

"The rest of your life."

"That's too long. What if I want to get married or have a family?"

"What do you suggest then?" he asked. "I will be losing one of my companions, someone who has been with me for years, whom I consider a friend."

She looked out toward the sea, thinking about it. "Have you ever seen a Door open into death?" She glanced at him.

Now he looked intrigued. She pressed on.

"I let you come on three jobs with me. You can make your own Door to get there, but you can see how it happens. Then, I have dinner with you once every two weeks."

"For life?"

"How about for a few years?"

"Twenty."

"Ten," she said. "Ten and I make you an original piece of art."

He paused for a long time. "Done."

The next morning, she watched as the Seelie girl embraced Yelbeghen, kissed his cheek and wiped her eyes. "I'll come visit you. Or you must visit me," she said.

"I will do my best."

But Astrid knew the truth. The Seelie girl would most likely never leave her people's world and the drake was not likely to visit her there. The girl was free, but it didn't seem to make her any happier. She hung her head as she held Yelbeghen's hand and he made a Door. He returned alone.

A little later, Astrid stood near a high window and looked out over the sea. Skidbladnir's red and white striped sail billowed in the moonlight. She called Hazel, who audibly sighed with contentment when she saw her ship. Hazel grabbed her things and rushed out, calling out to Astrid to tell her that they'd wait for her on shore.

Yelbeghen met her near the tunnel that led to the path out to the beach.

"I'll see you in two weeks. Don't forget."

CHAPTER 41

HUGINN WATCHED AS ASTRID FILLED the black marble bowl with water and waited for it to settle into glasslike stillness. Once it did, she tried over and over to make a Door to Elliot.

"It's not working," she said. "Even if I treat it like a mirror, and that's the easiest thing for me to make into a Door."

"What if you asked another Door to help you?" said Huginn. "When Red Fawn helped you, you were able to make a brief Door into the Library."

"We still don't know if it was the library we wanted. Just that it was a library."

But if she thought about it, Elliot must have received her old sketch book. How else could they have sent words through her drawings? That meant that the library must have been close to her world once again.

"Still, could you get help?" said Huginn.

"None of the psychopomps would help me. I'm not supposed to use my abilities this way. Only for official work."

He watched her, knowing she was thinking the same thing he was. He wondered why she acted as if he meant the psychopomps.

"Yelbeghen could help you," said Huginn. "Hazel says he likes you."

"Yeah, and I hope I get to like him, because I'm going

to be dining with him regularly for the next decade. I don't want his help."

"I would venture to say that the situation does not call for what you want, but what Elliot needs. And what Neil needs as well."

She glared up at him and zipped her jacket closed. "Yeah, I know. I guess I'll head to Yelbeghen's place when you all are ready to go to ancient Egypt. I have to stay in my own time, and either I go to the Time Corps house or the drake's."

"My friend," he said, as gently as he could, "please do not be unhappy. You are doing the best thing under bad circumstances."

"Yeah. Well, don't we always?" she said, with a little rueful smile. "I think I'm still upset that I had to send Sister away."

"You will see her again."

"And Elliot is stuck in the Library because I did my best under bad circumstances."

"He's alive, and we know he'll get out. We've met him when he's older."

"I know," she said. "I'm not ready to give up yet. Elliot can be saved. So can Neil, I hope. Sister can be brought back. Maybe, with Yelbeghen's help, the Seelie could be sealed into their world permanently."

"Anything is possible," said Huginn.

"Well, not much is going to be possible unless I can use this bowl," she said.

Two hours later, the crew's preparations for extended time travel were complete. Never before had anyone used one of the machines to travel so far from their point of origin.

Astrid said her good-byes and made a Door to the drake's home. Hazel warned the crew, and then threw the switch to activate the time machine, then sailed the ship through the time rip. When they exited, aside from a nauseated sensation, Huginn could detect no difference. The sea and sky were as they always had been, blue and gray green, windy and cool.

Hazel leapt up from below decks with a big smile.

"I double and triple-checked the coordinates. We're a few years after the destruction of the Library."

That was the plan. Ignorant of the exact day of the fire, they had decided to go a bit later and Yukiko would ask around to discover the date they needed. Then, they'd travel back in time and arrive at the correct date.

This was the tedious portion of time travel, thought Huginn as he watched Yukiko and Pangur Ban head up the beach from the ship and toward Alexandria. There were investigations, questions and lots and lots of footwork. Yukiko could communicate with any human, and though Pangur Ban could not, she was intelligent enough to stay out of trouble, most of the time. That afternoon, they returned with the proper date and Hazel calculated and then set the new coordinates.

This time, the feeling of nausea was not so intense and after Hazel verified their date, they brought the ship to shore.

"A week from now, the library will burn," said Hazel to her crew gathered on the beach. "Do not try to intervene."

She folded the ship, pressing its sides while standing in the surf. It shrank and then transformed into a folded piece of brown cloth which she handed to Mr. Escobar. As long as the ship was not stolen from the captain directly, it would not become anyone else's. But if a pickpocket took it from the captain, they would become the owner of the ship. The other consideration was more grim. The crew could go home and live out their lives if Hazel and the group did not return from the Library.

Pangur Ban and Yukiko accompanied Hazel up the same road that they had traveled before with Huginn flying overhead. When he circled back, he still spied some of the monkeys racing toward a cluster of date palms and acacia trees. It was remote enough from human civilization that they would not be troubled by anyone. Huginn flew as the group walked the rest of the way to the city of Alexandria, passing the harbor full of ancient ships, which Huginn noticed Hazel eying thoughtfully. The stone lighthouse stood in the distance, gleaming white in the sun.

In a way, Huginn pitied Yukiko and Hazel. When he and Pangur Ban went on missions together, they did not need to take gold to convert to local currency for rooms or food, but hunted or scavenged on their own and slept where they pleased. They required no special clothing to disguise themselves as natives and even when they did not speak the local language, they knew enough about humans and their ways to discern trouble. Hazel and Yukiko required so many things, and spent the larger part of the first day acquiring them.

Plenty of money and a woman who could pass as a local got them a room in a comfortable inn suitable for two women traveling alone. They chose a room on the top story with a window that Huginn and Pangur Ban could use as an entrance. Not that they spent much time there. As the days passed, they spent their time at the library.

Hazel could not go in without Yukiko, as she did not speak the language and had no way of convincing anyone she was a scholar. Yukiko used her magic to alter their appearance, changing their ethnicities, ages and sometimes their sex. Huginn sometimes joined them and Yukiko created an illusion to allow the people to overlook a large bird on her shoulder.

Using Yukiko as a translator, Hazel questioned people relentlessly, searching for information on golems, mud men, any kind of life created in an unnatural fashion. Aside from myths and legends, they found nothing. They asked about a Jewish section, as the Jews were the originators of the term "golem" and the letters in Neil's mouth had been in Hebrew. They found very little they did not already know. There was nothing on reviving a dead golem.

Huginn and Pangur Ban decided to do what they did best: find things that were difficult to find. In this case, that was the goddess Seshat.

It took until midday on the last day for them to locate the librarian. She only came now and again, they had learned, and kept no set schedule. But between a cat and a raven, no area of the library was truly out of their reach. After days of wandering and searching out hidden corners and rooms, they discovered a scroll-lined room with a single high window and one door. The door led out into the rest of the library, but when they tried to find the other side of the door, they found only a blank wall.

"A one-way door," said Pangur Ban. "You would have to know it was there to use it."

"And one might not be able to open it without some special skill or knowledge. Perhaps a word."

It hardly mattered, as they did not need to use the door. Huginn waited, perched up on the high window sill, until a woman carrying an armload of scrolls entered. She was young, younger than Huginn would have thought, dark skinned and petite. Her clothing was ordinary for this time and she wore her hair braided in a simple style.

She glanced up at him without alarm. Perhaps other birds liked to come and perch near her sanctuary.

"I do not know you," she said. "Are you kin of my husband?"

"No. I'm a foreigner. But I am seeking information."

"Then you are like me. I am always seeking information. Would you like to come in?"

He accepted her invitation and took a perch on the back of a chair.

"These are my newest acquisitions," she said, setting down the scrolls. "I seek to collect knowledge of all kinds. Some day, I would like to collect all of the world's information."

"Then perhaps you can help me. I am looking for information about golems. Men of earth that are brought to life."

He explained the situation, and she listened patiently, asking a few questions.

"The name of a god ..." she said.

"It's supposed to be the name of the single god. The one god."

"It's impossible then. There are many gods."

"But if you had to guess, what would you pick?"

"There are believers in a single god, yes. I know of them. It's an intriguing question," she said. "Would you wait here? I could ask my husband. He may know."

She left the room's door open, but none of the people passing by in the next room seemed to notice the door had not been there a moment before.

Then, Huginn smelled smoke. The humans hadn't noticed it yet and were still studying, reading and speaking quietly together.

He had to warn Seshat. He had to tell the people to get out and to inform Yukiko and Hazel. He flew through the door, noting that windows were few in this portion of the building, and those he saw were shuttered. He was as trapped as they were, and smoke rose, so unless he wanted to hop along the ground, he needed to get to a safe place before the smoke grew thick. For now, it was only a faint, faraway scent.

He flapped through the rooms, looking for Seshat, but he could not find her. The humans were still milling about, selecting scrolls and scratching their beards. He felt bad frightening them, but this was no time to worry about delicate human sensibilities. If they were upset by a talking bird, they'd be far more upset in a few minutes.

"Fire!" he cried. "Get out! There's a fire!"

The people listened then, looking around them to check what the other people were doing about this supposed fire. Some even thought another human had called out. Foolish things. He continued to look for Seshat, and it wasn't until the people smelled the smoke themselves that they really began to move. They poured out of the rooms, while Huginn went farther in. If he wanted to stay in the Library while it slipped into the void, he knew he should stay with Seshat, and if he had to guess, she would be close to the fire, trying to put it out.

He ducked under doorways and darted over cabinets and between shelves. Then, he noticed that two people, both elderly men, were rushing in the same direction he was. But one was dragging a large trunk on wheels and they were moving far too quickly for their age. A white cat trotted at their heels.

"Yukiko! Hazel!" he called, and they glanced up at him.

Pangur Ban darted on ahead, and then called over her shoulder to help the two women know which way to go.

The smoke was heavy here, and Huginn flew low to breathe, veering around furniture and fleeing people. His eyes stung now, and he landed on Hazel's shoulder, gripping hard, for he could no longer see well enough to fly.

To one side, he saw a petite woman and a tall, thin man.

"Seshat!" he cried and flew toward her.

"It's burning. It's all burning!" she cried.

Through an open doorway, he saw the yellow flicker of fire illuminating the adjoining room. Yukiko, Pangur Ban and Hazel had all followed him, determined, just as he was, to stick with Seshat and the man who must be her husband, Thoth.

They followed the pair into the room with the flames, and shoved the trunk with the time machine up against a wall. They would use it to get out of the Library with Elliot, if luck was on their side. But after a few moments, they had to pull back. The gods could stand the temperature and lack of air, but they could not. Seshat and Thoth beat the flames, trying to smother them as the mortals were forced outward, away from the flames as they spread. They kept low, trying to stay as deep within the library as they could.

But it did no good.

There were screams from within, first a woman and then the voice of a man. Huginn and the others had to flee, finding a door to the outside. They slipped into the fresh air, hoping they could catch their breath and return, but the choking smoke only grew thicker. They watched as the fire consumed the building. They drew back, joining the watching crowd.

The library never moved. No door to the void opened to take the building from this world. It simply burned and crumbled amid smoke and screaming, the crash of the ceiling collapsing and the relentless roar of the advancing flames. People arrived with buckets of water, but everyone knew it was too late.

"I was going to learn the name of the one god," said Huginn. "So we could bring back Neil."

Huginn saw the tears in Hazel's eyes. Of all of them, she loved Neil best, and now her best hope of reviving him was gone.

CHAPTER 42

ELLIOT KNELT BESIDE THE BLACK water-filled bowl in his room, the sketch book open beside it. After a few minutes of gazing into the bowl and even speaking to it, he knew the act was futile. He had written and erased words on the mirror picture in the sketch book so often he thought he might rip through the paper if he tried again.

He could sit here all night with the two objects, but he knew nothing would come of it. More than a week had passed with nothing happening, and he thought he knew why.

From far above, he felt the tug of the forbidden area, the area of the time anomaly. It pulled him, and he knew that if he brought the bowl there, and perhaps the sketch book, he would have a greater chance of success. The anomaly itself, connected to the bowls, would hopefully give them some kind of boost that would help Astrid find him. Then, the Time Corps could use her bowl's reflection to get a lock on his location and time.

He poured the water from the bowl into an old water skin he had found in the kitchen, slung the strap over his shoulder and took the bowl and sketch book up the stairs. He was less afraid this time. The ibis was there, waiting, but facing the creature was less terrible than endlessly failing at using the bowl.

The outer rooms were just as he had remembered them, filled with junk and clutter. The floor mosaic now pictured a white comet burning across a star-filled night sky. He moved on to the room with the columns. This time, the faces at the tops of the columns were of an ape, a raven, a fox and a cat. He set the bowl down on the floor and poured in the water. It took a while for it to settle into stillness, and he studied the column heads. All had their eyes open, but did not seem to be watching him with any malevolence. For the first time, he felt almost comfortable there.

He listened for the ibis, but heard nothing. Then he whispered Astrid's name to the bowl. Nothing. He carefully erased and redrew Astrid's name on the picture of the mirror. But even if she did see it, what more could he tell her that would help her find him? He had given her all the information he could. He had to focus on the bowl and the time lock.

The other rooms silently called to him, and he felt them in his mind in that way the Library had of intruding into his thoughts. The rooms pulsed softly, welcoming. Was this some kind of trap set by the ibis? Or was the Librarian in another part of the Library, and this was Elliot's chance to go farther, to discover how far the time anomaly went? Before, he had felt fear. Was this new sensation of tranquility only a trick of the mind, part of the anomaly, or was he able to detect the ibis's absence?

He emptied the bowl back into the skin and carried it through the rooms, passing sitting rooms and reading areas. The long dining table stood empty. The ibis wasn't here. He knew it with certainty now. He could feel a palpable difference in the place.

He climbed a staircase, then another, moving higher until he was sure he must be close to the top of the Library. Pausing on one of the landings, he thought of pulling out the bowl, but he knew he could get even closer to the anomaly, right up to where it might actually rip time and allow the bowl to work. The fabric of the rug underfoot changed as he watched, from black with roses to a green and gold geometric pattern to plain orange. The banister went from marble to wood and back again.

He walked down a hallway, and he knew what he sought waited at the end. The anomaly tugged at his mind, like when he had looked out into the void. Malachy had said that people went mad looking out into it, but it had never affected the tortoise. But Malachy was a solid, earthy being. Elliot knew better than to think that he would be immune.

He turned the ornate handle of a white and gold door. The room inside was an ordinary sitting room, but a fire crackled in the fireplace. A book lay open on a side table, as if its owner might return any moment, but Elliot did not take more than a moment to register this. What drew him were the large open French doors.

They opened into the void.

A huge round balcony spread out beyond the doors, the largest he had ever seen. And above it and below stretched the endless, lightless black of the void. The balcony was like a second room, it was so large, filled with plants, a low stone table, two chairs and even a small fountain. It would have been a lovely place to relax if it hadn't been hanging out into pure emptiness. Also, most pleasant balconies did not include a deathly still woman lying on a cushioned platform at the center.

The woman was petite with dark skin and hair and she lay on her back, holding a scroll to her chest, as a corpse might clutch a lily. The cushion she lay on was oval, and all around her lay rolls of parchment, papyrus, thin sheets of wood and pieces of ordinary paper. All of them had writing on them, though from this distance, Elliot could not read them.

He walked out to her. Though he was deep into the anomaly, none of the plants on the balcony changed as he watched, and the papers near the woman remained fixed and still. He looked back into the room and saw the painting at the far end change from a seascape to a still life of a dead pheasant. The fire burned green for a moment, then returned to normal orange and yellow. Nothing at this side of the room changed, and the balcony felt eerily still.

This was the eye of the storm.

This was the center of the anomaly.

He pushed aside a few pieces of papyrus and set the bowl on the stone table beside an old-fashioned oil lamp, the kind that looked like a stone version of Aladdin's lamp. A tiny flame burned from the tip. Elliot was torn between filling the bowl and approaching the woman. He poured the water.

"Try to be quick," said a female voice in his head. He spun around to find her eyes open, but not watching him. She looked like a drowsy person stargazing.

"I sent him away, but he'll return," she said, and he understood that her voice was coming into his mind through the part of his brain dedicated to the Library. It was as if the library was a separate room, and a window opened into the rest of his mind. Her words were little birds, slipping inside.

"Who are you?" he asked. The water needed time to settle, and he took a step toward her, not wanting to get too close.

"I am the Librarian's wife. Thoth's wife. I am Seshat."

"And you're the center of the time anomaly."

She did not answer.

"You're also the thing that watches in the Library, aren't you?"

"I am."

She did not need to say any more. He knew with perfect clarity that she was the Library's heart, the center of the entire thing. She was the living catalog that touched every mind within the place, the thing that grew inside his mind with time. But there was more. She was more than the heart and mind of the place, the collector of information. She was the embodiment of the idea of the Library.

These ideas came to him in a rush, overwhelming him for a moment. Seshat had allowed the information transfer. She had willed it.

It also meant that she was the watcher from the pillars. It meant she was the one who controlled where the library went.

"Can you move the Library?" he asked. "Can you move it to touch the human world?"

And then, she changed. One moment, she was young and alive, although eerily still, and the next she was charred, the top layer of her skin blackened and cracked, revealing blood red tissue beneath. Her lips were gone, her charred teeth exposed in a death's grin, her features burned away, leaving only a skull covered in the remnants of flesh. A second later, she was alive and healthy once more, gazing at the sky.

"Why did you change?" he said as calmly as he could manage. His heart was pounding hard.

"I am as I have been these many, many centuries."

"Burned and alive?"

"Yes."

He had a moment when he wanted to simply ask her to take the Library to his world, but a tiny ounce of chivalry remained inside him.

"Can I help you?"

"No. I am both and neither, but I live still. I do not wish to die."

"Oh, I didn't mean I was going to kill you," he said. "I just thought maybe—I don't know. If there's something you need, maybe I could do something."

"You did not come here to help me."

It was true.

"I want to go home. To the human world. Can you get me there?"

"I can."

"Then do it. Take me back to when this place touched the human world. That was in Egypt, right?"

Once in Alexandria, he could find a way to communicate with the Time Corps. He saw something in the void then, a luminous thing, like a crack. He rushed to the edge of the balcony.

"Only a void wyrm," Seshat said. "It will not come close."

He watched the thing, long and serpentine, move farther away, no doubt in search of other food. Something else moved closer, and he knew it was the yellowish light of day from his own home world.

"I know you," she said. "But you did not come here from Alexandria."

"No, but you can leave me there. I can find my own way home."

"Your friends came to that old library," she said and Elliot turned to look at her. She was blackened again, but it did not frighten him as it had before. "The girl with the ape feet, the cat, the raven and the fox. They looked and looked for a way to get to you."

Was that why the heads on the columns had been an ape, fox, cat and raven? Hazel and the Professor both had the strange primate feet of humans from their home world. Yukiko was a fox, and Pangur Ban and Huginn might have been with them. Had Seshat pulled those images from his mind, or was she showing him his friends from Alexandria?

She continued. "They also looked for a way to save the earth man."

"What earth man? We're all from earth."

"The man who became earth, the one they wanted to revive."

Elliot didn't know what she meant, but he could find out everything when he got home. If the Time Corps had been to ancient Alexandria already, then it meant they could travel farther than they had when he left. Getting him home would be a snap.

As the Library drew closer to the human library, he could make out the interior of a room, a place of seated scholars and shelving filled with rolled scrolls and folded documents. Others were open and in use. This was the Library before it had grown into its current form. Seshat was not taking him outside, into the city, but straight into the building.

"Not there!" said a man, and Elliot turned to find the Librarian. This was Thoth, the ibis, though now a simple man, tall and slender with brown hair and eyes. He looked every bit like an ordinary man of about forty in his black suit and loafers, but Elliot was far beyond judging by appearances.

"The boy who took the bowls," said Thoth.

Elliot resented being called a boy, as he was in his twenties, but no sooner had that thought occurred to him than he questioned it. How old was he, really? How long had he been in the Library? Could he age backwards here? No, that thought was ridiculous, and his body was just as he expected it to be. Except for the tail which curled, snakelike, brushing against his ankles.

No. He couldn't have a tail.

Thoth was watching him with a thoughtful look, and an idea flew through Elliot's mind, one that caused everything to make sense, but it was like words flying by on a computer screen, like a scroll being unrolled too quickly, and he could not catch it.

The tail was gone.

Thoth was now a giant ibis. He was tall and lean, like a stork, with the long, curved beak and wide-splayed toes common to wading birds. His feathers were white, but his head and legs were black, as were the tips of his wing feathers. But the next moment he was a man. Seshat was one moment a beautiful woman and the next a burned and tormented horror. Elliot clutched the railing and he remembered the black bowl, sitting on the table. He glanced away quickly, hoping that ibis would not notice it. The water would be settled now, but there was no opportunity to use it. It was a telephone, wasn't it? Or something similar. A television screen, but made of water? It was hard to remember.

His thoughts halted when he saw the creatures teeming around Seshat. Her eyes were wide open in terror now, and her mouth was frozen open, as if she was calling out. She was back to her smooth-skinned self, but the creatures, insects, rodents, tiny serpents, all crawled and scurried and slithered over her body. They had been bits of paper, papyrus and wood before, but now he saw their true forms. One bit her throat, another dug its pincers into soft flesh at the inside of her elbow. Another, this one iridescent and insectile, leapt onto her cheek and crawled toward her mouth.

Elliot ripped the thing from her face and hurled it away. He scooped and threw the tiny horrors onto the ground, away from the paralyzed woman. There was a sound in his mind, a high keening noise, which could only be Seshat screaming. Elliot threw more and more of the creatures away, though they cut at his hands like tiny bits of glass.

But no sooner than he had cleared a few away, than they crawled back. He thought of the void. He would throw them there, where they could freeze or burn or suffocate or just hang in limbo until a void wyrm ate them.

He hurled a few over the railing, but though only two of them had wings, they all floated back, like leaves on the wind, only to alight on the ground and return to their relentless march toward Seshat.

His hands were bloodied and stinging. As he continued to fling the things away, he glanced inside. The fireplace.

Fire. Everything was afraid of fire.

The Librarian, now a man, stood between him and the

open doorway, doing nothing more than watching with his arms folded. What was wrong with the man? His wife was being attacked and he simply stood there.

But the fireplace wasn't the only source of flame. The little stone oil lamp sat beside his bowl and the pieces of papyrus on the table. He could hurl it in among the skittering creatures, but he didn't want to hurt Seshat. And throwing the lamp onto the ground might break it, but it might not. He snatched up a piece of papyrus, rolled it and held it into the flame.

Thoth leapt forward to stop him, but the papyrus caught quickly and Elliot dodged beneath the man's arms to hold the flame in among the largest clump of monstrosities on the ground.

How quickly they caught fire.

How surprisingly quick.

They curled and blackened, some sliding away as if blown by the wind, and igniting others. The fire spread.

Thoth howled and tried to gather them up, but dropped the burning things just as quickly. Elliot crawled up beside Seshat, and pushed handfuls of creatures onto the ground where they burned with their brothers, slithering and skittering and rolling together as they died.

"This is the place," said Seshat, and Elliot realized that the screaming inside his head was still going, the high-pitched minor note like an endless train whistle. The sound was not coming from Seshat.

The Alexandrian library, the one in the human world, was close now. Only a few more moments, and the Library would be touching it. But it was not as it ought to be. The people inside were only partially human, though they changed as he watched. The walls undulated and music came to him, high piping that blended with the sound in his mind until he could not tell the two apart. Colors shifted and blended until he couldn't make sense of what he was seeing.

The moment the two libraries touched, a harsh wind pulled at Elliot, rippling his clothing and pulling all of the burning creatures away, through the gaps in the railing and over it, through the few feet of space until they landed on tables and chairs, on shoulders and hair, and all along the shelves and cases housing the texts of antiquity.

Thoth roared then, and launched himself over the balcony, becoming the great slender white bird with black-tipped wings, gliding downward. Elliot was about to follow, but Seshat yelled a commanding, "Stop!" and all sound ceased, including the screeching in his mind. The human library pulled away while the flames grew and people fled. Thoth, half aflame himself, leapt amid the chaos, trying to save his library.

And then all was silence and the human library withdrew into the void.

"Again, it burns," said Seshat. "It always burns. He does not wish to be there. I should not have taken you there."

"I needed to go home," he said. "I still do."

He looked at her, and now all the corpses of the tiny evil creatures were gone. All of them had been nothing more than paper, papyrus and thin slices of wood. Now all that remained were charred curled bits crumbled on the ground.

"What was on those papers?" he asked.

"Words. My husband created many words for me. As long as information comes to me, I live."

"And if the information stops?"

"My husband sees to it that it does not. It is all he can do for me."

"He drove me mad, didn't he?" Elliot asked.

"He did not permit you to leave. But in his madness, he drove you to set fire to his writings and then the Alexandrian library. There was only one way it could be. It was always thus."

"Will he return?" he asked.

"He always returns."

"What about my friends?"

"They did not perish in the fire. They were outside the Library."

But if that brief moment when the flaming papers had flown into the human library was the only time this place touched his world, then the Time Corps had missed their only opportunity to save him.

CHAPTER 43

"WELL, NEIL," SAID HAZEL. "I don't know what to do."

She pushed aside the cover on his crate and pulled back the cloth covering his face. It was unchanged.

"I don't know about this name of God business," she said. "You had 'truth' in your mouth, not the name of God. And Huginn says that Seshat didn't know of any name of a single god. We've tried everything. I have no other ideas."

She sat beside the crate and sighed. Tears blurred her vision as she blinked and studied him. He was dead. Her friend, the man who had saved her life in so many ways through the years, was gone. From freeing her from her cruel uncle as a child to saving her life a few times in the Time Corps, he had been her faithful colleague, loyal crewmate and closest friend. He had always been there, silent and steady. He loved her, she knew. She couldn't doubt it, though she wondered why he had never acted upon the feeling.

Up until now, she had pushed the thought aside, focusing on her missions with the Time Corps, her crew, her ship. Emotions and entanglements made one weak, though she knew her own passionate nature enough to admit that she loved people, and fiercely. She also knew it was a vulnerability.

She understood now, as she looked at the thing in the form of a man before her, that he was gone forever. Their mission to the Alexandrian library had failed and as the place went up in flames, so went her hope of reviving him. His absence tore open a wound inside her so deep that she was shocked at the intensity of the pain.

Gone. Neil Grey was gone. Not waiting in heaven, but erased forever from existence. Her Neil, whom she loved. Yes, she loved him. There was no sense in denying it to herself. She had never pictured herself with anyone else. In all her visions of the future, Neil had always been at her side. He knew her, her past, her failures, her weaknesses, and he loved her still.

She loved him, and he was dead. Unable to bear looking at him, she rested her head on her arms and wept. She cried for the past and all of the things unsaid between them, for the future, grim and empty, and for the present and the knowledge that she was now starting upon a new path alone.

Later that night, rain thrashed against the outside of the ship. She had cried until she was emptied and calm, the storm inside her quieted into a black despair that had no more words or tears. Now and then she heard the crew shout to one another. The ship was in no danger. They would call her if they required her help.

She glanced at her computer, at her books. There had to be something else, something she was missing. Through the pain, she had to make herself think.

Mr. March was no devout or holy man, so the notion that he created Neil through heavenly means was perhaps misguided. Maybe he had done it through evil and nefarious means. But that didn't help her at all. What was she going to do, perform a wicked blood ritual or a human sacrifice? Even if she were willing to do such a thing, she wouldn't know where to begin.

"Do you remember that Italian gallery we visited?" she said softly. "And how you admired the sculptures.

'Capturing life in stone,' you said. They almost seemed alive. Too bad you didn't get to become something you considered beautiful. Just a lump of earth. Dust to dust."

Dust to dust. Adam, the first man, had been created by God out of earth. Then at death, to dust he returned, as would all his countless children. Neil's transformation had simply been quicker than that of the average person.

Ah, but perhaps she was looking to the wrong culture when trying to revive Neil. He may be a golem, but that didn't mean she had to solely consider the Hebrew stories. She naturally had felt drawn to them, her own eighteenth-century French Catholicism finding a comfortable spiritual home within the idea that God could create and that His name held the power to bring life, even to a lump of earth.

But she had met others who followed different gods. She had managed to keep her faith by acknowledging that this world, like so many of the worlds different from her own, had other traditions, practices and creatures. It also had gods that lived and breathed, and she was friends with two of their servants. She did not disbelieve Yukiko and Huginn when they told her that their masters were real. The other gods might not be the one God, but perhaps were part of His overall plan.

How many ways were there to make life, beside the ordinary human one? What things did most rituals include? She thought about it. Symbolic objects, words, fire, blood. Yes, blood might be involved. A human birth was always accompanied by blood.

She pulled open her desk drawer and extracted a pen knife. Locking the door to her quarters, she knelt beside Neil and made a small cut in the pad of her index finger. She squeezed it hard, and a little dark globe of blood appeared on her fingertip. Then, holding her finger over Neil's mouth, she squeezed the sides of her finger hard. The pain was nothing, and she watched two, then three drops land on his tongue.

He lay unchanged.

She put away the pen knife and sucked her finger as she paced and thought. Waking the dead, reviving the dead, how did one go about it?

Gods and goddesses, spirits and fair folk, they all were real. Doorways both natural and mechanical, people who could change appearance at will. Sea folk with the bodies of humans and the tails of ocean animals, sidhe with animal body parts, animals who spoke. All were real. Some she had met, and some she had heard about from others. Even dragons were real, and they still craved young maidens. She wondered if there were no longer any real princesses left for them to snatch.

Princesses. Now princesses were truly a rare thing. She thought about it. What had happened to Snow White when she had lain dead? And Sleeping Beauty?

A kiss? She glanced at Neil and returned to her position beside him.

"Do you remember how every time we met, you asked how old I was?" She paused, as if he might answer. "What were you waiting for? What am I going to know when I'm older that I don't know now? Or was it something else?"

His dead, dry mouth lay open. He had no real lips to speak of. But still, she leaned over and kissed his forehead, his eyes, his cheeks and then his mouth. Then she pressed her forehead to his and sighed.

"Did you ask my age because it'll take me years and years to figure out how to bring you back? Will I be an old woman by the time I manage it? Or will I never manage it at all?"

She covered him back up and replaced the crate's lid, then got ready for bed. And when she slept she dreamed of growling dogs and rolling trains, earthquakes and other low, rumbling things.

When she woke, she wondered if the tossing of the storm had caused the lid of Neil's crate to slide askew. She glanced around the room, but nothing else had moved. Her door was still locked, so no one else could have disturbed the crate.

She pushed back the crate's lid, and when she saw Neil, she cried out in horror.

He was alive and moving. He had torn most of his wrappings off and they lay in tangles around his body. He had even managed to push the lid back. But he could do no more. He exhaled a rattling breath and Hazel put her hands to her mouth as he struggled to sit, writhing in place, his chest rising and falling and his mouth working without forming words.

How had this occurred? Had it been the blood? The kiss? Had he heard her voice and somehow returned to her?

A fresh wave of horror struck her, the horror of what she had done. She had taken a dead man and brought him back to life into a body of crumbling stone.

CHAPTER 44

When Yelbeghen took Astrid's hand, the world exploded into sensation. She held her breath as colors leapt into vividness so bright it was painful. Sound became magnified, not only louder, but more detailed. From the swish of the curtains blowing in the sea air to the robin's egg blue of the sky, all of it was too intense to bear.

She pulled her hand away.

"I can't do this."

The bowl sat between them on the kitchen table, beside Yelbeghen's open hand.

"When Red Fawn helped me, it made it easier," she said. "I could concentrate. But you make it worse."

He didn't apologize, but she didn't expect him to. It wasn't his fault that together they were even less successful in making the bowl work. Besides, Red Fawn specialized in creating illusions and fooling the human mind. Not that Astrid was entirely human, or that Yelbeghen wasn't good at illusions. After all, she didn't think he had been born looking human.

"Perhaps Red Fawn should help you again," Yelbeghen said. "I don't think there is much I can do."

Astrid poured the water out into the kitchen sink and wrapped the bowl in a towel.

"Do you have time to stay for dinner?" he asked.

"Not this time. I know my cousin is outside of time, but every minute counts. I don't know how soon it'll be until

Hazel and everyone come back from ancient Egypt. I need to have a functional bowl if they fail."

"And if they do not return?"

"Then I need to get all of them out of the Library. I know they brought a time machine in, but who knows if they'll be able to use it."

"Your cousin has caused a lot of trouble for his friends."

"Most of it because of me."

"I wish I could help you more."

"Why?"

He paused, as if startled by the question. "I'm not sure. I suppose I withdraw the offer."

"Fine. But thanks anyway for trying. At least now I know that doubling up on the people making Doors doesn't make the Doors work any better."

"I could have told you that. There was a time when there were more of us."

"When? And why? The population of earth is at its highest level. Were souls more sticky and likely to become geists? Is that why they needed more psychopomps?"

"Perhaps souls were more sticky," he said, "but not all Doors were psychopomps." He then rose and held out her coat for her.

She took it from him and put it on herself, still uncomfortable with his occasional over familiarity. She thanked him, and taking the bowl and her bag, she made a Door to the Time Corps house in Los Angeles.

An hour later, the Professor had all of his instruments set up around the bowl on the dining room table. Cables and wires ran between various boxes with exposed electronics and other devices with wind-up parts and cranks. All of them culminated in a single receptor device, shaped roughly like a cone, but made of black metal, suspended over the water-filled bowl. If things worked correctly, it would be able to pinpoint the time and place of the transmission and get a time lock. Or so the Professor claimed.

Red Fawn sat on the sofa, telling a story to both of the kittens and Astrid felt Sister's absence keenly. The girl would have been with the cats, listening, or just watching from the sidelines, pulling absently at the tassels on her shawl.

Felicia set up a video camera, which Astrid hated. She had no desire to be recorded making a Door or even just sitting still. But she couldn't deny the logic of having the thing record her. If they could freeze images, like the unknown library though her previous Door, they could perhaps identify specific items.

"Ready when you are, lass," said the Professor.

Red Fawn slipped into a chair beside Astrid and took her hand. Once again, the room and people in it faded away until only the bowl remained. Astrid vaguely noted the click and whir of the Professor's machinery and the glow of the red recording light on the front of the video camera, but in a few moments, even those faded from her consciousness.

The water in the bowl was perfectly still, reflecting a ghostlike version of her own face. It was like she was looking up at herself from below, from the bottom of a deep, dark, quiet lake. It was lovely there, like the void, silent and serene. From the dark place, she reached out to the surface of the water and then beyond it, feeling the place on the other side.

That was when she felt the other bowl.

There were two. They were a set.

That was why the writing on the bowl said bowls were mirrors. Not a single bowl. Bowls. Plural. The bowls were twins. Like Astrid and Sister. Like Huginn and his brother. Like the twin ravens carved into the rim of the bowl.

She registered movement around her. Perhaps the Professor was adjusting some equipment. Or a kitten might have leapt up onto the table to investigate. Red Fawn's hand was soft and warm in hers. Again, she felt the twin bowls, and then she saw the opening, the tiny dot in the center of the water that opened, dilating, until she saw the ceiling of a room.

And then there was a face. Elliot's face. He saw her at the same instant, and said something, but she couldn't make it out. She heard sounds and knew they were speech, but it was like he was speaking gibberish. It didn't matter. Someone would tell her later, or the video camera would record it.

The image vanished, then reformed, then disappeared again.

"We're losing it," said the Professor, and this time, she understood the words.

If only she could use the bowl to step through, or to get Elliot through. Instead, it only allowed an image and words to travel.

The bowl was black now, the Door gone, and Astrid blinked and took a deep breath.

Red Fawn patted the back of Astrid's hand. "I think you got what they needed."

She hoped so. Felicia and the Professor were examining readings together and taking down notes. The Professor looked like he was about to jump out of his skin with excitement and Felicia beamed at Astrid.

Astrid watched Felicia as she worked with her husband and wondered if there was a way to use this information to get Felicia home. Astrid could open Doors between worlds, but Felicia's world was very difficult to reach. Unlike Astrid's world, the hub world, it did not sit cheek by jowl with many other worlds. But what if, with time, Astrid could help her?

"It'll take me a few hours," said the Professor. "I need to go over the readings and recalculate a few things. But

I think we'll get a solid time lock. I think between my machines and your Doors, we can do it."

Diego leaped into her lap and purred, rubbing his forehead against her stomach. He might not understand what was going on, but he knew it was good. She petted him while Felicia unhooked the cables and rolled up the wires. Red Fawn went into the kitchen to make coffee, as the Professor would be up late, and Astrid sat looking at the black bowl with the twin ravens and her name on it.

Her phone rang. It was Hazel.

"Are you okay?" said Astrid.

"We're all alive," said Hazel. "We couldn't get into the Library, and it burned, just like in the history books. But we all are fine. Well, almost. I managed to bring Neil back. But it's bad. Is Julius there?"

Astrid called Julius and put the phone on speakerphone so they could all hear. Hazel said she was sending a picture of Neil and Felicia and Red Fawn gathered around to see. A few moments later, a picture came through, a picture of a man made of stone sitting on a chair.

"He's getting better, I think," said Hazel. "He can move more."

"What did you do?" asked Julius. "How did you do it?"

"I'm not sure. I put some blood in his mouth. And I—I kissed him. But nothing happened. Then, this morning, he was moving. I think he might be getting better."

"Is he in pain?" asked Felicia. "Is he flesh in a stone casing, or is he stone all the way through?"

"I don't know," said Hazel. "I didn't dissect him. But he can hear a little now, and he can nod and shake his head."

"She brought back a golem," muttered Julius. "She actually did it."

"You said he's getting better," said Felicia. "What did you mean?"

"He has some normal skin between his fingers now.

And his eyes look a little moist sometimes. So does the inside of his mouth."

"Then he's returning to human form," said Julius. "Wait. I'm not sure if that's good or bad."

"It's good!" said Hazel. "He's back alive and that's most definitely good. And I don't want to hear any nonsense about golems turning on their masters. I'm not his master. He's a free being."

Astrid wondered if this was so. She hoped Hazel was right, for all their sakes.

Then another thought occurred to her.

"I wonder if he can still travel within ten miles of himself," Astrid said. "Because the Professor is working out the numbers for a time lock. With my Doors and his machines, I think we can do it. And if we can have ten or twenty golems with us, that could only help."

"I'm not sure," said Hazel. "But give him a few days. How is the Professor going to manage it?"

Hazel and Felicia were the two people who best understood the Professor's calculations and machines. Either of them could operate them nearly as well as he could. But to Astrid, they seemed as strange and impossible as her own abilities must seem to them. Felicia told Hazel a few of the details.

"I'm going to work with him," said Astrid. "I think he has a way to guide the Doors I make."

"The dynamic time lock," said Hazel. "He developed a new method using some complicated algorithm."

"Yeah, I guess that's it."

"But I thought you couldn't use your Doors to go to other worlds and definitely not to the Library."

"Well, I couldn't, but now I think I can," said Astrid. "With the time lock and the machine, I might be able to."

"Isn't there some rule against it?" asked Hazel. "Won't the psychopomps send you to psychopomp hell or some such?"

"There is no psychopomp hell. At least I hope not. But whatever they do to me, I don't care. I'm tired of the Seelie with their tasks and drakes with their deals and psychopomps with their rules. I'm a Door, and I'm going to get Elliot out of that Library."

CHAPTER 45

"We're going to run a test," said Hazel. "A scientific test."

Neil sat motionless, but she knew he was listening. He nodded once.

"I'm going to order you to do something, and we'll see if you are compelled to do it."

He dipped his head again.

"Stand up!" she commanded.

He remained seated.

"I said, stand!"

Still, he stayed in his chair.

"I think this is good," she said. "But I'm not sure. What if I really have to mean the command? Perhaps I didn't truly want you to stand, because I want you to be free. So maybe by having my will oppose my words, I'm doing it incorrectly."

Neil blinked slowly, and the tissue of his eyelids looked softer now, like discolored skin caked in gray sand. She knew he had thoughts, that he wanted to communicate them, but it would have to wait.

They stayed in the early twenty-first century Mediterranean, where the Time Corps could easily reach them by phone. A week passed and they took on supplies. Once Neil could move his hands he could write in a rough fashion. His desires were mainly for water and a comfortable chair. A few times, he asked Hazel to play violin for him. As the days passed, his mouth softened and became wet, as did his eyes and he regained the ability to speak.

"I order you to give me that cup," said Hazel.

Neil shook his head. "I refuse."

Hazel thought she saw a tiny smile, but it was hard to tell.

"I think this exercise is futile," he said. His voice was low and dry, as if he were recovering from laryngitis, but to Hazel it was beautiful. "There are two possibilities. Either I am free, and that is that. Or, if you are my new master, then your will is for me to be free. Unless you change your mind, then I am truly free."

She supposed it would have to do. But there were so many unanswered questions. What, precisely, had she done to bring him back? And could he be killed again, and if so, by whom?

By the time a fortnight had passed, Neil was back to normal except for rough earthen patches on some parts of his extremities. His fingers were stiff, but usable. His vision was completely clear and he could move with his usual strength and agility.

It was time.

She called the Time Corps house, and then a Door appeared on deck. Felicia and the Professor stepped through with Astrid, all of them bearing bags of equipment.

"It's going to be dangerous, Professor," said Hazel. "Are you certain you want to come?"

"First off, I could say the same to you. You worry me sick out on the sea in that ship with only monkeys for company."

"Neil is on board too, sometimes."

"Yes, and I can't say I sleep as easy as I once did. I thought he was some kind of genetically modified human man."

"You know him as well as I do, and he'd never do me harm. Right now, he's getting ready to go save his partner, at great risk to himself. And he has helped us both countless times."

She watched the Professor take a deep breath and look out over the ocean.

"I know he's not a bad person," he said. "But I'd rather you weren't so attached to him. Someday, I'd like you to find a nice man. Don't you want that?"

Hazel watched him study her, gauging her reaction.

"Well, I think Santiago is handsome," she said, keeping a straight face. "Do you think he fancies me?"

"Dear mother of—you know what I'm talking about."

"Right now, we are talking about going into the Library."

"So we are," he said. "Now, Felicia and I aren't going into the Library at all. We will stay here. Then, if Astrid can't make a Door out or your machine doesn't work, we'll see what we can do on our end."

That was sensible, Hazel supposed. It meant that their rescue crew included their top infiltrators, Pangur Ban and Huginn, Yukiko as translator and illusionist, Astrid the Door, the many copies of Neil and then Hazel. She was the only one with no special skills or abilities, and for a moment she lamented the fact. But then, what difference did that make? She'd fight as hard as any of them. She checked her pistol, made sure she had extra ammunition in her gun belt and pulled on a coat.

They docked the ship, disembarked, and Neil took one of the time machines up the beach. He made a time rip and stepped through. A minute later, he reappeared, a day or a week older, Hazel could not guess. He shoved his hands into the pockets of his duster as various other Neils began to gather, some from up the beach, some from over a nearby hill. Each of them but the youngest had been through the Library and returned to this moment to do it all over again. She watched as the Neils spoke to each other.

Mr. Escobar took the ship out to sea, where the crew

would wait for their return. Astrid and the Professor discussed the logistics of using Astrid's Door with the Professor's machine while Felicia and Hazel set up the machinery.

Hazel's stomach twisted in knots at the thought of the Library. Sure, she had traveled in time before. She had taken Skidbladnir from the nineteenth century to the twenty-first. But when she had, she knew from Felicia and Neil that the future world was a decent place to go. A miraculous one, to her way of thinking, full of fast cars and faster planes, telephones and radio, motion pictures and computers. But the Library was different. It was outside of time, and if Astrid had trouble making a Door there, then she might not be able to make one out. A time machine might not work either since all of its calculations were based upon having a starting point as well as a destination inside space and time. What if they couldn't find Elliot? What if they all ended up trapped there?

Hazel ran cables and checked the machinery. Astrid put her hand on Hazel's shoulder and leaned in close to her ear. "Thank you," she said softly.

Hazel looked up in surprise. "For what?"

"For going. It's dangerous, and Elliot isn't even your family."

"Neither is the Professor, technically. But he's family to me. Elliot is my friend and colleague."

"But it didn't occur to you to leave him? Or to just let everyone else go after him? After all, Pangur Ban and Huginn are pretty old. Even Yukiko has lived beyond a normal human lifespan. You're still young."

"You're younger than I am and you're going."

"Yeah, I guess so. But you have your ship and crew and Neil and the Professor. You have a whole life."

"That's an odd thing to say. So do you."

"I don't have family except for Elliot. I do, but they won't speak to me."

"Are you talking about your parents?"

"My mother and aunt. I don't know where my father is."

Hazel tried to think of something to say, but came up with nothing. She knew precisely where her parents were. They were buried in a small cemetery outside of New Orleans.

"You have the other psychopomps," said Hazel. "And you have your art school to go to."

"I guess so, but that all seems so far away now."

"Well, it's only going to get farther once we're through the Door. Can you fasten that coupling there?"

Astrid did, and the two finished setting up the machinery in silence. Hazel considered Astrid. The young woman was sullen and quiet, the complete opposite of her sunny, ever-cheerful cousin. And even if Astrid hadn't protested enough over the delivery of the triplets and was overly familiar with the drake, Hazel knew she was a basically decent person at heart.

Hazel hadn't understood until now that Astrid, in some ways, was more of an orphan than she was. Hazel had the Professor and Felicia, her crew and Neil. Astrid had no one other than Sister and Elliot, and both of them were in other times. While Hazel was free to do as she pleased aboard her magnificent ship, Astrid's life was consumed by the demands of the psychopomps and the Seelie, and now the order from the drake to have dinners with him. In some ways, this twenty-first-century woman's life was far more constrained than the lives of Hazel's fellow Southern women during the Civil War.

Hazel glanced up as a shadow fell over her. It was Neil, probably the oldest one of the batch. He would have all the memories of the others. She checked the last fastener, stood and brushed off her pantaloons.

"We're going to survive this, aren't we?" she said.

"Is your gun loaded?"

"Yes, and I brought extra ammunition."

"Good."

They backed up as the Professor hurried around the devices, powering them up and checking various readings. Astrid stood in the center of the machines, her navy blue jacket zipped up to her throat. She looked small and young and frightened.

At last, she made the Door. It flickered between various locations and the Professor adjusted a few of the machines. After a few tries, the Door held steady. The Professor took readings, confirmed them with Felicia, and then he stepped back with a grin.

"The readings match. It's the Library."

Pangur Ban went through first, followed by Huginn and Yukiko and then the Neils. Hazel counted fourteen of them. She and the oldest Neil went through last, dragging a trunk with the time machine.

Once through the Door, the first thing that struck Hazel was the feeling of space inside the Library. She had been on a beach a moment earlier, the sky open and clear, but the Library felt even more open. The ceiling soared overhead, supported by massive columns with countless shelves, three stories of them, lining every inch of wall space.

The next thing she noticed was the intensity of the light. Hazel had grown up in a time before electricity was common, and she still noticed luxuries like indoor plumbing and central heating. The light here was bright and diffused, pouring through multiple translucent white panes up along the top edges of the room.

"We need three teams," said Neil.

"No, we stay together," said Hazel. "We all stay with the Door."

Then she understood. This was the oldest Neil, the one who knew what the Library held. Only the youngest one was as lost as they were. "Very well," she sighed. "Which way?"

"Some of us will go with Pangur Ban and Huginn. Others will go with you, Yukiko and Astrid. And a few are on their own. They'll be looking for information on golems."

"Why? Why split up? If you know where Elliot is, let's get the golem information, get him and then go."

"He's on the move. He doesn't know we're here yet. And there's something Huginn needs to find. It's necessary to get us out."

"Are you going to tell us where to go?"

"I can't. You know how it is."

She did. If the oldest Neil told them everything they needed to do, then the information would form an unstable time loop, going from the older Neil to Hazel and the Time Corps. Then the youngest Neil would learn from Hazel only to pass the information on to Hazel once more.

They agreed to meet up in that exact spot in an hour.

"And you?" Hazel asked Neil. "Which team will you be on?"

As the oldest of the Neils, he would be the most experienced and therefore the most valuable.

"Yours, of course," he said.

CHAPTER 46

Ready to take flight at any moment, Huginn rode on the shoulder of one of the four Neils that joined him and Pangur Ban. Occasionally he flew upward to look down an upstairs corridor or peer through an opening here or there that was large enough for a bird or cat, but not for a man. He flew upward to examine a high opening, but it turned out to be a storage area filled with torn pages and damaged books.

"You said I needed to find Elliot, right?" Huginn asked Neil, returning to his shoulder.

"I said there's something you need to find."

Huginn pondered this. What else could he want to find? A group of three Neils had already gone to find golem information, and seven Neils had accompanied Yukiko, Astrid and Hazel to locate Elliot. What else could he hope to find?

Pangur Ban fell into step beside Neil.

"Perhaps we ought to be searching for a way out of the Library," she said.

"Then why did we need to leave Hazel?" asked Huginn. "She has the time machine with her."

There had to be something else, but Neil couldn't tell him without creating an informational time loop. Huginn imagined that he were Julius, a being dedicated to research and learning. What would Julius look for here? What would he seek? Huginn wished he had his brother's memories. Then he could search them and come up with an idea.

"There's not much time," said Neil.

"Until what?"

Neil tipped his face upward, ever so slightly, as if smelling something. Huginn smelled nothing, and his own sense of smell was excellent. Pangur Ban had not mentioned a strange smell either.

"We should just hurry," Neil said. "The Librarian—"

A giant tortoise stepped out in front of them.

"New arrivals! And so many," he said. He squinted as he examined the four identical Neils.

"What sort are you?" the tortoise asked.

"New arrivals, as you said," Pangur Ban said. "We're here as a group from the Americas. We have research to accomplish."

"And your topic of study?" asked the tortoise.

The Neils moved to stand together silently, perhaps with the intention of appearing as one being in four parts, which, Huginn thought, they were. He wished he could think of a kind of being that came in quadruplets, but he could not remember.

"We seek information about a Norse raven, an old one," said Huginn, a sudden flash of inspiration coming to him. "His name was Muninn, and I believe he is dead."

"Dead in what time?" asked the tortoise.

Ah, yes. He would not know what time they came from unless he tried to guess by the Neils' clothing.

"We do not know when he died, but he was still alive a thousand years after the first Library of Alexandria burned."

"So he lived in a time of written records."

Huginn tried to remember. "Yes, we had writing. But we did not begin that way. We began with stories told by one person to another."

"I see," said the tortoise. Huginn imagined that if the

creature had hands, he would have scratched his head. "You might try the Northern archives. Four stories up and about four minutes that way." He motioned with a paw.

Then the tortoise jerked his head, as if he had just heard his name called. "No," he said, almost to himself. "No, down two floors and five rooms along the corridor to the right. The Room of Speech."

The tortoise muttered something to himself and then looked up at Huginn, studying him with one shiny black eye. "I can hear it, but it's not the one here."

"I am here," said Huginn.

"No, the other one," said the tortoise, who then turned and shuffled a few feet away and looked up into the face of a Roman bust in a display niche. "It's too much. It's too many of them."

"I think his mind is touched," said Pangur Ban.

"No," said Huginn. "I know insane, and he's not insane. He's hearing things. He's talking to someone we can't see."

"I believe that would be the very definition of insanity," said the cat.

The Neils remained silent, and Huginn wondered why fourteen of them had come. Why not fewer or more? What need had he and Pangur Ban of four unnaturally strong bodyguards?

"We go where the tortoise said, to this Room of Speech," said Huginn.

They went downstairs, found the room and stepped inside. All along the edges and sitting on long tables running the length of the room were statues. Some were crudely carved wood, others polished marble. Some were weathered bronze and others faceless figures of chiseled stone.

"A display area. Like a museum," said Pangur Ban, walking down the length of the room.

Huginn flew over the statues, landing and examining a few, and then moving on.

"Huginn," said Pangur Ban. "You ought to come see this."

She sat in front of a raven statue made of dark wood. Its wings were folded and it perched on a round object, like a small globe. It was precisely his own size and shape.

"Do you suppose this is you or your brother?" asked Pangur Ban.

"I don't know," he said. And then he thought he understood what the room contained. "Statue, are you capable of speech?"

The beak opened. "I am."

Huginn took an involuntary hop backwards and a shiver passed through him. The voice was his, but not his.

"Are you Muninn?"

"No. But I possess some of his information."

"Only some? Not all?"

"I do not contain all of his information, no."

"Do you know where he is now?"

"He is dead."

The words hit Huginn like a wall of frigid air. He had not realized how tightly he was holding onto the hope of seeing Muninn again. And now, that hope was dashed. Without his brother, he was truly lost. Without his memories, what was he?

"When did he die?" he asked. "And how?"

"He died in the early twenty-first century, Gregorian calendar, in Los Angeles, California, United States, Terra, Sol System."

Well, that was terribly specific.

Something stirred inside him, a feeling, a very familiar one, as if a key had slipped into a lock and was turning, but had not yet clicked into place.

"How did he die?" Huginn asked.

"Unknown."

"Why did he go to Los Angeles?"

"Unknown."

"Where was he before that? Where has he been these long years?"

"Unknown."

"Gods! What good are you then?" Huginn cried. The stupid thing was useless and rage roared to life inside him. He wanted to tear at the statue's face, to peck out its eyes.

And with that thought, the key clicked into place in his mind and the lock snapped open.

Too many ravens near the Time Corps house, the angry crows had said.

Two too many.

Two ravens.

He had been there when his brother died. He remembered now and the memory was fresh and clear. His brother had died up on the roof of the Time Corps house, lying on the cool overlapping tiles.

The door opened completely in his mind now, and the memories flooded back. But how? How did he have memories?

Muninn had come. It was recent, so very recent. Only a month before. For years, Muninn had been seeking their master, the Wanderer, the Tree Hanger. The god had vanished long before, but no one had witnessed his death. Muninn had sought him, eventually seeking out the information in the Library. He had not been admitted as a scholar, for though his memories were perfect, he did not have a creative mind, one that could connect ideas in new ways. He had entered the Library as a scholar's pet, but upon discovery, had fled.

He had managed to escape. At the time, Muninn had not understood why he was not driven insane like others. But Huginn could figure it out. As Muninn was the embodiment of Memory, his memories were not a part of what he was, but were his entire self. The Librarian must have attempted to extract his memories, but had instead done grave damage to the raven's very self. He had escaped intact, but mortally wounded.

When he found his brother in Los Angeles, Muninn was weak. Huginn remembered the croak of his voice. He could barely speak. Muninn told him what had happened, and that Huginn would go on living without him. Memory was of the past. But Huginn was of the future and the present, of ideas and possibilities. He was Thought, and Thought did not age as Memory did.

"It is long past time for me to join our master," whispered Muninn. One moment he was crouched on the roof, then he lowered himself, sighed and was gone.

Huginn had not wept. He was not human. But even if he had been, he knew that the pain of this loss was deeper than weeping. Tears would not cleanse his soul, for half of it was now gone.

Muninn was still warm, and Huginn ate his brother's body. He took his skin, his tongue, his flesh. With utmost love and respect, he took his brother into himself, absorbing him and becoming one.

And as he consumed him, he received memories of their past. Some were to be locked away, but some were kept out, like objects on a table: the white Bast statue, the Nordic couple that looked like Santiago and Sister, all the things that Huginn had been able to remember in the past few weeks.

And now more memories came flooding back. Their voyages and long flights together. How they had loved to explore and soar, high on the icy wind, dipping down and spinning up into the sky again. He would never fly with his brother again, but there was more. Memories of adventures and quiet times, of friendships and losses, memories of the long years since their birth. All of them flew through his mind now, stopping and forming themselves into orderly thoughts. Coherent memories.

This statue with his brother's voice, this infuriating

thing that he had wanted to tear the eyes from had unlocked it all. And had he not also eaten his brother's eyes?

Something crashed into the room and Pangur Ban arched her back and hissed. The Neils rushed toward the commotion, but Huginn was aware of only one thing. He was now whole. He had his memories and his thoughts. The two pieces were one.

Born of the same egg, now inside one body and one mind, the twin ravens lived again.

CHAPTER 47

"THERE ARE TOO MANY OF some sorts of people," Malachy said to Elliot.

"What do you mean?" Elliot sprinkled the dough with more flour and kneaded it.

"Copies and copies. The Library was even confused."

Now that got Elliot's attention. He hadn't heard Malachy speak of the Library itself as a person. The Librarian, yes. But never the Library itself. Or herself. For still, Seshat slept and burned upstairs, and the Librarian had returned. Why he had not come after Elliot, he could not guess. Perhaps Seshat had done something. The Librarian was insane and Seshat might be able to keep him under control to a degree.

He didn't want to think too much on the topic. His minutes of induced insanity disturbed him. If he couldn't trust his own senses and perception of reality, what could he trust?

"What do you mean, copies?" Elliot asked.

"Twins, but doubled. And then a half of a set of twins. Doubles and halves. The Library told me."

Elliot wiped off his hands. "I don't understand."

"We librarians can feel things within the Library. We know where things are. Your ability to do this will grow in time. Well, I could feel copies where there shouldn't be copies. That was the men. And then there was half of two that should have been copies. That was the bird."

"Have you been near the Librarian? Did he do something to you?"

"No. I have not seen him. Did you say you were from America originally?"

"Yes."

"Well, they are from an American delegation. A raven, a cat and four identical men."

They were here! They had come for him. Pangur Ban and Huginn and Neil and his duplicates. Finally, at long last, they had come.

"Where? Where are they now?" He tore off his apron, considered running to his quarters for his old shoes, and then decided against it. There was no time.

"They sought something in the Room of Speech."

Elliot was about to ask where it was, but the location clicked into place within his mind. "That way?" he asked, pointing.

"Yes."

He didn't know why they'd want to visit that particular room. But it didn't matter now. They had come for him.

He left Malachy in the kitchen and raced toward the Room of Speech. By the time he reached it, it was empty. Many of the statues inside were toppled and a few lay in pieces on the floor, shattered stone mixed with a few black feathers. This was very, very wrong. His friends would not destroy things without cause, and unless Huginn was molting, something had ripped out some of his feathers.

He started back down the hallway, but then paused, feeling, hoping to catch a hint of where his friends were. Duplicates and halves, Malachy had said. He felt for these things, and a tiny sensation, like a whisper, led him upstairs and down a corridor in the direction of one of the larger chambers of the Library.

When he heard a woman scream, he ran. Then came the gunshots, five of them.

He raced through the doorway where a heavy cloud of

dust filled the chamber, obscuring the group of people. It didn't matter, as he knew each and every one of them, even the multiple copies of Neil. It looked like there were about thirty of him. When he saw the giant sandstone scorpion with Hazel standing over it, gun drawn, he knew where the dust had come from. She leapt nimbly away as it attempted to crush her with a giant open claw. She called out to it, luring it away from a figure on the ground.

It was Neil, and he wasn't moving. That was what had caused Hazel to scream. But as Elliot watched, Neil rose to his knees. Another of the Neils helped him up, while five others placed themselves between the scorpion and Yukiko. She held the handle of the rolling trunk that Elliot knew held a time machine. Hazel joined Yukiko as they tried to back up toward a doorway that was blocked by a snapping stone crocodile.

"About time," said one of the Neils, noticing Elliot. "Here." He handed him a gun.

"I don't think this is going to do us much good against statues. It doesn't look like Hazel did much other than make a bunch of dust."

"Well, it can't hurt either," said Neil.

Too true. Statues of two identical lions and three women, all ten feet tall, nude and bald, entered through two of the doors.

Hazel reloaded her gun. "Get the machine out of here!" she called to Yukiko. "Hey, Elliot's here!"

Yukiko looked confused for a second, and then she spotted Elliot. Her face broke into a smile of such pure pleasure that it distracted him for a moment. Neil shoved him aside and kicked the legs of one of the bald women hard, knocking her to the ground.

Elliot glanced back at Yukiko and jerked his head to the side, to remind her to get the machine out of there. Then he fired on the statue, blasting away part of its head.

Not long ago, having Yukiko smile at him would have

made his day. She was pretty and seemed to like him. And he was happy to see her. But something had changed, and he knew what it was. She wasn't Bennu.

He spun to fire his gun into the face of a stone crocodile, blowing off half of its upper jaw. It thrashed toward him, attempting to snap at him, but he jumped clear. Two Neils lifted the crocodile off its feet and smashed it into one of the thick columns nearby. It shattered into four large hunks.

"You guys outnumber the statues ten to one," Elliot shouted to Neil. "Why don't the others do anything?"

"All but fourteen are Yukiko's illusions."

"I can't tell the difference."

"The ones actually killing the statues are me."

"Where's Astrid?" Elliot asked.

"Up there near Huginn."

The black raven swept down on the statues, flapping in their faces and tearing at them with his claws. Though he did little damage to them, it did serve as a fine distraction and gave the Neils more opportunities to knock the statues to the ground or shoot them enough times to immobilize them.

Hazel shot one of the lions, and then the section of floor beneath it shimmered and the creature fell through the floor, into empty black space.

Astrid was on the second story, and as he watched, a giant scarab beetle vanished through another Door just beside her. Elliot leapt up the stairs toward her.

"Took you long enough," he said.

"Hold on," said Astrid. "Pangur Ban is leading one of them to a clear area."

The white cat darted here and there, an ostrich statue on her heels. She took a great leap over an empty section of floor, and the moment she did, a Door appeared under the ostrich and it fell through.

"Where did you send it?" he asked.

"The void, I think."

The statues moved toward to the doorway to the next room, and Elliot knew that Yukiko and Hazel must have gotten the time machine through it and the statues were following.

"We should follow them," he said. "Unless you can get us home on your own."

"We all go together," she said, heading down the stairs. "I need the machine and a quiet place to set it up. That's how we got here."

The statues clustered around the doorway, and others joined them, peacocks and hippopotamuses, even an asp. The group closed in, completely blocking the door. Huginn came to perch on the banister beside them.

"Elliot, is there a way into the next room that isn't through that door?"

"Yeah, but it'll take us a while. We have to go up and around."

"I got it," said Astrid. She called to Pangur Ban and made a Door. The place beyond the shimmering oval looked just like the next room, complete with Hazel and Yukiko heading down a hallway. Elliot stepped through, followed by Huginn and Pangur Ban, then Astrid.

Then he had a terrible thought, one that might put them all in even further danger, and it would all be his fault.

"Astrid, I need the books. If I get out of here, I need the fairy tale books and the metallurgy book that I give to us when we're younger. They're back in my room."

He was grateful that she understood immediately. He would have no other opportunity to retrieve the books, and this was their one and only chance to preserve their past timelines and keep them stable.

"How far is it?" she asked.

"Ten minutes, if we run."

Pangur Ban and Huginn had already joined the rest of the group, and Elliot grabbed Astrid's hand and ran.

"Wait, tell me where it is."

"It's near the kitchen. That way." He pointed.

She narrowed her eyes, and created a Door. Though the Door in front of them flashed through a series of rooms, none of them were his quarters or the kitchen. Then, a room adjacent to the kitchen appeared.

"That one!"

She stopped and they ran through. Elliot raced up to his room and grabbed the books. Then he took her to the kitchen where he put the books into a cloth bag that he normally used to carry things from the market and slung it over his shoulder.

"I have an idea," he said.

He grabbed an oven mitt and pulled open the wood-burning stove. Then he pulled a log from a wood stack nearby and handed one to Astrid.

"The Librarian hates fire," he said. "I think he hates it more than he hates all of us."

She caught on immediately, and they held the wood in the flames for the interminable time it took for them to catch fire. When the flames were strong enough, they took the logs into the nearest room.

He pulled books from the shelves and held them to the flames. Once they caught, he flung them against the bases of other bookshelves. In a minute, he had a few fires going. He continued to toss a few other books into the flames, careful not to smother the fire.

"I hate to do this," said Astrid. "I hate to destroy all these antiquities."

"Not too long ago, I would have agreed with you," he said. "But today, the Library burns."

CHAPTER 48

ASTRID HAD TO FORCIBLY PULL Elliot away from the series of fires he had set. The expression of determination and fury on his face frightened her. He had always taken things in stride, remaining optimistic in the face of difficulties. But now, something had changed in him. He was two years her senior, but his time with the Time Corps meant he was even older according to his personal timeline. He didn't look much older, but he had aged. The man whose arm she now pulled was a darker being.

"We have to find everyone," she said. "Now that we've found you, we need a place to set up the machine so I can make a Door back home."

"Something is coming," said Elliot. His tone was grim with satisfaction.

Astrid knew they wanted to draw attention away from the others with their fires. But Elliot seemed inordinately pleased with this new development, even eager.

"I don't hear anything," she said.

"You can't feel the place like I can. The Library is angry with us now."

"And it wasn't before?"

"We didn't set it on fire before."

Well, she wouldn't wait any longer. She made a Door to the room where the statues had been attacking her friends, but it was now empty. She moved the Door to a nearby room, searching for a place that looked safe before stepping through. Then she heard rushing footfalls nearby and five men tore into the room. Two of them set to putting out the fires, while the others raced toward Astrid and Elliot. She and Elliot leapt through the Door and she closed it just before they reached them.

"Those are a few of the librarians," said Elliot. "Seshat must have sent them."

"Is Seshat the main Librarian?"

"No, she's his wife. I thought she liked me, but I doubt she's so fond of me now."

They headed into the next room, and the next, following the trail of broken statues and destruction.

"The Librarian's name is Thoth," said Elliot, "and I think he is the one who sent the Library into the void. He made a duplicate or broke off part, I'm not sure. But it grew into what it is now. I think he did it to save Seshat. She's here burning and dying upstairs, but she's also alive and healthy."

"How can she be both?"

"I think it's because of the void. And because they're gods."

"If Thoth can move things into the void, then that means he's a Door," said Astrid.

"A psychopomp?"

"I wouldn't know," she said. "But I've learned that not all Doors are psychopomps." For some reason, she didn't want to tell him about the drake just yet. It could wait until they were safe at home.

They turned a corner and Astrid picked up on the sound of shouts. They raced down a few more corridors and found six of the Neils destroying a giant cobra statue.

"We need an undisturbed place to set up the machines," said Hazel as she holstered her pistol.

"They're sending actual people after us now," said Elliot. "Living people. We ran into a few. I don't think we'll want to kill so many unless we have to."

Astrid caught the look that passed between Hazel

and Neil. She knew that Hazel had killed once, and she wouldn't want to do so again. Neil too would be hesitant to kill unless they were under the direst of circumstances.

"We need somewhere remote," said Huginn from a spot atop a nearby bookshelf. His normally glossy black feathers were dulled with dust. "If they're heading here now, then we wait until they come. Then, when they're gathered here, we hop through a Door to another place in the Library far from here. That'll give us time to set up the machines and get home."

Making Doors here in the void was easy, Astrid thought. Her lessons with Graciela had helped her become more accurate, and her natural affinity for the void meant that creating Doors through a defined physical space, like the Library, was fairly simple. If they hadn't been pursued by murderous statues and avenging librarians, she might call it fun.

"I think I know a place," said Elliot softly. "But I think the Library can hear us. She'll send people there too."

"Whisper it to me," said Astrid.

"It's more complicated than that. I can feel where it is, but I can't explain how to get there. It's been a while, but no one goes up there."

Then Astrid had a thought. If making Doors was easy here, then her other abilities might work equally well.

"Can you think of this place?" asked Astrid.

"Yeah, of course."

"Then I'm going to try something. I'll pull a thread in your mind. It won't hurt. At least, I don't think it will."

He nodded once and she reached into his mind, just as she did with the dead, finding a jumble of thoughts, words, sensations and images. She had to be careful, as Jeff had warned her not to disturb the minds of the living. She didn't want to hurt him.

"Think of the place clearly," she said.

Then, one thought emerged, glowing and bright. She touched it and knew the place at once.

"I think I have it," she said. "Did you feel anything?"

"It was like a little red spark," said Elliot. "It didn't hurt."

But he looked at her with a new expression, one of wariness and fear.

"I can't do it normally," she said. "Only with the dead. And here in the void, I seem to be able to do things I can't do as easily in the ordinary world."

"Someone's coming," said one of the Neils. "There are eight or nine of them."

Astrid made the Door to the room. It was nearly empty, with only a chair beside a window open into the void. Along with its appearance, Astrid also knew Elliot's thoughts on the place. It was dark and quiet, like a little piece of the void within the Library's walls. Perfect.

Astrid closed the Door once all of them were through.

"I'm going to wait outside," said Yukiko. "I might be able to fool a few of them and give us more time." She looked exhausted, and Astrid knew there were limits to her power. After making multiple illusions of Neil, she must be worn out.

Pangur Ban, Huginn and all but one of the Neils decided to stand outside as sentries while Hazel gave instructions on how to set up the machine. Elliot threw down his book bag and got to work. Astrid was about to help when she glanced out the window into the void.

The black stillness was hypnotic and beautiful, more lovely than any dance or symphony or piece of art. It went beyond expressing the ideas of a single artist's heart and mind, instead expressing the complete totality of all minds and all souls. It was whole and complete, but empty at the same time. A paradox, but one that felt true.

Long ago, when she had sent Elliot to the Library, the Piper had told her that he thought he heard the sound of wings about her. It made some sense, at first, since her aspect was the owl. But an owl's wings were silent. It was one of the things that made them stealthy predators.

Somewhere outside were the void wyrms. She knew that they waited in the dark. Like her, they were things of the void. And if Yelbeghen was a Door, then so was he. She had never heard a drake fly, but a being that large must have to displace a lot of air to keep aloft. Its wings must make a sound.

But she was no drake. She was certain of that. Still, something in the void silently called to her, pulling her heart toward itself.

Elliot grabbed her arm.

"Are you okay?"

She blinked and took a breath, suddenly aware of the air around her, the sensation of her clothing on her skin and the grip of her cousin's hand.

"Someone told me people can go mad looking into the void," Elliot said.

She knew it wasn't true of herself. The void was her home, and if anything, she felt the real world was the place of madness. But she didn't wish to worry Elliot, so she helped Hazel connect the last of the devices. She glanced up at Elliot, who had a distant look, and she knew he was feeling the parts of the Library.

"It's him. He's coming," he said. "Quick, turn it on."

Hazel flipped a switch just as one of the Neils came in.

"Yukiko is trying to stop it by making more fire illusions, but there's a bird coming," he said.

"An ibis," added Pangur Ban, slipping in behind him. "Six feet tall."

"We can't get hold of him," said Neil, "but the others of me are distracting him. It won't work long."

Astrid tried to make a Door, but it simply flashed through areas of the Library.

Hazel cursed. "I'm trying to get the settings right. Hold

on." She worked at the knobs and counted on her fingers to do calculations.

The sound was louder now, and at long last, Hazel flipped the switch.

But it was too late.

The ibis stood in the doorway.

CHAPTER 49

"You have what is mine," said the ibis.

Huginn's mind raced, pulling up details and connections, old memories and newer ideas. This was Thoth, the Librarian, the ibis, the Mad One.

"He's not yours," said Hazel. "Elliot belongs back in his home world."

"He has what belongs to me," said the ibis.

The Neils did not move to attack the ibis, and Huginn understood why. The oldest of them knew what was going to happen, and all but the youngest had been through this before. Overcoming the Librarian with force was an impossibility. He could change or move or create any illusion. If Yukiko's abilities allowed her to temporarily bend reality, then the ibis was capable of creating entire new realities, each within a different person's mind.

All of this came to Huginn in an instant, his brother's thoughts and his own now working in harmony.

"He means the books," said Pangur Ban. "Especially the one listing the fine."

"You cannot leave now," said the ibis. "I will not allow it. You must stay. You brought things that cannot leave this place."

"What things?" asked Elliot, striding up to the ibis and standing face to face. "What can you possibly want from me or from them? We're of no use to you."

Huginn was only partially shocked at his boldness. Elliot stood eye to eye with the great bird, but he seemed smaller, less powerful, though they were close in height. He also noted that Elliot had positioned himself between the ibis and the rest of the group, leaving only the Neils outside.

"I want what's mine," said the ibis.

"You mean the books?"

"You already took those. You owe me more."

"Then take it!" he cried, spreading his arms wide. "What else can you do? You took Imee and drove her insane. Now she's somewhere in Thessaloniki. And what about Bennu? You kept me from her. You keep people inside this place and transform them into parts of yourself. Malachy hears the Library talking in his head. How long until that happens to me? What do you want? My life? Then why didn't you kill me when I arrived?"

"I do not want your death," said the ibis. "You owe me. It's why we brought the Library near to you. And you came through a Door to us. It was your choice."

"I had to go through that Door to save my skin. And if you want me to pay a debt, I've paid. I've spent months serving you, cleaning and cooking, helping with research."

"You also tried to burn the Library."

"There's that, yes. I don't like a cage. But I've done my time in it."

"I do not want your present or future time. I want past time. I want what you already have."

"My past?"

"You must give it to me to pay your debt."

Then Huginn understood, and the full horror of it struck him.

"He means your memories," Huginn said. "The information you have. The Library craves knowledge."

"You want my memories?" asked Elliot.

"I do. It is for my wife. She needs what you have. What you owe. You took the books, which have the thoughts of others. And now you owe that many thoughts back.

The fine is stated inside the cover. You owe one hundred years."

"I thought it meant the years I have left until I die. That is what Malachy said. But if you want my memories, I only have twenty-five years of those, and the early ones are hazy at that. And the fine says one hundred."

Huginn had an idea. "What if we each give a few years of memories, equaling one hundred? Surely that would pay the debt."

The ibis appeared to be evaluating the idea. And as he did so, Huginn felt something brush against his mind, like the tip of a feather.

"No," said the ibis. "The duplicate men have too few memories and they are so fresh, so green, with half of them stolen. If the Door, the small freckled woman and Elliot give me all their memories, plus all of the duplicate man's, it will still be short. Now, the Kitsune, she has a century of memories. And the cat even more. Those two will do."

"Then we can pay it," said Huginn. "I can give extra to make up for the younger ones."

"I do not think you understand," said the ibis. "Elliot owes a hundred years. The rest of you do as well. A hundred each."

"But that's not fair," said Elliot. "They didn't take any books."

"They added to the Library when they came. They brought their stories. They cannot take them back again. They belong to us."

"No one belongs to you," said Elliot. "Don't you understand that? They came to help me and I came here by accident."

"Nothing is an accident."

"Not to you maybe, but to us humans, it is. Imee didn't choose to come here through a bathroom door in Manila.

I didn't choose to come here. And neither did Malachy or the other librarians."

The ibis listened and then stretched his neck upward and ruffled his feathers.

"What do you think happens to librarians when they die?" he asked.

"I suppose they're free of you," said Elliot.

"No. They become part of the Library. Just as you must. Now, give me what is mine, or I'll take it from you."

Then Elliot leapt back as if something was on the ground at his feet. He pulled at his shirt, grasping at something that wasn't there. Then he pulled up his shirt and clawed at the flesh of his stomach. Neil grabbed him, pulling his arms behind him to restrain him from harming himself. He cried out in frustration and Huginn saw Neil whispering something in his ear.

Astrid looked like she was concentrating, but instead of looking at an empty space before her, as she did when she made Doors, she was watching the Librarian.

"Don't attempt that with me, little Door," said the ibis. "Your clumsy groping for threads in my mind is like an ape trying to weave a tapestry."

"Enough!" cried Huginn. "Stop it now, Old One. I've known others like you. And I've outlived them all. You're a relic, a thing that will live here in the void, but never return to the ordinary world. Now, stop toying with the humans and we'll settle this ourselves."

Then the Librarian turned to Huginn and his blood ran cold. He knew what he needed to do. If any of the others gave up a century of memories, they'd be left useless and insane. He knew what that was like, and he would not wish it on anyone. He also knew that of the group, he was the only one who would survive such a thing. All the others would be driven insane, for the Librarian did not leave amnesiacs, but tore the memories violently from the mind, leaving only a trail of confusion. He knew this because his brother had known it. Perhaps he had heard it or read it, but Huginn now understood it too.

"There are seven of us," said Huginn. "Seven hundred years, then."

"The duplicate man is fourteen people. Fourteen sets, even if they are copies. Then the Kitsune, the Door, the cat, Elliot, small woman and you. That means twenty centuries."

The ibis must have ceased tormenting Elliot, as he was now calm. "You knew," Elliot said to Neil. "You knew he'd count you."

"That's why I only came fourteen times," said Neil. "It was the least I could do and have us survive the statues," he looked at Huginn. "I'm sorry."

Huginn's mind raced. How long had he been alive? When had he been born? Time had been marked differently then, with no universal calendar, but he knew he was over a thousand years old. Probably over two thousand, if he counted his years with the Time Corps and his brother's long years as well. How many memories would the ibis take?

"All of them," said ibis, answering Huginn's unspoken question.

"I cannot allow it," said Pangur Ban. "This raven has suffered enough. He has only gotten his memories back recently. He is only now whole."

"You, little white cat, would take his place?"

His partner's face did not show fear, but her fur was puffed and her pupils were dilated.

"If you will allow it."

"No," said Huginn. "I have lived a long time without my brother. I can live that way again. It was not so bad, really."

He knew that Pangur Ban would recognize the lie, but he said it anyway. It felt like a little betrayal, as the two of them did not indulge in human customs and tell the little untruths that lubricated human social interactions. But in this case, he had no other way to tell her that he would give this piece of himself for her and for the others.

"You will be half a soul, forever lost," said the Librarian. "And you would willingly do this?"

"I will."

The ibis regarded him with interest. "Your brother will be preserved," said the Librarian. "He will exist here forever."

That was cold comfort, as Huginn would never return to this place again. But while his brother was already dead, the people in front of him were very much alive. He was a creature of the present and future, and if he could purchase the lives of these people, he would do so.

Then the room swirled and went black. The emptiness inside him blotted out everything and he slammed into the hard, cold floor. He maneuvered his wings and got his legs beneath him, then he felt gentle arms scoop him up. He was in a woman's arms, and a white cat leaned close to him.

"I pity you, Nightwing," said the ibis. "For I too know what it is like to never be whole. As my wife burns, I am in your place, living a half-life."

"Then go to her," said Elliot. "Go and let us go home."

Without another word, the great bird turned and left.

The cat touched her nose to Huginn's forehead. He knew who the cat was, and that she was his friend. There was something else, something important that had happened, but he could not remember what it was. The young woman who cradled him in her arms was a friend, as were the other people who leaned over him.

"I am trying to find something," he said, clicking his beak, trying to recall. "I am looking for someone."

The cat spoke. "I am not your brother, but I will help you remember. You will not be alone."

A small thought came into his mind. Her name.

"You are my good friend, White Hunter."

CHAPTER 50

Astrid looked Sister up and down. The girl wore a belted pink cotton dress and her blonde hair was pulled back with a simple matching ribbon. But aside from her clothing, Sister had a different feeling about her. She embraced Astrid.

"How long has it been for you?" Sister signed.

"Only a few weeks."

"It has been two years for me. I enjoy living with Hazel in New Orleans."

Astrid wanted to speak with this older version of Hazel, the retired older woman who lived in her home city in another world. But the elder and the younger Hazels could not be within ten miles of each other and Astrid could not time travel without abandoning her psychopomp responsibilities. Even now, she dreaded the inevitable call from Jeff castigating her for being absent.

Neil had been Sister's escort for this trip from Hazel and the Professor's home world to this one. He shut down and put away the time machine, leaning the trunk that housed it against the kitchen wall. How casually it was done, thought Astrid. As easy as leaning a bicycle against a wall.

"Are you attending art school?" asked Sister. "I remember you wanted to."

"I rented an apartment near school, but I split my time between Los Angeles and New York. And you?"

"The civil rights movement is heating up," said Sister.

"Hazel got thrown in jail during a protest and I had to bail her out. She said it wasn't her first time behind bars either, but the jails are nicer. I'm getting a good education and there is much work to be done in helping others who are deaf or who cannot speak. I am happy."

"I take it you want to go back?"

"I do. I'm making a home there, a good life. I miss everyone here, but I understand that it's not safe for me here."

"Not yet. But once I finish my third task for the Seelie, it might be."

"I'll consider it."

Just then, the two kittens bounded into the kitchen. Frieda and Diego skidded to a halt at Sister's feet and she dropped to her knees to pet them.

Astrid's phone rang, and her stomach lurched when she saw it was Jeff. Well, no sense in putting off the inevitable. She left Sister with the kittens to take the call.

"You know what I'm calling you about, don't you?" he said.

"I left my post."

"Yes, exactly. You're fortunate that Gopan was able to handle the geists that you left behind."

"I'm sorry I left, but I had to get Elliot out of the Library. I couldn't leave him there. Besides, I technically didn't go into another world, I went into the void. And I didn't time travel. I just slipped from here to the void and back."

"I ought to report you to our superior."

"He doesn't already know? I thought he was all-seeing or something."

"I don't know. Maybe he does know. He hasn't said anything to me about it."

"If he doesn't know, how did you find out?"

"I thought you might try it. After asking all those questions about going outside of your own time, it only made sense. And when Gopan was getting pulled by your leftover geists and no one could get hold of you, we all knew what you had done."

"I'm not going to make a habit out of it. Besides, look what I've accomplished. I've completed two tasks for the Seelie, which means I'm nearly done and free. I have friends among the Time Corps, including a golem who can duplicate himself. And I've struck an alliance with a drake. No geists were harmed. So what would this superior person do to me anyway? Ground me? Force me into some new form of service? Because I'm not going to be forced into anything anymore. I can leave this world and time and you'll never find me again."

"Now, Astrid, I'm not threatening you. I'm not unhappy just because you broke a rule and Gopan had to pull double duty. If one of us is very sick or injured, we can cover for each other. It's something else, something the elder did mention to me, an instability between the void and our world. By making the first Door there to send Elliot to the Library, you made a hole, like a wound. And then you tore another wound in and another out. When there's a wound in the human body, it attempts to repair itself. The void is no different."

"That's a good thing, right?"

"Well, yes. But there are things in the void, bad things. And I'm not sure if the void can heal itself properly. We don't know what stabilizing force might be unleashed. So for God's sake, don't go into the void again. Stay away from it completely. For your own sake and for the safety of everyone else. Promise me."

"I promise," she said, and meant it. As alluring as the void might be, she had no desire to put anyone in danger. Besides, she never wanted to encounter the Library or void wyrms again.

Jeff was silent for a moment, but Astrid could hear him breathing.

"I'm sorry," she said. "I didn't mean to cause any problems."

"I know you didn't. And the wounds may still heal themselves. Doors occur naturally on their own, without any human intervention. Those heal up fine. And you're a natural part of the world, unlike the Time Corps, who forcibly make time rips. So perhaps your natural rips will heal themselves. "

"Well, we used the Professor's machine along with my abilities to get to the Library. I couldn't do it on my own."

"I see," he said. "I suppose that explains the instability that our higher-up mentioned."

"So are you going to report me?"

She heard him sigh.

"I don't see what good it would do. The deed is already done and I'd hate to see you get punished for it. But if the instability persists and if he asks, I'll have to tell him."

She felt bad for Jeff, trying hard to keep the world stable and do his job. He was careful and conscientious, and she had just made his job a lot harder. But like he said, the deed was done.

"Hold on," Jeff said. "I have to sign for a package."

She waited and then heard him pick up the phone. "It's from your address in Los Angeles."

"I didn't send anything," she said.

She listened as he opened it.

"Look at that. It's Dickens."

That didn't seem so extraordinary to her. The man ran a bookshop.

"It's a first edition. My God, it has the Boz title pages and the fireside plate. All the volumes. Original publisher's binding. And it's in perfect condition, like it was printed yesterday. Hold on, there's a card. It's a thank you card from the Time Corps."

"For what?"

"For assistance and favors, it says. Did your cousin send this?"

"Possibly. Or someone else. A bunch of people in the Time Corps travel to the eighteen hundreds, and some were born there."

"Well, tell them thank you. I hope you don't think this gets you off the hook."

"I told you I didn't send it. And honestly, what hook would that be? Between the Seelie and the drake, I'm in enough hot water."

"I have to agree. Just promise you'll try to behave."

"I'll try. I really will."

Neil was barely back to his normal self and Elliot had already planned out their next job.

"There are two women," said Elliot.

"Sounds like a recipe for trouble."

"Not like that. One is a friend from the Library. Her name is Imee. She escaped from the Library, but the Librarian took her memories and left her insane. I know she was near Thessaloniki when she got out. A scholar told me she was in an asylum, but I don't know what year."

"Thessaloniki?" said Neil. "Hazel and I got images of a painting from that area. An ibis burning. It was painted by some ancient seer."

"I wonder if that might be Imee," said Elliot. "Maybe that image was seared into her mind when she left. Well, whatever happened to her, we'll find her and return her to her family in the Philippines. Insane or not, they'll want her back. It's not really enough, but it's the best I can do for her."

"And the other woman?"

"Now that we have a machine that can go back thousands of years, there's someone I want to find. She went to Huginn's old country, and Yukiko and Pangur Ban even know which town."

"Is she insane too?"

"No. She left the Library with permission, but I need to find her."

Elliot caught Neil studying him. "You care about this woman," Neil said.

"Yeah, and shut up. She was promised in marriage to some chieftain, but she didn't want to go."

"Now you're using time travel to further your love life."

"Fine, don't help me. I don't care. I'll go alone."

"I didn't say that. I'll help. I want to meet this woman. But there's something I want to do first. I want to find out where I came from, who made me and why."

Elliot looked at Neil, now in his forties. "How long have you known what you are?"

"A while."

"And you didn't tell us?"

"Unstable time loops are bad, stable timelines are good. You know the routine."

Elliot did. So much of their relationships, from their first meetings to later encounters were dictated by trying to avoid unstable time loops. Every idea and piece of information needed a natural origin. So if Neil told the Time Corps what he was, but later learned from them that he was a golem, the information formed a loop.

Neil asked so little of Elliot, very rarely asking for anything personal, that it would be a betrayal of their friendship to deny him this wish to discover his origins.

"If you want to find where you came from, I'm up for the trip," said Elliot.

After dinner, Hazel found Neil in the backyard. He wasn't reading or looking at anything in particular, just standing and watching the crimson light of the smoggy Los Angeles sunset.

"Will you tell me now why you always asked me how old I was whenever we met?" she said. "You don't do that with anyone else. Not even Elliot."

Neil didn't turn to look at her, but she saw him take a deep breath. She wondered if he treasured the feeling of breathing again.

"I wanted to make sure you had a choice," he said. "That you knew what I was."

"I'd be your friend no matter what you were. And why would my age matter?"

"How did you bring me back to life?" he asked.

She felt her cheeks go hot, but she didn't want to lie to him. He had the right to know how she had brought him back from death.

"I'm not completely certain. But I placed three drops of blood in your mouth."

"And?"

"And I kissed you."

There, she had said it.

"And that was all?" he said.

"I talked to you, but I had done that before already."

He shoved his hands into the pockets of his duster. "I think you did more than talk. I've been thinking, and I think you breathed into me. Maybe when you kissed me, maybe after. But I don't think it was the blood or the kiss."

She remembered then, resting her forehead against his, speaking to him and sighing. But how could something so simple and ordinary bring him to life?

"In the Old Testament, Adam was a golem, in a way," said Neil. "His name means 'earth.' And God breathed life into his nostrils."

"I'm no god."

"I never thought you were. But perhaps I may truly be

free. If that method of lifegiving grants free will, I should be. I don't know yet, but I mean to find out."

"What does this have to do with asking me how old I am?"

"I've been waiting for something." He took her hand, then slowly pulled her to him, giving her plenty of opportunity to pull away. Then he kissed her.

A minute later, she was breathless and a little dizzy, but in a pleasant way.

"You've been waiting twenty years to kiss me?" she asked after a few moments.

"No. I've kissed you countless times. This is just the first time you've kissed me. Well, the second if you count when I was dead."

"And once when you were twenty."

"Right," he said. "So three for you. But to the point, I wanted you to know what I was before you made any decisions. It's only fair."

"I wouldn't have cared."

"I'm not even a human being. I don't have a soul."

"You don't know that for sure."

"Maybe. But you deserve to know what I am."

"So you waited twenty years?"

"No. Every time we meet, I ask how old you are, and if you're older than you are today, twenty-three years and six months, then I know where we are on your personal timeline."

"So I'll see you again when you're younger and I won't scandalize the Professor by getting romantically entangled with a much older man?"

"We have twenty years of adventures in my past, and still more to come."

"And you won't turn on me? They say every golem turns on its creator."

"Never."

Huginn ruffled his black feathers and preened, running his curved beak over his wings and breast, enjoying the sensation. The ritual soothed him, and sometimes, when his memory was particularly bad, it was all he could think to do. It was familiar and comforting, like the presence of Pangur Ban.

He and the cat sat up high in their favorite tree, while Pangur Ban told him a story. He knew she had told him the tale before, and as she told it, he remembered bits and snatches of it. When she finished, they sat for a long while in silence.

"Do we have a new job lined up?" asked Huginn after a while. "I'm itching to get back to work. My mind needs something to chew on."

"Not yet, but soon," said Pangur Ban. "The humans don't feel it yet, but I can. Something has loosened. Slipped. It's so slight that I don't know if the Twelve or Santiago and Yukiko can sense it yet. But there has been a shift."

"I don't feel anything."

"That's because you can't remember how it was before," she said gently. "Something is waiting."

"Is it death?" he asked, but he didn't know why this thought occurred to him. It was simply the first one that popped into his mind.

"Death comes to all of us, one way or another," she said. "Even those as old as we are. But no, it's not death."

"Tell me about your kittens' father," he said. "Was he like us?"

"Do you mean was he a common animal? No, he was like us."

"Where is he now?"

"I do not know. But cats are not like humans and

ravens. We do not mate for life. I doubt I will ever see him again."

Then she looked at him. It made him uneasy, the way she watched him.

"I have never asked you," she said. "Did you ever have a mate?"

A little jolt of sensation went through him and he waited a few moments for it to pass. "I don't know."

"I do not ask you to trouble you, old friend," she said. "Only because I wonder if there are others like you. Other ravens. If you have children, then you might have grandchildren and great-grandchildren."

He had never thought of it before. Or, if he had, he could not remember thinking it. Perhaps it was true. But he had no way of knowing. And a moment later, he found that he did not care. If he found others, then that would be a fine thing. But sitting here, in this tree, with his closest friend beside him and his other friends in the house below, he was content.

And then he remembered other trees and other pleasant times. Evenings near a warm fire, conversations and delicious meals, bright mornings with clear skies. The memories were few, but they were strong.

Ah, so his brother was not totally gone. The Librarian had not taken everything. Damaged and broken as he was, his brother had not completely left him. A few little fragments of him remained, his memories like dandelion tufts, floating in the recesses of his mind.

AUTHOR'S NOTE

I love hearing from my readers. To drop me a note or to learn about my other books, please visit www.heatherblackwood.com.

If you enjoyed this book, please post a review on the retail site where you purchased it.

www.ingramcontent.com/pod-product-compliance
Lightning Source LLC
Chambersburg PA
CBHW020252200626
46816CB00001BA/246

* 9 7 8 0 9 8 8 8 0 5 4 4 6 *